IN
Places
Hidden

Books by Tracie Peterson

*with Judith Miller **with Judith Pella ***with Kimberley Woodhouse

GOLDEN GATE SECRETS

1

Places Hidden

TRACIE
PETERSON

BETHANYHOUSE
a division of Baker Publishing Group
Minneapolis, Minnesota

© 2018 by Peterson Ink, Inc.

Published by Bethany House Publishers
11400 Hampshire Avenue South
Bloomington, Minnesota 55438
www.bethanyhouse.com

Bethany House Publishers is a division of
Baker Publishing Group, Grand Rapids, Michigan

Printed in the United States of America

Library of Congress Cataloging-in-Publication Data
Names: Peterson, Tracie, author.
Title: In places hidden / Tracie Peterson.
Description: Minneapolis, Minnesota : Bethany House, a division of Baker
    Publishing Group, [2018] | Series: Golden gate secrets ; 1
Identifiers: LCCN 2017035830| ISBN 9780764218996 (trade paper) | ISBN
    9780764230653 (cloth : alk. paper) | ISBN 9780764230660 (large print)
Subjects: LCSH: Frontier and pioneer life—Fiction. | GSAFD: Love stories. |
    Christian fiction.
Classification: LCC PS3566.E7717 I49 2018 | DDC 813/.54—dc23
LC record available at https://lccn.loc.gov/2017035830

Scripture quotations are from the King James Version of the Bible.

This is a work of historical reconstruction; the appearances of certain historical figures are therefore inevitable. All other characters, however, are products of the author's imagination, and any resemblance to actual persons, living or dead, is coincidental.

Cover design by LOOK Design Studio
Cover photography by Aimee Christenson

18 19 20 21 22 23 24   7 6 5 4 3 2 1

To Camri and Caleb and Kenzie

Grow strong in the Lord and seek Him first. There may
be rough roads in life, but nothing takes God by surprise.
He's already made provision for your every need.

CHAPTER

1

Late November, 1905

*S*an . . . Fran . . . cisco! Next stop, San . . . Fran . . . cisco," the conductor called in a slow, elongated manner.

Passengers throughout the car began gathering their things, and the volume of conversations grew as the train slowed.

Camrianne Coulter smiled at the two women sitting opposite her. "Thank you both for making this such a pleasant trip. I believe God put us together for a reason."

The redheaded woman who'd introduced herself three days earlier as Kenzie Gifford nodded. "I don't imagine I've been good company, but I'm grateful for your friendship."

"You've been through a great deal, Kenzie, and despite that, you've been lovely to talk to." Judith Gladstone pushed an errant strand of blond hair under her hat and smiled at Camrianne. "I'm not all that knowledgeable about God, but as my mother used to say, 'I feel that fate has brought us together.'"

Camri nodded as some of the male passengers moved toward the end of the car. The aisles were narrow, and as the men jostled Camri, they tipped their hats and apologized. She paid them little attention. She'd grown up in Chicago and was used to crowded situations and people who were always in a hurry.

Seeing no need to compete for a place on the car's platform, Camri merely checked the buttons on her gloves and continued her conversation. "I knew when I started this journey that God would provide for my every need. Because of my education, some people think it strange that I put my faith in an unseen Deity, but I believe trusting God is a choice based not only in faith, but wisdom. I personally don't believe in fate or luck, but I'm very thankful that you both agreed to help me. I'm glad to help you in your searches as well."

Kenzie gazed out the train window. "I am too. Although my search isn't a physical one, like yours. I'll be content just to find some peace of mind and heart."

"I'm sure you will," Judith said as she strained to look out the dirty train window over Kenzie's shoulder. "And Camri, I'm sure we'll find your brother."

Camri's journey was not one of joy and excitement, as it had been just a year ago when she'd traveled from Chicago to San Francisco with her parents. They had stayed with her brother, Caleb, for several weeks, and Camri had helped him put his house in order.

Now her parents were ill, and Caleb had disappeared.

She frowned. He had been missing for over three months, and no one had any idea where he'd gone. Until August, his letters had always come like clockwork on the first of every month. One letter came for their parents and another for Camri. He even managed to write their older sister, Catherine, who was married and lived nearby with her family. It was a routine Caleb had never wavered in since moving to San Francisco five years earlier.

Until now.

"Are you certain your brother won't mind us staying at his house?" Judith asked.

The train conductor passed through the car again. "All out for San . . . Fran . . . cisco!" He edged through the men standing at the end of the car and moved on to the next.

Camri raised her voice to be heard above the din. "I can't imagine he would. He's always been kind and generous." She retied the ribbons of her simple travel bonnet. "He has a nice house with four bedrooms, so there will be plenty of room." Especially since he was not even there. Camri left that thought unspoken. She had already spent the entire trip dwelling on or discussing her missing brother. "Since we've all come to San Francisco with a particular goal in mind, I'm glad we can pool our resources."

The train came to a jerky stop with the screech of metal wheels on metal rails.

Judith sighed. "I'm glad not to have to go to a hotel. My funds are quite limited."

"As are mine," Kenzie said, turning to face Camri, "although I'm hopeful my mother's cousin will honor his word and put me to work at his candy factory. I'll ask him about jobs for you both."

Camri nodded, although with her expanded college education, she found the idea of working at a factory a bit beneath her. Education had always been important in her family, and that, along with women's rights, had taken all of Camri's attention the last few years. She had hated leaving her teaching position at the women's college in Chicago. Her teaching ability was highly regarded by the college administration, and her work with the suffrage movement had garnered respect from men and women alike.

But Caleb's welfare was much more important. Something had to be desperately wrong, or he would have written.

She couldn't help but sigh. The stress and worry had taken such a toll on their parents that both had taken to their beds with various maladies, and the doctor was concerned. Camri had decided, at their urging, to look for Caleb. She'd left their parents to the care of her elder sister, hoping against hope that she'd arrive in San Francisco to find that Caleb had merely been too busy to write. Of course, she was certain that wouldn't be the case. Since even his household servants, Mr. and Mrs. Wong, hadn't seen him, she knew he had most likely met with harm.

The real question was whether or not he was still alive.

Now that the train was stopped, passengers flooded the aisles. Camri knew better than to be in a hurry to disembark. She had no desire to be pushed and prodded by others as they rushed to exit the train.

Judith was the first of the trio to stand, reaching down for her small carpetbag. From the looks of it, the bag was ancient, but Camri knew it was one of the few things left to Judith. According to her sad tale, most of her family's assets had been sold off to pay the debts left by her deceased mother and father.

Kenzie was next to get to her feet, pulling a dark veil on her hat down over her face. It was in this state that Camri had first met Kenzie in Kansas City. While she'd waited for her train west, Camri had shared a table with Kenzie in the crowded depot restaurant. At first Camri had thought the redheaded woman to be a widow in mourning, but she'd soon learned that Kenzie Gifford had been stood up at the altar on her wedding day.

Camri gathered her thoughts along with her things. It was important to stay focused. She tucked her large leather satchel under one arm and clutched her purse close with the other. One could never be too careful in big cities, and she wasn't about to become the victim of a pickpocket.

They were helped from the train and instructed where they could hire a porter and cab. Camri was used to traveling and easily managed the arrangement. A large uniformed black man took their information and collected their trunks while the ladies waited in the comfort of the depot.

"I'm so glad you recommended we take the train from Los Angeles rather than coming into Oakland," Kenzie said as she glanced around. "I doubt I could have managed the ferry ride over. I'm already somewhat motion sick."

"The other route is much longer." Camri and her family had taken the Oakland route last year, and it had seemed to take forever. Caleb had learned only after their arrival that it was much easier to come by way of Los Angeles.

The porter finally returned and announced that their trunks had been loaded into a hired carriage. Camri tipped him generously and motioned to the other ladies to follow her.

Outside the depot, San Francisco was damp and chilly and noisy. The carriage driver helped them board and hardly waited for them to settle before putting the horses in motion. He paid little attention to the conveyances and people around him, almost as if he expected the traffic to magically part for his horses. It was quickly apparent that travel through the city was pretty much a free-for-all. Camri watched in silence and not a small amount of fear as horses and carts darted between automobiles and cable cars with a daring that should have been reserved for a circus act. Added to this were people who crossed streets and maneuvered in and out of traffic as though they had no fear of death.

The noise of a city was something Camri had missed. Long hours on the train traveling through wide-open farm country and prairie wastelands had left her longing for the city and its clamor. Vendors hawked their wares, cable-car drivers clanged their bells while newsboys sounded the headlines of the day, and annoyed freight drivers hurled insults at preoccupied pedestrians. It was a musical symphony Camri understood well.

Caleb's three-story house was set in a fashionable neighborhood just west of downtown. It wasn't where the elite of the city had their palatial estates, but it was near enough that respectable folk could approve. Caleb had boasted that one day when he became a famous lawyer, he might own one of those grand mansions on the hill, but for now he was content with his stylish home.

"Goodness, I had no idea this city was so hilly. It must be exhausting to walk anywhere," Judith declared as she gawked around like an excited child.

"You should try riding a bicycle here." Camri smiled at the memory. "Caleb and I did just that, and I never exerted more energy."

"I like bicycles," Kenzie murmured. "I used to go riding with—" She stopped abruptly as if the memory were too painful to speak.

Camri swooped in to fill the awkward silence. "I think you'll both enjoy the city. There are so many things to do, and once we're settled in, we can take a walk."

Kenzie brushed dust off her dark blue skirt. "Right now, I just want a bath."

"Well, you won't have to wait much longer. There it is." Camri pointed to Caleb's house. "It's the ecru-colored one with the bay windows trimmed in white."

"Ecru?" the driver called back.

"Beige," Camri clarified.

He threw her a blank stare.

"The light brown."

He looked back at the row of houses and nodded.

Kenzie and Judith gazed about them while the driver pulled to the curb. No doubt they were impressed with this beautiful little neighborhood and its lovely houses set up off the streets. Camri certainly had been when she'd first come here.

The driver helped them from the carriage, then began to unload the trunks. Camri made her way up the stairs. The first steps rose up from the sidewalk in a set of twelve. She paused on the landing, then turned to climb another six. At this landing, she waited for Judith and Kenzie to catch up.

"Isn't it a charming house?" She gazed up at the two white pillars that framed the small portico. The double entry doors were artistically designed with stained-glass inserts. "I fell in love with it when we visited last year."

"It's charming," Judith agreed. "The entire neighborhood is more beautiful than I expected. It doesn't even seem like it's in the city."

"And much quieter than I thought it would be," Kenzie added.

"I think the trees and shrubberies help," Camri replied before moving up the final six steps. Her thoughts were on the last time she'd been here and Caleb's enthusiasm about his house. Now he was missing, and though the house and neighborhood was just as she remembered, Camri couldn't help but feel Caleb's absence.

She paused at the door and squared her shoulders. Nothing about this trip was going to be as simple and entertaining as her last visit to San Francisco.

"Well, here we are." She turned and looked at her new friends. "Welcome home."

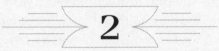
*C*amri knocked on the door, and it was only a moment before Mrs. Wong, the housekeeper, appeared. The older woman was dressed in a simple black gown with a white apron. Her once-black hair was now salted with gray and pinned in a sedate manner at the nape of her neck.

She smiled at Camri and gave a little bow. "Miss Coulter, it is good to see you. We were glad to get your letter." She looked behind Camri at the other two women on the porch.

"Mrs. Wong, I've brought a couple friends to stay with me. I apologize that I couldn't offer some warning." Camri turned just enough to give introductions. "Miss Gifford, Miss Gladstone, this is Mrs. Wong. She is the housekeeper, and her husband is the groundskeeper."

Again Mrs. Wong bowed. "I am pleased to know the friends of Miss Coulter. I will make bedrooms ready for you." She stepped back and gestured for them to enter, then moved to slide open the pocket doors to the front sitting room on the right.

"Has there been any word from Caleb?"

"No. No word." Mrs. Wong lowered her head. "No word."

Camri motioned her friends into the sitting room. "I will

pay the driver and then give you a tour of the house while Mrs. Wong makes up the bedrooms."

"Husband can take care of the driver and luggage," Mrs. Wong said, her head popping up. She disappeared for only a moment, then returned with Mr. Wong. He was a small man dressed in a suit, and he wore his hair in a braided queue. Although born in America, he followed this style in honor of his deceased father and the traditions that followed him to America.

He bowed. "You are welcome, honored sister of Mr. Caleb. I see to your things."

"I'm glad to finally be here." She handed Mr. Wong money to pay the driver, then joined the girls in her brother's sitting room.

"I have tea to serve. You would like some now?" Mrs. Wong asked.

"Tea would be lovely. Then we will probably want a nice long rest before dinner."

Mrs. Wong nodded and scurried off.

Camri gazed around the sitting room, desperate to sense her brother's presence. A piano stood in the far corner, its rich ebony wood polished to perfection. She could still remember Caleb sitting at the keys, playing his favorite Chopin nocturnes. He would get so caught up in the music that he'd forget anyone else was in the room.

Not far from the piano was the fireplace. On the mantel stood a framed photo of their parents. The reminder only made Camri all the more desperate to find her brother. Their parents had been devastated with worry, and when she'd said good-bye to them a week earlier, they hadn't even been well enough to go to the train station. Her brother-in-law had driven her instead.

"I love the rug," Judith said, interrupting Camri's thoughts. "I've never seen anything like it.

The fringed Turkish rug in reds, blues, and golds covered most of the floor. Her brother had purchased it during his travels abroad. He had been so proud of it, for he had bargained with the seller for nearly an hour to reduce the price by half. Even now, the memory of him telling the tale made Camri smile.

"It's one of my brother's prized possessions."

Judith made her way to the piano. "He has very good taste. This piano is made by the best in the business."

"Do you play?" Camri asked.

Judith nodded. "It's my one proficiency. I never was all that good at book learning, but music is my dearest love." She touched the keys. "My mother taught me. She played amazingly and knew a great deal about pianos and music."

"Playing was something I never mastered," Camri admitted. "I suppose it's because I always had my nose buried in books of all kinds. I loved learning. I still do. You and Kenzie should consider furthering your educations. In this day and age, a woman must learn to do for herself. There won't always be a father or husband to care for you."

Judith frowned and left the piano, taking a seat on the sofa beside Kenzie.

Camri worried she'd offended her new friend and hurried to smooth things over. "My passion for education gets the best of me. Each person should do what's right for them, of course."

Judith nodded, and her frown disappeared. "I doubt I'll ever go to college. I was schooled at home, and such places seem intimidating."

"And I have little use for furthering my education. You hardly need much book learning to package candy," Kenzie added. She lifted her veil, then removed the pins that held her hat in place. "But I do enjoy reading. I was the assistant to the librarian in my hometown." For the first time since Camri had met her, Kenzie smiled.

"I believe you mentioned that when we first met. I adore libraries."

Kenzie nodded. "I do too. So quiet and restful, yet full of wondrous adventures through books."

Judith shrugged. "I suppose I'm the only one who doesn't care to spend all my time reading."

"That's all right." Kenzie nodded toward the piano. "You can play music while we read."

Mrs. Wong returned, pushing a tea cart. Not only had she brought tea, but there were a variety of cookies as well. "You want me to pour?"

"No, Mrs. Wong. Thank you. We can manage." Camri untied her bonnet.

Mr. Wong and the driver passed the sitting room doorway, each loaded down with a trunk or suitcases. Mrs. Wong took this as her cue to leave and without another word hurried from the room.

Camri put her bonnet aside, then unbuttoned her wool coat. "She always seems to be in a rush."

"They seem very nice," Judith declared. "I've never met any Chinese people before."

"There are a great many of them in San Francisco." Camri put her coat across the back of a wooden chair and began to pour the tea. "They're quite oppressed, as most Americans would prefer the Chinese be driven from the country. However, Mr. and Mrs. Wong are first-generation Americans. Their parents arrived here during the gold rush after selling everything they had to come to America. The two women were expecting and had their babies within days of each other. Mr. and Mrs. Wong grew up together and eventually married, as was the wish of their families."

"If they grew up here, why is their English . . . well . . . why do they speak differently than we do?" Judith asked.

Camri had never really thought about it. "I suppose because they were raised in Chinese communities. I know they generally

18

speak Chinese when alone." She looked up and motioned to the cart. "Would either of you care for sugar?"

Kenzie was first to reply. "No, thank you."

Judith shook her head as Camri crossed the room to hand them each a cup and saucer. "Mrs. Wong makes the most incredible tea. It tastes like flowers." She went back to the cart. "Would either of you care for cookies?"

When both women nodded, Camri brought the plate to the sofa, and Kenzie and Judith each chose from the assortment. Camri took up her own tea, then joined her friends. She sat in her brother's favorite chair, a leather wingback, and sampled the tea. It was just as she remembered.

"The Chinese have had a very hard time here. All manner of laws have been passed to remove them from America, but perhaps that is more strongly addressed here on the coast than in other areas of the country."

"I've read about the troubles," Kenzie admitted. "They were blamed for epidemics of the plague."

"The plague?" Judith asked in disbelief. "I thought that was something from the Middle Ages."

"It was, but unfortunately it's still around." Camri shook her head. "They now know, however, that the disease is carried by rats, and the Chinese live in the poorest areas, where the rat infestations are generally quite bad."

"Goodness. I never would have expected such a thing."

Camri suppressed a yawn. "It's a hard life for the poor."

Judith had just taken a bite of her cookie, but nodded.

Kenzie put her cup and saucer on the table beside her. "While I've not suffered such poverty, we were by no means wealthy while I was growing up. My father was a shopkeeper. His uncle owned an emporium, and he hired my father to manage it. When I was young, I used to go there and help when I wasn't in school. I learned bookkeeping and eventually handled all of the receipts and billing. When Father's uncle passed away, he left the shop and an inheritance to my father. We lived comfortably after that." It was the most she'd spoken of her past the entire trip.

"But why did you work if your family had plenty of money?" Judith asked.

Camri was surprised by the question and spoke before Kenzie could reply. "Because being a woman independent of one's family is important. Far too many women don't have that advantage and find themselves forced into marriage at a young age."

Both Kenzie and Judith looked at Camri as if she were speaking a strange language. It wasn't unusual for her to be received in that manner. Most women didn't even realize how oppressed they were or that marriage was often just another form of servitude. Camri quickly sipped her tea.

"I didn't work to prove anything to anyone," Kenzie said after several uncomfortable seconds of silence. "I loved working at the library, and it filled my days with something other than sitting at home. I didn't make enough money to truly support myself, but I did manage to set enough aside to pay for my travel here. My parents helped with that as well."

"My folks were never ones to have much money," Judith admitted. "My father worked wherever he could—mostly cowboy labor jobs. He had to quit school at a young age to help support his family. My mother took in laundry and sewing. She said when they started out, they had enough money that they could get a mortgage on a little ranch. It wasn't much. Father had a couple of hired hands who worked for room and board most of the time. When he sold the steers, he paid them in cash and bought Mother and I some necessities. It was never much, however. We did better at raising sagebrush and tumbleweeds."

"Did you have any brothers or sisters?" Camri asked.

"No. I was an only child. In fact, my parents swore there

were no other family members alive on either side. But now I know that wasn't true."

Camri nodded. On the train, Judith had told them about a letter she'd found after her mother died, addressed to her mother's sister but never sent. Judith had come to San Francisco to find the aunt she'd never known she had. "What of you, Kenzie. Do you have siblings?"

"No, not living. My mother wanted a large family, but she didn't have an easy time being with child. She miscarried several times and, when I was five, gave birth to a stillborn son. We were all devastated. Especially my father."

"That's very sad," Judith murmured, looking as if she might cry.

Mrs. Wong arrived. "Rooms ready now."

"Thank you." Camri got to her feet, glad to have something else to focus on. "I don't know about you, but I think we should freshen up and rest. Kenzie, I know you wanted a bath."

The other two women nodded and rose.

"I'll give you a quick tour as we go upstairs." Camri pointed to the closed door not far from the piano. "There's a smaller sitting room through there. Across the hall from that is a large dining room." She motioned Kenzie and Judith to follow. "The Wongs live downstairs. The kitchen and laundry are also down there." She paused at the staircase. "Farther down the hall past the stairs are my brother's study and the back stairs that lead to the lower level."

She began to climb the steps. "Upstairs are four bedrooms and a bathroom. My brother has the largest of the rooms at the end of the hall. I'll take the room opposite his, and you ladies may have the two bedrooms at the other end."

They reached the top floor, and Camri pointed to the door directly ahead. "This is the bathroom. It has all the modern conveniences." She turned to the right and opened the first door.

"Those are my things," Judith announced. "This must be my room." She looked around at the stylish furnishings. "It's so beautiful."

Camri smiled. She had stayed in this room when she visited with her parents. "It is. It was rather bland before, and I made a comment about it to Caleb. He immediately took me shopping and suggested I make over the room any way I liked. Once we started on this room, it seemed only natural that the other rooms also get dressed up a little."

"Well, I'm going to be very comfortable here. Blue is my color. It matches my eyes." Judith sat on the edge of the bed. "This feels amazing. It's fit for a princess." She'd no sooner sat down than she popped up again. "And look!" She rushed to the bay windows, where a cushioned window seat awaited. "Oh, this is wonderful. I can sit here and look out on the world."

"I found it a lovely place to read." Camri immediately wished she'd kept the thought to herself. She didn't want Judith to feel she was purposefully bringing up the topic of reading again. She stepped back into the hall. "And over here is the other bedroom."

"I'm glad we haven't far to go," Kenzie said. "I'm more tired than I realized."

Pushing open the door, Camri stepped back. "I picked out pale green and pink for this room."

Kenzie stepped in and surveyed the entire room before commenting. "It's like a garden. So lovely. So peaceful."

Camri smiled. "I'm glad you like it."

Judith had followed to peek inside the room. "I love the flowery wallpaper and matching drapes."

Mrs. Wong appeared and offered a smile, but it didn't quite reach her eyes. She bowed her head as she always did before speaking. "When you like dinner?"

Camri took out her pocket watch and checked the time. It was nearly three. "Would six be all right?"

Mrs. Wong nodded. "Six. Good time." She left as quietly as she'd come.

Camri turned to her friends. "Well, ladies, I will leave you to rest."

Without another word, she made her way down the hall to her bedroom. She started to open the door, then turned instead to enter her brother's bedroom. It was just as it had been when she'd last been here. He liked dark shades of forest green and had done up the room to suit his preferences.

The shades were pulled, but there was enough light that Camri didn't bother to raise them. The room bore just a hint of her brother's cologne, and the smell brought tears to her eyes. It was the first time she'd really been able to think about him since they'd arrived.

"Where are you, Caleb? Are you hurt? Are you sick?" Camri went to his dresser, picked up a folded handkerchief monogramed with CC, and held it to her nose. There was only the faintest scent.

She shook her head and used the handkerchief to blot her tears. The task her parents had given her was not only daunting, but frightening in a way Camri couldn't explain. There were so many possible explanations for Caleb's sudden disappearance, and none of them were good.

CHAPTER

3

*T*he next morning all three women agreed there was no sense in wasting time. Kenzie telephoned her mother's cousin George Lake, who sent someone to pick her up while on his delivery route. Meanwhile, Judith and Camri sat down at the mahogany dining room table and spread out several newspapers that Mr. Wong had acquired for them. They began to scour the ads for jobs in case Mr. Lake had no extra positions.

"Here's one for a nursery attendant," Judith said, shaking her head, "but I doubt I'd be any good at it. I've had no experience with children."

"There seem to be plenty of light housekeeping positions, but the pay is a fraction of what I made teaching." Camri pushed one paper aside and took up another. "Once we locate Caleb, I'll go back to my previous position. It wouldn't be fair to apply to teach here, only to leave in a few weeks." She opened the back of the newspaper and began to scan the columns. *At least I hope it won't be more than a few weeks—a few days would be even better.*

"There are quite a few requests for seasonal work. Some of

the restaurants want cooks and girls who can wait tables." Judith looked up. "I could probably do that. I know how to cook."

"But from the looks of it, the pay would scarcely be enough to buy food, much less pay the Wongs and perhaps a man to help with our search." Camri sighed in exasperation. "There are some spots available at a soap factory, but it doesn't say how much they pay nor what one has to do to earn that pay."

"Can you sew?" Judith asked. "There are a number of dressmaker positions. One place offers excellent pay if you have experience in formalwear."

Camri shook her head. "I can mend but was never all that capable of actually creating a garment."

Without warning, the chandelier overhead shook enough to draw attention.

Camri felt the sensation of brief, but certain, movement. "Was that an earthquake?"

Judith shook her head. "I don't know. I thought they would last longer."

Camri nodded. "Maybe it was just a little tremor." She'd heard Caleb speak about earthquakes and tremors, but during her previous visit to the state, she hadn't experienced any.

They continued to pore over the papers, marking any position that sounded the least bit promising. When the clock chimed the noon hour, Mrs. Wong appeared to clear the table in order to serve lunch.

Camri walked over to a large mirror on the wall and attempted to resecure her hair. At home there had been a number of people to help with her clothes and hair, but here there was no one. She didn't feel it would be right to impose on Mrs. Wong, especially since she'd learned the night before that the couple hadn't been paid since Caleb's disappearance.

It wasn't the first time she'd had to do for herself, and it probably wouldn't be the last. With great care, she adjusted the hairpins.

"I can help you with that," Judith said, jumping up from the table. "I used to do my mother's hair all the time."

Mrs. Wong entered the dining room carrying a tureen. "Duck soup," she announced.

Since they'd had roasted duck the evening before, Camri wasn't surprised. She turned to Judith. "Maybe we can help each other after the meal. We should look our best before going out to apply for jobs."

Judith followed Camri back to the table. "Mother and I always did for each other as best we could. We never had servants."

Camri murmured her acknowledgment. The weight of the situation rested heavily on her shoulders. She had done a quick inventory of the pantry that morning only to find there was nothing much to count. There was still plenty of flour, coffee, and sugar, but little else. The Wongs explained that with Caleb gone, there was no money for their salary or household needs. They had relied on the charity of extended family to provide an occasional basket of food, while Caleb's employer had managed the utilities. The first order of business that morning had been to send Mr. Wong to the grocer for supplies, which had used up a good portion of Camri's savings.

Savings she'd hoped to use in finding Caleb—not just to support a household.

She took a seat at the table as the housekeeper returned with bread and butter. Camri smiled in appreciation, but the hopelessness of the moment left her with little joy.

When Mrs. Wong had once again departed, Camri looked at Judith. "Shall we pray?" Judith bowed her head, and Camri did likewise. "Lord, we thank thee for thy bounty. Guide our steps and show us the way you would have us go. Please help us find situations that pay well. Above all, please help us find those we seek. Amen."

"Amen." Judith reached for the bread. "I don't think we should worry. I feel confident Kenzie will secure us jobs with her cousin."

"What gives you such confidence?"

Judith shrugged and handed Camri the bread plate. "I guess I just feel in my heart that things will work out. Usually when I feel like this, things go well."

"I hope you're right." Camri chose a piece of bread and set it aside before ladling soup into her bowl.

Judith waited until after she'd had her turn with the soup tureen before continuing. "I know you're very worried about your brother. In my short time of knowing you, I've come to worry about him as well."

Camri smiled. "He's a good man, and I know he wouldn't make us worry unnecessarily. That's what makes me certain something has happened to keep him from contacting us. I fear he might be sick or injured."

"Maybe he fell from his horse and hit his head and doesn't know who he is anymore. That happened to one of my papa's friends. He never regained his memory either." Judith covered her mouth with her hand, seeming to fear she'd said too much.

"It's all right. God knows I've thought of such possibilities as well as things much worse. It's hard not to imagine the worst." Camri bit her lower lip to keep from saying anything more. If she dwelled too much on the terrible things that might have happened, she'd soon be in tears.

Mrs. Wong brought a lovely china teapot to the table and began to pour a cup for each woman. Camri decided that rather than wait until after she'd eaten, she'd pose the questions on her mind now.

"Could you sit with us a moment, Mrs. Wong?"

The older woman looked momentarily startled, but nodded and quickly finished with the tea. "You have problem?" she asked, taking a seat at the table. She sat rigidly on the edge of the chair, her hands folded in her lap.

"I suppose I do," Camri said, putting aside her spoon. "I tried to get into my brother's study this morning, but it's locked. I wondered if you might have the key."

Mrs. Wong shook her head and a brief look of worry passed over her face. "Mr. Caleb only one to have key."

"I was afraid of that. When did you last see my brother?"

Mrs. Wong looked down at her hands. "He went out on business August twenty-five. He not come home."

"Did he leave in the morning or the afternoon?"

The older woman continued to stare at her lap. "He go out in evening. He go to his study, and I see him there at his desk. He tell me that he had . . . to do business." She chose her words in a slow and deliberate manner, almost as if she wanted to make certain she didn't misspeak. Camri wondered if there was something the housekeeper wasn't telling them.

"Mrs. Wong, do you have any idea what his business was that night?"

The housekeeper shook her head. "Not my business." She stood but continued to look at the floor. "I have work now."

Camri nodded. "I'm sorry for detaining you. I'm just trying to gather all the clues that might help me find my brother."

Mrs. Wong gave a little nod, then left the room in her usual hurried fashion.

Camri looked at Judith. "Did she seem upset to you?"

Judith shook her head. "I wasn't really paying attention. I find her hard to understand sometimes." She shrugged, as if that explained everything, then went back to focusing on her meal.

Judith seemed so naïve, yet perfectly content to be so. It was possible that with such a lack of education and social life, she truly didn't know to want more. Wasn't that exactly what Camri had found with so many young women when trying to talk to them about their rights? Perhaps the best thing to do was enlighten Judith a bit.

"I know I've told you about my education," Camri began.

"Yes. You went to college." Judith's blue eyes twinkled. "You're the smartest woman I've ever known. When I think of all the books you've read and the studying you've done . . . well, it's so impressive for a woman."

"Women are no different than men when it comes to desiring knowledge." Camri spread some butter on her bread. "And while it's true that some people want to learn more than others, I think it's most important to know what options are available. In your situation, you were probably never told about the possibilities."

"My situation?" Judith frowned, as was her habit when confused.

"Living in the middle of nowhere on a cattle ranch wouldn't allow you to speak with many people or attend lectures where education was being discussed. And even if you'd lived in town, you might not have had many opportunities to hear about the current political events that involved women."

Judith looked as if she was considering this. Camri hoped she hadn't offended her new friend again. Judith was far and away the sweetest of young women, Camri didn't want to hurt her feelings.

"Growing up," Camri continued, hoping to move the focus back on herself rather than Judith, "we were encouraged by our mother and father to do whatever we wanted with our lives. My sister Catherine became a scientist, as is her husband. She continues to work, even though they have two children. My brother Caleb became a lawyer, although he studied a great deal of theology as well. And I became a teacher as well as an advocate for women's rights. My mother was a great supporter of the cause. In fact, whenever someone was speaking about women's suffrage or the various movements to better women's lives, she insisted I attend. My mother and father are very progressive in their thinking, as were their parents. They all support women getting the vote and having all the legal rights afforded to men. They want to see women have more opportunities."

"Opportunities for what?" Judith asked.

Camri smiled. "For their futures. My parents want me to have whatever kind of life I want, even if it has nothing to do with marriage and having children."

"But why wouldn't you want to marry and have a family? I've wanted that all my life. I want a big family." Judith blushed. "I suppose that sounds bold, but it's true. I grew up without anyone but my mother and father. It was lonely, and I always longed for brothers and sisters. I hope one day to marry and have a dozen children."

"A dozen?" It was Camri's turn to frown. "But this is the 1900s. You should know that there are other opportunities."

"But what if I don't want other opportunities? If your goal is for each woman to be able to choose her future, shouldn't I be allowed to choose mine?"

She was right, and Camri was once again trying to impose her beliefs on others. "I'm sorry, Judith. I don't know what's gotten into me lately. I suppose being surrounded by students and other women who believe as I do has made me pushy when it comes to educating others. I'm often hired to speak at ladies' functions, so I just naturally lecture."

"It's all right." Judith smiled in her sweet fashion. "I think your ideas are wonderful. I truly admire your passion. But it's *your* passion. Not mine. I hope you won't think less of me because of that."

Camri felt ashamed, because she *had* thought less of Judith for her simple desire to be a wife and mother. "Again, I apologize. I'll try to rein in my thoughts."

"You don't need to do that," Judith countered quickly. "Just don't be offended if I don't want the same things you do. Right now, all I really want is to find my aunt. I hope you understand."

"I do, and I appreciate that you're willing to help me with my search for Caleb first."

"What you said on the train made good sense. If we pool our resources and efforts, then we have two other people to count on. Three can cover much more territory than just one. And I don't mind at all that I have to wait a little longer. Your brother might be in danger, and it's far more important that we find him first."

"Thank you, Judith. You're such a kind soul. I can learn so much from you."

Judith giggled. "From me? Goodness, I don't think so."

Camri smiled. "I do, and I think God has put us together for that very reason."

They finished their lunch in relative silence. Camri was humbled by Judith's spirit. Here she was supposed to be the Christian full of grace and kindness, yet Judith was far more gracious and kind. She was content and patient, while Camri knew a despairing restlessness that grew a little stronger every day. She had told herself it was just her worry over Caleb, but perhaps it was something more. If she was completely honest with herself, she had to admit she was lonely. Teaming up with Judith and Kenzie had alleviated some of that feeling, but only to a small degree.

Mrs. Wong came and cleared the table. She kept her head down, signaling that she had no desire for conversation, and Camri felt even worse. If she wasn't careful, everyone in the house would come to dread her.

She decided to focus on searching for the key to Caleb's study. "I'm going to search my brother's room. I can't imagine that he'd just carry the key to his study around with him all the time."

"Might I help?" Judith got to her feet. There was no hint of dismay in her countenance. She was all forgiving and sweetness.

Camri smiled and nodded, and they made their way to her brother's room. "Caleb was always very particular about his room and study. He's very orderly." She opened the door to the bedroom.

"Oh my, it's a perfect room for a city gentleman." Judith appeared completely enthralled by Caleb's room. Camri couldn't help but smile as Judith made her way around, touching the drapes and furniture. "At least what I would imagine a city gentleman would like," she quickly added. "After all, I've never really known any."

Camri raised one of the large window shades. "I tried to get him to lighten things up a bit, but he loves this dark green."

"I do too. With the wood furniture, it's like being in a forest." Judith turned to gaze at the fireplace. Two chairs sat in front of the hearth. "I can just imagine sitting here on a chilly evening with a lovely fire."

Camri's emotions were triggered by memories of Caleb doing just that. "The house has a furnace system that generally keeps it warm, but last summer there were several cool evenings, and Caleb had a fire laid. I remember one night after our parents had gone to bed, I couldn't sleep. I found Caleb here reading, and he encouraged me to join him. We sat until the wee hours of the morning, discussing the future."

Judith smiled. "How wonderful to have a brother who would do such a thing. He sounds amazing."

"He is." Camri wiped away her unbidden tears. She went to the far side of the bedroom and began to search through the drawer of a nightstand.

"Should I go through the pockets of his clothes?" Judith asked.

Camri glanced over to find her friend standing in front of the wardrobe. "I hadn't even considered that, but it makes sense. Please do." She was glad to give Judith the job. She was afraid if she did it herself, she would break into sobs.

After an hour in Caleb's room, leaving no item unturned, pocket unsearched, or drawer unopened, Camri and Judith still had found no sign of a key.

"Once, when my papa had a door lock that wouldn't budge," Judith said, looking thoughtful, "he just removed the hinges."

Camri had never heard of such a thing, but it made sense. "That's a brilliant idea. Thank you. We'll go talk to Mr. Wong and see if he might lend us a hand."

They quickly made their way downstairs and found the Wongs sitting together in the kitchen. They were speaking softly in Chinese and seemed caught up in their conversation when Camri knocked on the doorframe.

"Please excuse the interruption," she said. The Wongs sat up straight and nodded but otherwise said nothing, so Camri continued. "I've been looking without success for the key to my brother's study. Judith had a thought, and I wondered if you might help us, Mr. Wong."

He nodded again. "I am pleased to help."

"We want to take the door to the study off its hinges and get into the room that way."

"I can do that. Let me get tools." He left the room momentarily, then returned with a hammer and slender chisel.

Camri led the way upstairs to her brother's study. Her hopes were high until they reached the door. "Oh no." She felt immediate defeat. "The hinges are on the inside."

Mr. Wong shook his head, as did Judith. It was apparent neither one had any further ideas.

Frustrated, Camri and Judith returned to the dining room table. Their lack of success was a serious damper to Camri's mood. She had to find a way to get into that study. She was certain that if there were clues regarding Caleb's affairs, they would be in that room. She sank into her chair and picked up the newspaper, flipping to the back to look despondently at more job listings.

A loud knock sounded at the front door, followed by the doorbell. Mrs. Wong rushed down the hall, and Camri heard her open the door. A moment later, Kenzie came into the room.

"I'm so excited. Mr. Lake said he has jobs for both of you." She began to unbutton her coat. "You start tomorrow."

Camri put down the newspaper. "Well, that certainly worked out better than I anticipated. I must say, I'm surprised."

"Not only that," Kenzie said, pulling her hat from her head, "but he's going to pay you more than he might someone else. I told him what we were up against, and that while we did have a place to stay, we would need to be able to put our money together and support ourselves and our causes. What with it being the holiday season, he's overwhelmed with demands for his candy and desperate for people he can trust."

Camri considered her words. "Why is trust such an issue?"

"I'm not entirely sure, but apparently there has been some sort of trouble." Kenzie placed her hat on the table and then discarded her coat. "But Cousin George, as I'm allowed to call him, is a nervous, fussy man. I think he would probably perceive trouble even if there were none."

"I'm so excited," Judith declared. "I love sweets, and working at a candy factory sounds like a great deal of fun. Don't you think, Camri?"

"I wish our door troubles could be so easily mastered," Camri replied.

Kenzie gave her an odd look. "What door troubles?"

"The door to my brother's study is locked. Mrs. Wong said Caleb had the only key, but Judith and I searched through his bedroom and found nothing. I'm starting to fear he had the key on him when he disappeared."

The redhead glanced around the room as if assuring herself that no one else was listening in. She leaned down, putting her lips only inches from Camri's ear. "I can open it."

Camri straightened. "How?"

"Well, you know how I helped in my father's store? A boy who worked in the back . . . he taught me how to unlock doors without a key."

"You mean you can pick a lock?" Camri asked in a hush.

She nodded. "I can. It was just a game to me—a puzzle to learn."

Camri jumped to her feet. "Then come quickly and open the door!" She reached out to take hold of Kenzie's arm. "Please."

The trio made their way to the office door. Kenzie glanced around once again, then quickly went to work on the lock with two hairpins. It took only a few seconds.

"There," she said, stepping back as the door swung open.

Camri stared into the office in disbelief. The room had been ransacked. Papers were strewn everywhere, and some of the furniture had been overturned. Books had been torn from the shelves and left in heaps on the floor.

Behind her, Mrs. Wong gasped. Camri hadn't heard the older woman join them, but it was obvious that Mrs. Wong was just as surprised at the chaos.

"Mr. Caleb not do this."

"No, I don't imagine he did." Camri turned back to look again at the disorder. "Now we just need to figure out who did. And why."

4

*G*eorge Lake was a man of limited stature and patience. He handed each of the women an apron while he told them about their duties. Kenzie slipped the apron over her head.

"There is a great need for secrecy and cleanliness. The chocolate must be manufactured under constant scrutiny lest the secrets be revealed. There are a variety of candy makers in this town, and I'm certain they would like to put me out of business. You must pledge your loyalty and secrecy, or I cannot allow you to work here."

The girls all nodded in unison, and Mr. Lake continued. "I'm particular about how I manage my factory, and I'm sure Miss Gifford has informed you that I have been inundated with orders for Christmas."

"Yes," Camri replied, and Judith nodded.

"Good, then you will understand the need to get to work immediately. I'm putting you in the packaging department. I can move some of the men there to production, and then hopefully we can increase the amount of candy we make each day. Come this way."

Kenzie wasn't sure what to make of her mother's cousin. He

seemed constantly fearful and anxious. His gaze darted around the room from behind his wire-framed spectacles as if he expected to be attacked at any moment. The poor balding man had the demeanor of a mouse about to be pounced on by a cat.

Cousin George droned on and on, giving instructions that Kenzie listened to only halfheartedly. He'd already told her most of this when he'd toured her through the factory the day before. She was to sit at the end table, where she would put the final pieces of chocolate into the box, then wrap it in her cousin's trademark red-and-yellow ribbon. After that she would put the finished product in a packing crate.

"As you can see, there are more than ten different types of chocolates. Each has a unique filling, and different products will be packed in specific boxes," Cousin George explained. "The boxes marked *Variety* will have two of each type. Boxes that specify *Nuts* or *Creams* must be just that and nothing else. It's imperative you understand this. Goodness, we would have no end of trouble should you mix these up, and I won't be able to employ you if something so simple as that is a problem."

Kenzie shook her head. At least Cousin George and the candy factory would keep her mind off of Missouri and those she'd left behind. Or better yet—those who had left *her*. She tried not to think of Arthur Morgan stranding her in her wedding gown at a church in front of over two hundred guests. She tried to forget the pain of her father telling her that Arthur's family had sent word that the wedding was off and that Arthur had gone abroad. The pain in her heart was such that Kenzie had been certain it would kill her. Unfortunately, that hadn't been the case.

Because of Kenzie's misery and their own embarrassment, her parents had immediately taken her away to stay with an aunt. Soon after that, they conceived the idea of her moving to San Francisco, where no one would know her shame.

No one but me.

But of course, that had changed, much to her surprise. She hadn't meant to make friends with Camri and Judith, and she certainly hadn't intended to tell them anything about her past. But it had happened, and now, for what it was worth . . . she was glad. It was better to be in their company than to be alone.

"Now, take your seats," George Lake commanded. "I will demonstrate how to fill the boxes." He picked up one of the variety boxes.

The trio did as he instructed, each taking a chair at their appointed place. Kenzie sat at the end of the long table. Stacks of box trays awaited at Camri's end of the table, while the lids were with Kenzie.

Cousin George motioned to one of two young men who would be helping them. "David will make certain you have plenty of boxes in various sizes for the chocolates. He will also bring you spools of ribbon. Sam over there will bring in boxes of loose chocolates from the factory floor and will help take away the packed crates. David will do this also, if Sam gets behind with other duties."

The two young men smiled at Kenzie and her friends as if they were already making plans for the future. David even gave her a wink. Kenzie fixed him with a look of boredom, causing him to lose his enthusiastic grin.

For nearly an hour, Cousin George continued his tirade about the exact way the candies should be arranged. He even had each of the young women package and repackage the candies until he was satisfied that they could do the job. He took extra time with Kenzie, showing her how the ribbons should be tied.

"I see that you're right-handed," he said, "but if you would tie the bow as if you were left-handed, you will find it gives a flat and finished look."

Kenzie practiced several times, stopping momentarily to study the steps of her normal bow-making method in order to reverse them. Finally she created several bows using Cousin George's left-handed method.

"Good. Folks look for my ribbons in order to quickly identify my chocolates. It's critical that you secure them properly and make them beautiful."

"I understand." Kenzie quickly mastered the ribbon's placement, much to her cousin's relief.

Finally, Cousin George concluded his instructions and left the women to their work. Kenzie was almost certain she heard the other two sigh when he finally departed. She felt the same way. His nervousness was enough to make her reconsider working for him.

"Well, I suppose I am the start of this assembly line," Camri announced.

The plan was for her to take up a new box and load it from the loose chocolates that had been placed in front of her. Next, Judith would do the same with the chocolates she'd been given. Once the box was full, Kenzie would secure the lid and ribbon before gently placing it into a large crate that Sam periodically removed and replaced. It was all very orderly and allowed the men, who previously had helped with the packaging, as well as Cousin George, to return to full-time work on the factory floor.

Kenzie and her friends were able to package the chocolates with lightning speed. Even Cousin George was impressed when he returned to check on their work. He opened one of the boxes just to ensure the girls were packing them correctly, then praised their work before disappearing again. By the time the workday concluded, there were a great many crates full of Lake Boxed Candies and an ache in Kenzie's shoulders that left her longing for a hot bath.

On the cable-car ride back to their neighborhood, Kenzie sat wedged between Camri and Judith. She watched the world go by and tried her best not to think about Arthur. But no matter where she sent her thoughts, Arthur was there.

Why? Why had he left her at the altar? Why had he suddenly decided not to marry her when he had been the one to press for their union in the first place?

Kenzie had known from the start of their courtship that nothing would come of it. Arthur belonged to a family with old money and plenty of it. Their name made everyone sit up and take notice. He certainly wouldn't want a wife from a merchant family. Kenzie also had an obligation to care for her aging parents and had set her mind and heart on that task. She made all of this clear to Arthur.

Arthur, however, didn't care about social standing or Kenzie's plans for her parents. He insisted he could make her change her mind—that she would fall as madly in love with him as he had with her. She continued to resist his invitations and gifts until he finally claimed to accept her terms. They would just be good friends and enjoy each other's company. He wouldn't push her for marriage or mention his love again until the day that she declared her love for him. Which Kenzie felt certain she would never do.

It seemed a reasonable compromise, and she had been certain no harm could come of it. She was so very wrong. It was easy enough to remember the day, even the very hour, that she had realized the truth. The library was closing for the day, and she was putting away the last of the returned books when she spied a young couple hidden in one of the dimly lit aisles. The man and woman were in each other's arms, passionately kissing, completely lost in the rapture of each other.

Somewhere deep in her heart, an ache began, and Kenzie knew she'd lost control of her arrangement with Arthur. She wanted to be that woman. She wanted to be in Arthur's arms, lost in his kiss. Hopelessly in love.

That evening, when Arthur arrived to escort her to a concert, he almost immediately sensed that things had changed, but still Kenzie couldn't admit her heart.

It was only when her parents announced that her mother's poor spinster cousin planned to come live with them in return for seeing to her parents' needs that Kenzie began to reconsider. If her parents didn't need her to remain at home, then there was no reason she couldn't return Arthur's love and marry him.

"Are you coming with us, or do you plan to ride around the city this evening?" Camri asked.

Kenzie glanced up to see that they had reached their stop. "Oh, I apologize. I'm rather tired."

She followed Camri and Judith from the cable car and began the two-block trudge uphill to Caleb Coulter's house. The deep sadness she'd felt since Arthur's abandonment threatened to overwhelm her. She put her hand to her temple, as if to ward off any further thoughts of what might have been.

"Do you have a headache?" Camri asked.

Kenzie nodded. "I do. I think I shall just go right to bed. I'm not hungry, and the extra sleep will do me good."

Camri looked at her like she might protest Kenzie's decision, but she said nothing and kept walking, much to Kenzie's relief. The less that was said about her predicament, the better.

Camri knew her next move was to meet Caleb's employer, Henry Ambrewster. The only problem was that with her work schedule, it was impossible to meet him during the day. She decided her only option was to invite him to the house. She felt certain that if she explained the situation, he would understand. Caleb had spoken of him as a friendly and generous man.

She placed a call to Ambrewster's office and told the man who answered the phone why she was calling. "I'm Caleb Coulter's sister, and would like to leave a message for Mr. Ambrewster."

"You needn't leave a message, Miss Coulter. This is Henry Ambrewster. What may I do for you?"

She lost no time. "I'm here in San Francisco to look for my brother. I wondered if you might have time to stop by his house and visit with me one evening. I have some questions."

There was a long pause on the other line. Finally, Mr. Ambrewster responded. "I'd be happy to come. When did you have in mind?"

"The sooner the better. I've taken some temporary work here in the city, and it consumes my days. Otherwise I'd make an appointment to come to your office."

"Nonsense. There's no need for that. Are you free this evening? I was just leaving the office and could come by on my way home."

Camri breathed a sigh of relief. She wouldn't have to wait before getting to talk to one of the last people to see her brother. "Tonight would be fine. Thank you."

"I should be there in about half an hour."

She hung up and looked at the clock. She needed to change from her work clothes and clean up. It wouldn't do to meet Mr. Ambrewster looking as exhausted as she felt.

Upstairs, she found Judith ironing and made a request. "My brother's employer is coming here soon. Would help me dress my hair?"

Judith smiled and put aside the iron. "I'd be happy to."

"Just give me a few minutes to clean up. Oh, meanwhile, would you please find Mrs. Wong and let her know we're going to have a guest?"

"Of course."

Judith made her way downstairs while Camri hurried to make herself presentable.

With just a couple of minutes to spare, Judith put the finishing touches on Camri's hair. She handed Camri a mirror. "I hope this is acceptable."

"I wish it weren't such a bother. I've heard that many women are cutting their hair short. Can you imagine women wearing their hair cut like a man's? Sometimes I think it would be a wonderful freedom. I may try it."

Camri surveyed Judith's work. The style was elegant. Judith had managed to sweep Camri's long brown hair back, then make several braids, all of which she interwove and pinned into a neat bun.

"It's perfect. Thank you so much." Camri heard the doorbell chime. "I suppose that's him." She handed Judith the mirror, then glanced down at her gown. Fashioned from mauve silk in the latest princess-style, the gown was perfect for entertaining guests, yet reserved enough for church. The sleeves puffed out from the top and were banded at the elbow. She didn't bother with gloves, even though for some it was still very much the fashion.

"Miss Camri, Mr. Ambrewster is here," Mrs. Wong announced at Camri's open door.

"Thank you. Did you put him in the sitting room?"

"Yes. I bring tea and cake."

Camri smiled. "Thank you, that would be lovely."

She made her way down the stairs with Mrs. Wong following some paces behind. Camri paused in the doorway to the sitting room and took a moment to study the older gentleman who stood by the fireplace. He wore a double-breasted gray wool suit, white shirt, and dark burgundy tie. He was distinguished in appearance, looking well-bred and meticulously groomed.

"Mr. Ambrewster?"

He looked up and smiled. "Indeed."

Camri stepped forward. "I'm Camrianne Coulter, Caleb's sister." She crossed the room and took a seat in Caleb's leather wingback chair. "Thank you for coming, Mr. Ambrewster."

"Please call me Henry. Caleb always did, and I should very much like for you to do so as well."

"All right. You may call me Camri."

He smiled and took a seat on the sofa. "Camrianne. Such an unusual name."

"Yes. A combination of both parents', Cameron and Anne."

"Ah, yes. I like it very much."

She nodded. "So do I, but Camri suits me better." She smoothed the skirt of her silk gown. "Thank you for being willing to come. I've just arrived in San Francisco and am desperate to learn anything I can about my brother's disappearance."

"I would like to learn about it as well."

"So you know nothing?" She tried to keep the disappointment from her voice.

"About his disappearance? No." He leaned back and crossed his legs. "It's as if he fell off the earth. There's been no sign of him."

Camri tried to control her emotions. "I'm so worried. This ordeal has cost my parents their health, and our sister, Catherine, is seeing to them while I search for him."

The older man frowned. "This is hardly a task for a young woman."

"I believe a woman is just as qualified to set up a search as a man."

"I meant no insult. It's just that this town is full of dangers."

She nodded. "Be that as it may, I'm hoping you might tell me about the last time you saw my brother."

Ambrewster's bushy brows drew together as he frowned. "It would have been the Friday he went missing. He was at work, and we discussed several cases. Your brother was carrying a heavy load of work—we both were. Our office had been inundated with requests after your brother managed to have Patrick Murdock found innocent of murder."

"Patrick Murdock?" She tried to remember Caleb mentioning the name.

"Yes, he's a contractor. He and his father once owned a successful construction business, and we handled all of their legal dealings. When his father fell to his death, Patrick declared it murder and began to pursue the men he believed responsible. When one of those men turned up dead, Mr. Murdock was charged with murder. We generally don't handle murder cases. Our tasks are mostly directed at corporations and their legal affairs, but Caleb was determined to defend Mr. Murdock. It was quite the sensation at the time. There was noise made about graft and political influence, as well as substandard construction." Henry shrugged and smiled. "But when isn't there? This town runs rampant with corruption."

"Caleb mentioned that in his letters. I suppose all big cities suffer from such things. Chicago has more than its fair share of political corruption."

"I'm sure you're right." The mantel clock began to chime the hour. Ambrewster leaned forward. "I wonder, Miss Coulter . . . Camri. Could we perhaps continue our discussion over dinner? I'm famished and would be honored if you would accompany me."

Camri considered for a moment. It wasn't as if he were asking her out for a romantic interlude. "I suppose it only right that I accept. After all, I'm the one keeping you from your meal."

A smile spread across his face. "Wonderful. I have my car outside and know a lovely restaurant not far from here."

An hour later, they were seated in a nearby restaurant, enjoying a sumptuous dinner of creamed scallops and prawns.

"This is one of my favorite places to dine," Henry told her. "When my wife died, I found eating at home held less joy. I make the rounds most evenings to a variety of my favorite places."

"How long have you been a widower?"

"Four years. My Agnes died just a year before your brother joined my practice. I was difficult to work for after her death, and the two men I employed quickly found positions elsewhere.

Then your brother arrived and . . . well, I must say he was a breath of fresh air. His faith in God helped bring me back from the brink of despair."

"That sounds like Caleb." She smiled and enjoyed another bite of seafood before continuing. "I hope you don't think me insulting when I pose this next question."

"Of course not. You needn't fear. Be blunt with me." He smiled, and his blue eyes seemed to twinkle. "I doubt anything you say can put me in a bad frame of mind. This meal is pure pleasure to me."

Camri heard the flirtatious note to his voice. She didn't want to encourage him, but neither did she wish to alienate him. Despite what he said, she knew that men scorned could be just as difficult to contend with as women.

"Why is it you've done nothing to find Caleb?"

His right brow arched. "Who says I haven't?"

Camri dabbed her mouth with her linen napkin. "I'm sorry. That was presumptuous of me."

Ambrewster relaxed. "All is forgiven. But you should know that I did look for Caleb. At first I thought his disappearance had something to do with his interest in Patrick Murdock's sister."

"His sister?"

Ambrewster smiled. "Yes, I think they were taken with each other. Caleb seemed preoccupied with her—always wanting to do things for her. He would take time away from the office to escort her places. It was, I'm sure, quite respectful . . . but romance seemed obvious."

"He said nothing about having any interest in someone." Camri tried to imagine Caleb keeping such a secret from her. It wasn't at all like him. "But I can't imagine even that would cause him to become so irresponsible as to let his parents worry."

"You would be surprised the power a beautiful woman can have over a man." He gave her a surprising wink. "When he disappeared, I thought perhaps he had eloped. But when he didn't return, I feared there might be another reason."

"Did you ever speak to the young woman?"

"No. I spoke to her brother, though, who assured me they'd seen nothing of Caleb. After that I hired a man to search. He turned up nothing. He looked for leads, but as I said earlier . . . it was as if your brother vanished into thin air."

"But no one can really vanish. He has to be somewhere. Our parents are worried half to death." She put down her fork. "I have to find out what's happened to him. Even if . . ." She couldn't bring herself to finish her thought.

"My dear, don't fret. I'm sure now that you're here, we'll find him."

She lifted her face to meet his gaze. "I'd like to believe that. I must have hope, otherwise I fear I will despair. However, it isn't like Caleb to leave us guessing."

"No. He has always been a very responsible young man. Still, I don't want you to fret. I find you much too pleasurable a companion to allow you to brood. I will redouble my efforts and report directly to you on my findings. In the meantime, perhaps you would do me the honor of letting me take you to the opera on Friday night."

Camri shook her head. "Mr. Ambrewster . . . Henry, I appreciate the compliment you pay me, but I am not interested in anything more than finding my brother. When that task is resolved, my plan is to return to Chicago. I have a position there with a women's college and very much wish to take up my duties once this is resolved."

His expression grew serious. "This may take some time, Camrianne. You have to accept that your brother may not even be in the city."

"I realize that, but it doesn't matter. Until I know what happened to him, my focus must remain on my search."

CHAPTER
5

*T*heir first Sunday in San Francisco, Camri insisted they attend Caleb's church. She explained to Judith and Kenzie that they might find someone there who could give them clues about Caleb's disappearance. After that, if they desired to attend a different church of their choosing, she would completely understand.

The day was rainy and cold, but the girls made the short walk nonetheless. The miserable weather made them grateful for the warmth of the sanctuary, despite the curious looks of the congregation. Camri enjoyed singing hymns and listening to Pastor Fisher speak on Christ's birth. Prophecies from the Old Testament were the focus of his sermon. He stressed to the congregation the anticipation that the Jewish people would have felt, looking for their Messiah to come. They had watched and waited for years—centuries—and still nothing.

"But the Messiah didn't come to them as they thought He would. They expected a fierce king to come and set them free—to bring them success and prosperity—to set all that was wrong right again. They were watching, even searching, but they weren't looking in the right place."

His message about their hopes and desires struck a chord with Camri, especially Pastor Fisher's comment about the Jewish people not looking in the right place. Where was the right place to look for Caleb?

The sermon continued with the pastor sharing verses from Isaiah and other Old Testament books that gave insight as to where Jesus would be born. Camri glanced at Judith and Kenzie. Though they had come into her life unexpectedly, Camri already felt as if they had all been friends for a very long time. Still, she couldn't help but remember the last time she'd visited this church, when Caleb had been at her side instead. His absence at the house and now here at church left a desperate emptiness within her.

Camri tried to keep her thoughts on the spirit of the holiday to come. She didn't want her situation to cause Judith and Kenzie to think her less than joyful for God's blessings. She glanced up, determined to pay closer attention to the sermon, when the room began to shake.

Kenzie gasped, and Judith reached to take hold of the pew in front of them. This was nothing like the little tremor they'd felt before. This was a noticeable earthquake.

Pastor Fisher held fast to the pulpit and waited until the shaking stopped. He smiled down at the congregation. "As Luke tells us in the twenty-first chapter, 'And great earthquakes shall be in divers places, and famines, and pestilences; and fearful sights and great signs shall there be from heaven.' But we needn't be afraid. These things must happen, and though the very foundations be shaken . . . we will not be moved, for we are the children of God, and He will watch over us with tender care."

The people around her began to relax, and even Camri eased back in her seat and drew a calming breath. Her foundations had been shaken in so many ways, but God had brought her here amidst the quakes and tremors. He wouldn't leave her orphaned. Just as He wouldn't leave Caleb alone in his plight.

After the sermon, Camri made her way to where Pastor Fisher and his wife greeted their flock. "I don't know if you remember me," she said to him, "but I'm Caleb Coulter's sister."

"I do remember you," Pastor Fisher replied. "When I saw you in the congregation, I thought perhaps Caleb had returned." He clasped her hand. "Quite the welcome you had."

Camri nodded. "I've heard about earthquakes, but I've never experienced anything like that."

Judith and Kenzie came to stand beside her. Camri made the introductions. "This is Miss Judith Gladstone and Miss Kenzie Gifford. We came to town together, and they're staying with me at Caleb's house." She waited until the parties had exchanged pleasantries before continuing. "You mentioned thinking Caleb had returned. Do you have any idea where he's gone?"

The pastor shook his head. "No, but my son Micah was under the impression he had family business. Let me call him over." He looked around a moment. "Micah!"

A handsome dark-haired young man looked up from a circle of young women. He smiled and nodded at his father's motion to join them. Camri watched as he excused himself and made his way to where they stood.

"I don't know if you had a chance to meet our youngest son, Micah, when you were here before," the pastor said to Camri.

She smiled. Micah's piercing blue eyes held her gaze. "No, but Caleb wrote of their friendship." She extended her gloved hand. "I'm Caleb Coulter's sister, Camrianne."

"I've heard a great deal about you," he replied, taking her hand. "Caleb is a good friend."

"These are my friends." Camri introduced them, not missing the particular way Micah looked at Kenzie. It seemed the redhead had caught his notice. Kenzie, however, had no interest whatsoever in him and quickly looked away.

"You all look to have survived the quake," he said, grinning. "Just San Francisco's way of welcoming you."

"Micah was most likely away at school last year when you visited," Pastor Fisher explained. "He went back east to study surgery. Now he's returned to us and is working with a group of doctors here in the city. They specialize in helping the poor."

"An admirable position." Camri pulled back her hand. "We've been looking for some clue that will help us find Caleb. Your father says you believe him to be away on family business. Why did you assume that?"

"I didn't assume anything. Caleb's employer told me."

Camri fought to keep her expression fixed. "Mr. Ambrewster told you he was away on family business?"

"Yes. Caleb failed to join me for our regular Friday night dinner. I thought perhaps he'd had to work late and simply forgotten to call, but when he didn't show up to church on Sunday, I knew something was wrong. I went to his office and spoke with Ambrewster, who told me Caleb had some pressing family matter and had left the city. He had no idea when he would return. I asked where I could reach Caleb, but Ambrewster told me he didn't know. I'm sorry to say I've been so busy with my cases that I haven't had a chance to try to contact Caleb. I suppose I presumed he would soon return to the city."

"That is very strange. There was no family matter for Caleb to see to, and I'm not at all sure why Mr. Ambrewster would say such a thing. When I spoke with Mr. Ambrewster the other evening, he told me he had no idea where Caleb had gone. He thought perhaps he had eloped."

"Eloped?" Micah replied. "Caleb was seeing no one special, certainly no one with whom he'd elope."

"Mr. Ambrewster said he was quite taken with the sister of a man called Patrick Murdock."

"Yes, Murdock has a sister. Her name is Ophelia, and Caleb

knew her well, but I assure you that any feelings were all on the side of Miss Murdock. Caleb represented her brother when he was falsely accused of murder, and Miss Murdock saw him as a heroic prince rescuing him from certain death." Micah smiled. "There was nothing more to it. Caleb was kind to her—even helpful while Murdock was in jail—but I assure you he wasn't in love."

"Still, I would like to talk to her. Do you have her address?"

Micah shook his head. "No, but I believe I can get it for you. One of the doctors I work with is her physician."

"Thank you, I'd be grateful."

"Miss Coulter, it would be our honor to have you and your friends share lunch with us," Mrs. Fisher interjected. "It would be nice to hear of your journey."

"That's very kind, Mrs. Fisher."

"It's our pleasure," Pastor Fisher declared. "Let us finish saying good-bye to our friends here, and then we can walk over to the house."

Camri knew the parsonage was just behind the church and nodded. "Is that all right with you two?" she asked Kenzie and Judith as the pastor and his family moved away to speak to others.

"I'd prefer to return home, if you don't mind," Kenzie replied. "I can get there myself, so you don't need to give up your afternoon." She didn't wait for Camri or Judith's response, heading across the sanctuary without another word.

Camri looked at Judith. "How about you?"

"I'm more than happy to come," Judith replied. She lowered her voice to a whisper. "Luncheon with a handsome man is always preferable to my own company."

Camri smiled in spite of herself. "He is rather dashing, but I'm much more attracted to the fact that he was Caleb's good friend. Hopefully he'll think of something that will help our search."

Patrick Murdock sat across their tiny table from his sister, Ophelia. He was a tall, broad-shouldered Irishman whose quick wit could match any man's. In his younger years he'd been known to fight for money, but the appeal of that had faded with each passing year and new responsibility. And now that their father was dead, there were plenty of responsibilities.

"You're for sure gonna waste away if ye don't eat," Ophelia admonished.

He looked up and smiled. "And do I really look as if that's possible?"

She smiled. "I suppose not." She got up and went to the cupboard. "I'll be needin' more brandy for the Christmas pudding." She opened a bottle and poured the last few drops of its contents on a rounded bag where the pudding was keeping and curing for its unveiling at Christmas dinner.

In years gone by, Patrick had watched their mother do the same. Ophelia had copied her recipe and upheld the tradition in the nine years since their mother's passing.

"I'll see if I can't find ye a bottle," Patrick said, getting up from the table. "My thanks for the stew. It was hot and fillin' and all that a man could want from a meal." He could have eaten at least three more bowls, had there been any stew left. Their meager meals were necessary, however, due to his limited pay. Some days they had little more than oatmeal and soda bread purchased from his landlady.

Since losing the construction business his father had started, Patrick had done well just to keep a roof over their heads. Had Ophelia not hidden his tools when the creditors came, Patrick wouldn't even be able to complete the occasional odd job. Jobs doing what he knew and loved were now refused him. Construction jobs of any kind were only had with the approval of the powerful men who ran the city. They dictated who could work and who couldn't. Patrick had been lucky to pick up work here and there with friends since the conclusion of the trial. He was even luckier that Caleb Coulter had been able to save him from being branded a murderer.

"I'm gonna lie down for a spell," Ophelia said, coming to him. She stretched up on tiptoe and kissed his cheek. "Ye'd do well to take a bit of a rest yourself."

"Now, don't go worryin' for me." He smiled and kissed the top of her reddish-blond head. "I'm perfectly capable of seein' to myself."

She nodded. "Aye, that's true enough." She coughed and pulled her shawl a little tighter around her thin body.

Patrick watched her walk away. She went to the bedroom and closed the door, leaving him to wonder how much longer she'd be with him. She had the same consumptive disease that had taken their mother nine years earlier. Perhaps she'd even caught it from Ma.

He tried not to think about how life would be once Ophelia was gone. She was the last of his family. Oh, there were some aunts and uncles in Ireland along with their children, but no one Patrick knew all that well. His parents had married and moved to America the year before Patrick was born. He'd never even met his father and mother's siblings.

Settling into a wooden chair by the stove, Patrick frowned. Since Caleb Coulter had disappeared, Patrick hadn't had a moment without worry. His fear was that Caleb's disappearance was his fault. His friend had agitated the entire city on Patrick's behalf.

He might still be here if not for me.

It tormented Patrick day and night. Was Caleb dead? If not, then where was he? Had he been shanghaied and forced from the country? Everyone knew sailors and no-name men were drugged and forced to work as slave labor on ships bound for the Orient. Those ships were gone for months, even years, and the men were seldom heard from again. If that had been Caleb's fate, how would Patrick ever be able to prove it—to settle whether Caleb was dead or alive?

No matter how Patrick considered it, Caleb's ongoing absence only made the situation more desperate. He owed his life to this man, and yet he seemed unable to do anything to help him.

There has to be a way. I have to find him—even if he's dead. I have to find him.

CHAPTER 6

*T*he next day, after long hours of packing candy for Mr. Lake, Camri was surprised to arrive home to company. Henry Ambrewster's 1904 Winton and driver were parked along the curb, while Ambrewster waited for her in the front room. He had a huge bouquet of flowers in his hands and a smile on his face.

At Camri's appearance, he jumped to his feet. "I hope you will forgive the unannounced visit."

Kenzie and Judith quickly excused themselves and hurried upstairs while Camri pulled off her gloves. "What can I do for you, Mr. Ambrewster?"

He extended the bouquet. "First of all, I brought these for you. And second, I thought you were going to call me Henry." His tone was a mixture of enamored suitor and reprimanding father.

She looked at the lovely arrangement of flowers and smiled. "How kind. I'll ring for Mrs. Wong. Did she offer you refreshment?"

"She did, but I hope to entice you to join me for supper. I have reservations at the Cliff House. I don't know if you've yet eaten there, but it is one of the finest places San Francisco has to offer, and the view must be experienced to be believed. Sunset is the best hour. Not only that, but they have the most amazing chocolate drink. It's a Guittard creation. Are you familiar with Guittard chocolate?"

Camri hesitated to take the flowers. "Not really. I only know the name because Mr. Lake is certain they wish his demise."

As if anticipating her need, Mrs. Wong appeared in the doorway before Camri could ring.

"Mr. Ambrewster has brought these lovely flowers and I wondered if you would be so kind as to put them in water?" Camri asked.

Mrs. Wong nodded. Camri took the flowers, pausing only long enough to smell them before handing them off to the housekeeper. "Mmm, they have a very sweet scent."

"You eat here tonight?" Mrs. Wong asked.

"Yes." Camri glanced over her shoulder at Ambrewster. "I'm much too tired to venture out, I'm afraid."

"Mr. Ambrewster eat here too?"

Camri didn't give him a chance to reply. "No, Mr. Ambrewster has reservations elsewhere." Mrs. Wong gave another nod and hurried away. Camri could see that her conversation hadn't pleased the older man. "I am sorry, but I've been working since dawn and long only for a hot bath and a quiet supper." She unbuttoned her coat. "I also need to write a letter to my parents."

"I cannot pretend I'm not disappointed, but I do understand." He helped her with her coat and laid it over the back of the nearest chair. "It seems so strange to me that young women desire to work for themselves these days. In my younger years, we were taught that women were to be cherished and cared for."

"Yes, well, it's my opinion that both genders should be cherished and cared for in some manner." Camri gave him a patient smile. "What can I do for you?"

"I came hoping to discuss your brother."

"Have you learned something new?" She removed her hat and sat it on top of her coat, watching Ambrewster with guarded interest.

"Let's sit, and I'll tell you what I know."

She allowed him to lead her to the sofa but then took her brother's chair instead. "Please continue."

Ambrewster sat on the sofa alone. His expression changed to worry. "I'm afraid I don't have good news."

"Any news at this point is useful."

"Well, I went through your brother's papers and files in the office."

"You're only just now doing that? It's been over three months since he disappeared."

"I went through them before, but there were other records that I wasn't aware of. Caleb kept meticulous notes and ledgers, but it seems some of his dealings were less documented. Dealings in which I had no involvement."

"What do you mean?"

He leaned back and shrugged. "As I mentioned before, this town is full of deception and graft. I fear that it's possible Caleb was caught up in it."

"Are you suggesting my brother had illegal transactions?" She tried to keep the emotion from her voice. After what Micah told her on Sunday, she was suspicious of anything Henry Ambrewster had to say. However, she didn't want to reveal herself too soon. As Father had often said when dealing with dishonesty, *"Give a man enough rope, and he'll hang himself."*

"I don't know. I found some things that made little sense to me. However, the connection to certain nefarious characters can't be ignored. As I mentioned to you, Caleb represented a young man who stood trial for murder. Our firm handled their company's legal dealings, and when Mr. Murdock was arrested, Caleb insisted we help him. It wasn't in Caleb's normal duties to handle a trial, but there was no talking him out of it. At the time, I just saw it as a kindness. No one expected the young man to be found innocent."

"My brother must have, or he'd never have taken the case."

"Nevertheless, it's possible that the jury and judge were persuaded to find him innocent."

Camri shook her head. "Am I to understand that you believe my brother bought people off in order to win Mr. Murdock's freedom?"

"It's possible."

She'd heard enough. "You cannot say such things and have any real understanding of my brother's heart. Caleb is first and foremost a man of God. His faith isn't something he practices on Sunday alone. He lives daily with God's Word to guide him. He would never allow such corruption to enter into his life."

Ambrewster held up his hands as if to ward off her words. "I know this is difficult to imagine, but I wouldn't mention it if I didn't have proof. I was very fond of Caleb."

"Was? You speak as if he's dead. Do you know something more than you're telling me?" She fought to control her fears.

"Of course not. I didn't mean it that way. But people do change, and perhaps your brother set himself upon a different course. If he was involved with some of the men mentioned in his notes, then he might well have met with trouble, and sadly enough, it could very well lead to his death."

Camri felt her temper rise. "Mr. Ambrewster, I don't know what kind of game you're playing. I would like to know why you are telling me this now, when just a few months ago you told Dr. Micah Fisher that Caleb had gone home on family business."

Ambrewster dropped his gaze to the floor. "I'm not . . . well,

I'm not sure who this Dr. Fisher is or when I had a chance to speak with him."

"He's Caleb's friend, and he came to your office the Monday after Caleb went missing."

He looked up, nodding. "Yes. I remember him now. He came at the close of day and asked for Caleb. I had no idea who he was. I certainly wasn't going to tell him anything about Caleb. After all, he could have been there to cause him harm."

Camri raised a brow and cocked her head. "Why would you have thought anyone would want to harm my brother? You told me you've only just found these notes that suggest he was dealing with dangerous men."

"As a matter of practice, I don't give out information on anyone. I didn't know this Dr. Fisher, and it seemed wise at the time to suggest Caleb was merely away on family matters. If the doctor turned out to be the friend he said he was, then he would surely know how to reach Caleb in such an event. But instead he asked me for your family's address. I refused to give it, telling him I wasn't sure what the address was. I was merely protecting Caleb. After all, he'd just handled a difficult case weeks before, and some people were unhappy with the outcome."

"But you said nothing of this when we first spoke. Instead you suggested his interests were with a girl—that perhaps he'd eloped."

Ambrewster composed himself and smiled. "My dear Camri, you must understand. You are a member of the weaker gender, and I felt an obligation to protect you from the uglier aspects of life. I didn't wish to alarm you."

She stiffened. "Mr. Ambrewster, this is 1905, and I am neither weak, nor in need of protecting. I've spent my life in Chicago, and my work with the suffrage movement and women's concerns is well documented. I have seen more than my share of the uglier aspects of life. I've also become very good at discerning lies."

His brow furrowed as he frowned. For a moment, it seemed he would say nothing more, but just as Camri was ready to dismiss him, he got to his feet and paced back and forth in front of her.

"You must understand, I knew very little about you. Caleb had mentioned having a sister, but we spoke very little of his family. I was in Europe when you visited last summer, so I had no chance to meet any of you. However, I knew Caleb well enough to know that he would want me to protect you and your folks from any possible harm. Harm that might arise from his having made powerful men unhappy.

"In San Francisco, these men are not used to meeting with obstacles and being told they can't have their way. They do whatever is required to meet their desires. Your brother came up against them while helping Mr. Murdock."

"But if my brother was against them, why are you now concerned that he was working with them? Come, Mr. Ambrewster you aren't making sense. You're contradicting yourself at every turn."

He stopped midstep, and his face paled. "There are rival parties of politicians, and each has their supporters. These men are corrupt beyond comparison. It is possible that during the trial, one group struck a deal with your brother. I say this only because it was quite unexpected that Mr. Murdock was found not guilty. It's been suggested to me that your brother may have been offered something that he couldn't refuse, and in turn Mr. Murdock was found innocent. I'm sorry to say that juries and judges are bought off all the time."

Camri didn't like the way the conversation had gone. What if Ambrewster was right and Caleb had angered the wrong people?

Ambrewster sat back down on the edge of the sofa. "The powerful men of this town will stop at nothing to maintain their positions. Positions, I might add, that go all the way up to the mayoral office. Mr. Murdock meant little to them. I truly believe he was nothing more than an example to other small businesses that were considering opposing them. It's possible that they had a change of heart and paid off the jury and the judge in order to . . ."

He fell silent, but Camri could see the pain in his expression. Maybe she had misjudged him. Maybe he was telling her the truth, or at least his perception of it.

"In order to gain my brother's favor?" Camri asked.

He released a heavy breath. "I don't know. It's all speculation. I don't like to think of Caleb working with them, but there are things I can't explain."

"Such as?" She gripped the leather arms of her chair as her anxiety increased.

"As I mentioned . . . there are Caleb's notes and records." He lifted his face to meet her gaze. "There's also the matter of a great deal of money I found in your brother's desk."

She swallowed the lump in her throat. "What money?"

"Ten thousand dollars in a locked box in one of his desk drawers. When I initially looked through his things, I had no reason to open the box, but since your appearance I decided to be more thorough. Caleb had no reason to have such a sum. Unless, of course, you know something. Did your parents perhaps wire him money?"

Dread washed over Camri and threatened to cut off her breath. "No." She shook her head, but continued to hold Ambrewster's gaze. "They never sent him any such sum. They couldn't have afforded it."

"So there you are. The only thing I can assume is that the money came from those who could afford to spare it. The men at the top of this city."

She was still shaking her head. "But Caleb would never . . .

he wouldn't." She cleared her throat and got to her feet. "My brother would never work with dishonest men, not even to see an innocent man set free. He just wouldn't do that, Mr. Ambrewster." Tears came to her eyes, and she fought to retain control. "You'll have to excuse me. Please show yourself out."

CHAPTER 7

Henry Ambrewster didn't like the way things were shaping up in regard to Caleb. He had always been fond of the young man—had planned to make him a full partner. Even now the papers were signed and ready to present.

At the curb outside Caleb's house, his driver waited beside the open car door. "Good evening, sir. Shall I take you to the Cliff House?"

"No. Take me to my club." He climbed into the back of the Winton and tried to formulate a plan.

Henry knew the political machine created by Abe Ruef and Mayor Schmitz, and he'd had more than one run-in with their representatives. They were the strongest of all the political factions. If you wanted to succeed in San Francisco, you needed to court these men and agree to their terms. Henry had done all he could to avoid them. Still, at times he found it necessary to operate just inside of the law in order to meet their demands. It hadn't been easy, and it certainly hadn't always gone the way he wanted. Sometimes legalities were skirted. Other times they were ignored altogether, and Henry felt there was little he could do but go along with the matter.

In the past, money and political favor had soothed Henry's conscience. What little conscience he had. When his wife had been alive, he'd been more inclined to attend church and give the appearance of being a God-fearing man, but after her death, none of that seemed important. When Caleb came into his life, the young man reminded Henry of the things he'd left behind. Spiritual things—deep introspective desires to be a better man, to serve God. But now Caleb was gone, and his sister was here to search for answers, and Henry was awakened to another desire that had been left behind—for a wife and companion. Someone who could ease his loneliness. If he could find out what happened to Caleb, perhaps Camri would be so grateful that she'd see him as a potential mate.

The car stopped, and the driver quickly jumped out to open the door for Henry. He stood at attention while Henry straightened his necktie. "Pick me up at nine."

"Yes, sir." The driver waited until Henry had stepped away from the car to close the door.

Henry turned back. "Oh, and Charles, go to my tobacconist and procure some pipe tobacco for me. He'll know the kind."

"Yes, sir."

With that, Henry made his way into the club and handed his coat and hat over to the man handling the coatroom. A refined older gentleman greeted him almost immediately.

"Mr. Ambrewster, we're honored to have you with us tonight."

"Thank you, Masters. I'd like to take dinner."

"Very good, sir. We offer a seafood platter with scallops, mussels, and lobster, or a T-bone steak precisely two inches thick. Both are served with sides of asparagus and baked potatoes."

"I'll take the steak. Rare."

"Very good, sir."

"Oh, please call and cancel my reservation at the Cliff House." Henry started to go, then paused. "Who's here tonight that I might have business with?" It wasn't uncommon for newly arrived gentlemen to ask such a question. Masters kept a ready knowledge of who was in attendance and how they related to other members.

"Mr. Johnston is in the Green Room."

Henry nodded. "Then that's where I'll be. Have dinner brought there."

"Very good, sir." The refined butler gave a slight bow before departing.

The Green Room was located upstairs at the end of the hall. It was a room in which one could hold a private meeting or simply read the newspaper. Decorated, as most of the club was, in rich leather and wood furnishings, the room also boasted a private bar and a large stone fireplace that was always lit in the evenings no matter the weather or temperature.

Henry preferred this room to almost any other at the club. He had conducted many a business meeting here and had often taken his meals here as well. It was quiet, and any gaming attractions such as cards or billiards were off-limits.

A uniformed doorman opened the highly polished door as Henry approached. "Good evening, Mr. Ambrewster."

Henry nodded. He couldn't remember the young man's name, but Masters saw to it that the staff knew every member by sight. Henry was never sure how Masters did it, but if any staff member failed to acknowledge members by name, they were immediately dismissed without reference. If only all businesses and homes could be run with such efficiency. It was said that more than one member had tried to woo Masters away from the club with outrageous offers of money, property, and other benefits, but Masters was loyal to the club and his position. Henry also knew that the owner was privy to all those offers and saw to it that Masters was amply rewarded for his allegiance.

Frederick Johnston sat reading at the far end of the room, away from the fireplace and a gathering of several men. Henry had no desire to speak to anyone save Johnston and kept his distance, lest he have to acknowledge the other men's presence and join in their conversation. Thankfully, they were too caught up in their discussion to even notice Henry.

"Good evening, Fred. I wonder if I could take a moment of your time?" Henry asked, taking a seat opposite him.

He had known Johnston since long before Henry's sister Margarite had married Fred's younger brother, Nicholas. Frederick had a reputation for two things. Ruthless and underhanded business deals that always benefited his bank account, and a French mistress whose beauty was renowned around the world. It was rumored that she was of royal blood. It was also well known that when Johnston traveled, he took her along, whether or not his wife was also in attendance. Henry had heard that the amount of money settled on the wife for her cooperation was equivalent to the bank balance of some small nations.

Johnston put down his book. "What's troubling you, Henry?"

"I'll get right to the point. I had a young man working for me. Caleb Coulter."

"Yes, the one who went to battle for that Irish contractor accused of murder."

"Exactly. Well, he disappeared in late August."

"And you're just now curious as to where he's gone?" Johnston raised a brow.

Henry shook his head. "I've tried to find him. I'm convinced it wasn't of his own doing, but . . ."

"But?" Johnston eyed him curiously.

"But I fear the kind of trouble I might attract. It's recently come to my attention that Caleb was doing some work for your rivals. Given his background and character, I found this very hard to believe, but I discovered certain records."

"And you fear that something went amiss and your young man met with trouble?"

"I don't really know what to think. I hired a man to find Caleb, but he reported that there were absolutely no clues as to where he'd gone. The detective came highly recommended, and I'm afraid after he gave up, I was hard-pressed to know what else I could do. With Caleb gone, my workload doubled, and I had very little time to focus on the matter. But it wasn't for a lack of concern or desire to do so."

"If Ruef's people took him, there probably won't be any clues." Johnston pursed his lips, then ran a finger along his mustache. "I'll make inquiries, although I wouldn't hold out much hope now that so much time has passed. But why the sudden interest?"

"Caleb's sister has come to town to find him. Her parents sent her, and she is an independent and determined young woman."

Frederick's expression changed to one of understanding. "And is she also beautiful?"

Henry felt like an uncomfortable schoolboy. "Yes. She is that." He hesitated, then decided it did no harm to confess his feelings. "I find myself quite attracted to her."

"So finding her brother might well win you her heart."

"It might." Henry shrugged. "However, I care about Caleb as well. When he first disappeared, I gave his office a cursory examination. After all, I had to take up his cases and see that all matters were being handled properly. As I said, I've been busy. I've often worked until late in the evening, and with so much to handle, I simply stopped worrying about Caleb. I suppose part of me feared he was dead and that attempting further investigation might well bring me to the same end."

"Has anyone threatened you, Henry?"

"No, but now that I'm asking for your help, I fear they may."

Johnston frowned and studied Henry for a moment. His scrutiny made Henry even more uncomfortable. He supposed it would be best to tell him everything.

Leaning forward, Henry whispered, "Fred, I found ten thousand dollars in a lockbox hidden in Caleb's desk. There's no reason he should have had that kind of money. Someone is going to want it back."

Frederick nodded. "I understand." He steepled his fingers. "The matter intrigues me, and I love a good mystery. Very well, Henry. Don't worry about Ruef and his thugs. He knows better than to create problems for people close to me. While we are hardly friends, you could say Ruef and I are cooperative enemies." He got to his feet and straightened his coat. "I suppose the first order of business will be to find out who's missing ten thousand dollars."

———

Judith sneezed for the twentieth time in two hours. She felt miserable—bad enough that she'd remained home instead of going to work at the candy factory. No doubt Mr. Lake would be completely undone by her absence. The poor little man had stressed their deadline over and over.

She put a damp cloth to her head and closed her eyes. Hopefully the cold would pass quickly. Mrs. Wong had made her some tea that she swore had curative powers. Judith didn't know if this was true, but it tasted bad enough to be medicinal.

When the doorbell sounded, Judith got to her feet and set the cloth aside. Mrs. Wong had told her that she'd be busy with the laundry, and Judith had promised to see to anyone who came calling. She made her way to the hall, fighting off a wave of dizziness.

She opened the door to a rush of chilly air and Micah Fisher. "Mr . . . Dr. Fish . . . Fish . . . *achoo*!" She barely had time to cover her mouth with her handkerchief. "I do apologize. I've managed to catch cold."

"Good thing I'm a doctor." He held up his black bag. "Why don't you invite me in, and I'll see if I can help you?"

"You're welcome to come in, but I doubt there's much to be done. Mrs. Wong made me a tea that is supposed to help, and Camri admonished me to take a hot bath. I've done both, and neither seems to have made me feel any better."

To her surprise, Micah reached out and felt her forehead. "Good, you don't have a fever." He escorted her back to the front room and sat her down facing the window. He set his hat aside and unlatched his bag. "Now, open your mouth."

She did so and waited patiently as he peered inside. As bad as she felt, Judith found she wasn't even unnerved by how handsome he was. This only served to make her certain she must be dying.

Micah felt her face, pressing slightly on the ridges of her cheeks and between her brows. She winced.

"Painful?" he asked.

"Tender."

He nodded. "I don't think it's all that serious. I have some powders that might help relieve your misery. Mix them in a glass of warm water and take yourself to bed. You'll probably feel miserable for another day or two, but rest and fluids will soon get you back on your feet."

"Thank you." She smiled as he fished a packet of medicine from his black bag. "What brought you to visit us? I'm afraid I'm the only one home. Camri and Kenzie are both at work."

"Last Sunday I promised I would try to find an address for Ophelia and Patrick Murdock. I managed to acquire that today and thought I would bring it by." He handed her the medicine, then reached into his coat. "It's not in a very good part of town, so if Miss Coulter can wait until Sunday afternoon, I would be happy to drive her there." He gave Judith a folded piece of paper.

She opened the paper and studied the address a moment, but her eyes refused to focus for long. She refolded the note. "I'll give it to Camri the minute she returns."

He smiled and closed his bag. "You should just leave it with the housekeeper and take yourself to bed." He pointed to the medicine. "After you take that, of course."

Judith nodded. "I will do just that. Thank you for your kindness."

"It's easy to be kind when the recipient is so lovely."

She felt her face grow hot—no doubt as red as her nose. She started to reply, but before she could speak, she sneezed three times in a row. So much for being lovely.

Dr. Micah Fisher left as quickly as he'd arrived, and Judith found herself almost forgetting why he'd come in the first place. She looked at the note and packet of medicine in her hands and decided both required a trip downstairs to the kitchen. Hopefully Mrs. Wong would be able to help.

Judith made her way slowly down the back stairs, wishing she were already in bed. She paused at the bottom step, wishing that her vision would clear and the dizziness would leave her. Through the door, she heard Mr. and Mrs. Wong having a heated discussion.

"We cannot tell," Mrs. Wong declared. "Too dangerous."

"But if we not tell, then bigger trouble may come."

Judith frowned. What in the world were they talking about?

"You see what happened. You know danger," Mrs. Wong continued. "I think it our fault. We cannot speak of it."

Judith felt another sneeze coming on and did her best to appear as though she were just coming downstairs. "*Achoo!*" She entered the kitchen with her handkerchief up to her nose.

The Wongs looked up from where they sat at the table folding laundry. Mrs. Wong jumped to her feet. "You sick. You should go to bed."

"I plan to. Dr. Fisher stopped by and gave me this address for Camri, as well as medicine for me to take. He said I should leave the note with you and take this powder in hot water. He said rest and fluids would help me most."

Mrs. Wong's worried expression softened. She nodded and took the note. "I do that for you. You go to bed, and I bring hot water."

Judith smiled, trying her best not to give away her concern about what the couple had been discussing. Whatever the topic, they both seemed anxious. She had barely climbed to the third step when she heard Mrs. Wong start up the conversation again, this time in hushed Chinese. It was strange, but then again, everything seemed that way, given how she felt.

"It's probably nothing to do with the rest of us," she murmured upon reaching her bedroom. "Probably nothing at all."

CHAPTER 8

*I*t was late by the time Camri and Kenzie returned home that night. To appease Mr. Lake and keep him from firing Judith, they had agreed to stay and work an extra four hours. It wasn't entirely necessary, since both women knew that Mr. Lake's paranoia about who he could trust coupled with the large number of orders he had yet to fulfill would keep him from dismissing Judith. But it didn't stop him from threatening to, and Kenzie and Camri had agreed it would be best to make the offer. After the initial rant, Mr. Lake finally calmed and returned to his office, leaving them to get their work done.

And work they did. They didn't even pause for lunch, but ate apples and cheese at their workstation. Exhausted didn't even begin to describe how Camri felt. She longed for a hot bath but feared she might fall asleep in the tub and drown.

"Miss Judith say to give you this," Mrs. Wong told her as Camri shed her coat and hat.

"What is it?" She took the note.

"It address you wanted, but Mr. Wong say it bad place and you should not go alone."

Camri unfolded the paper. It was an address for Ophelia Murdock. "Oh, thank you."

"Husband say he take you if you need to go."

Camri nodded. "Well, it won't be tonight. I haven't the energy for it." She covered a yawn with her gloved hand. "Oh, I forgot about my gloves." She pulled them off.

"Where Miss Kenzie?"

"She headed straight upstairs. We agreed she could take a bath first. Do you suppose you could bring us a little supper on a tray? I think once I shed these clothes and bathe, I'm not going to have the strength to come back down to the dining room."

"I do that, sure." Mrs. Wong smiled and took the gloves Camri held. "You go now. I see to everything."

Camri nodded and made her way upstairs. She had planned to go directly to her room, but realized she should check on Judith. She gave a light knock, then opened the door without waiting for any reply.

Judith lay propped up in her bed with her eyes closed. She opened them as Camri peered into the room. "I'm not sleeping," she called out.

"How are you feeling?"

"A little better. Dr. Fisher said it wasn't all that bad. He gave me some medicine and told me to rest for a couple days and drink plenty of fluids."

Camri moved to the side of the bed. "Mrs. Wong gave me his note. Did Dr. Fisher say anything about it?"

"Just that you shouldn't go there alone. I guess it's not in a very good neighborhood."

"That's what Mrs. Wong said. She told me Mr. Wong would take me."

"Dr. Fisher said the same thing. He said if you could wait until Sunday afternoon, he would drive you there himself."

Camri shook her head. "I don't want to wait that long. I

feel like I've done precious little to find Caleb as it is. Work consumes much more of my time than I'd hoped. I may have to wire home for some money and quit the job."

"Maybe the Murdocks will be able to help you, Camri. Don't be too hard on yourself. You've done more than you realize."

Camri yawned and nodded. "I think I'll see if Kenzie is done with her bath. I'll tell Mr. Lake that you're under doctor's orders to stay in bed."

"No, I'm sure I'll feel more like myself tomorrow. I can't have you and Kenzie staying late on my account."

Camri smiled. "How did you know that's what we did?"

"Kenzie told me. She stopped by on her way to her room." Judith smiled. "I appreciate what you did to keep me from being fired."

"It's not a problem. We agreed to be in this together, and it has been such a blessing to me that you and Kenzie would allow my search for Caleb to come first."

Judith shrugged. "Well, he might be hurt or sick or in some other kind of peril. My search is not nearly so dire."

"Be that as it may, I appreciate it all the same. We will find your aunt as soon as possible."

She left Judith and made her way to her own bedroom. With what little strength she had left, Camri undressed and pulled on her robe. She put the address in her purse and then made her way to the bathroom. Thankfully, Kenzie had finished, and the room was still steamy and warm.

Camri drew a bath, poured in some salts, and then sank into the claw-foot tub. The hot water soothed her aching muscles. Teaching at the women's college had never required much physical labor. The candy factory, on the other hand, did. Today she and Kenzie had carried packing boxes from the warehouse to their work table. The young men who usually saw to that task were busy elsewhere, and there was no alternative. The same became true for loading the finished boxes on the pallets. All in all, Camri had never worked so hard in all her life.

"And I never want to have to again," she murmured. This was why an education was vital. Women should never have to work in factories.

Even as she had the thought, Camri had to smile. She had a master's degree and yet was working a factory job.

Difficult times bring about difficult solutions.

At least Mr. Lake was paying them well. He had accepted a huge number of orders, delighted to have taken business from the likes of Ghirardelli and Guittard. The only thing he hadn't stopped to consider was that he was hardly staffed for such an increase in production. At least the busyness kept him from focusing on his belief that he was being sabotaged by those rival gentlemen. But that paranoia also kept him from hiring additional workers.

Camri felt herself growing groggy and knew she couldn't remain in the bath or she'd fall asleep for sure. Reluctantly, she pulled the plug and climbed out of the tub. She dried quickly and pulled on her nightgown and robe. Back in her room, she found a tray of food left by Mrs. Wong, but instead of eating, she stretched out on her bed. Thinking of Caleb was the last thing she remembered.

Camri left work early the following day despite Mr. Lake's protests. She finally calmed him by promising to work late the next day. With Mr. Wong in the driver's seat of a small rickety wagon, Camri saw an entirely different side of San Francisco as they made their way to the address Micah had provided.

She had been warned about the decadence and perversion, and thankfully Mr. Wong did what he could to avoid those seedier areas, but the poor and dejected people could not be avoided. As they made their way deeper into the heart of San Francisco's poverty-stricken neighborhoods, Camri was reminded of the poor in Chicago. No matter where you went, the signs were the same. The buildings were unpainted and looked like they might be toppled by a good stiff wind. Children dressed in rags ran through the streets, chasing skeletal dogs. Women could be seen in various stages of work, many with a child on their hip and another two or three at their knee. Men were scarce at this hour of the day. Most were working at whatever meager living they could make, but no doubt a fair number were hidden inside their hovels, drinking to forget the conditions around them. What marked all of the people even more than the filth and disarray was the look of hopelessness in their eyes.

"This the place," Mr. Wong said, pointing to a three-story wood building.

Camri studied it for a moment, then climbed down from the wagon. "Wait here. I shouldn't be long."

"You want me go with you?"

She heard the wailing screams of a baby and the barking of several dogs. Somewhere nearby, a woman and man were yelling at each other, while all around the neighborhood, the noise of daily living filled the air. So too did the stench.

"No. I'll be fine." She straightened her shoulders and marched with determination toward the building. She was doing this for Caleb, she reminded herself.

The entryway to the building was surprisingly clean. The interior held the musky smell of unwashed bodies and garbage, but Camri had dealt with worse. She put her distaste aside and made her way to the apartment number given in the address. Thankfully it was on the first floor, not far from the entry.

For a moment she stared at the door. What was she hoping to find here? Despite Ambrewster's casual implication that Caleb might have forsaken his family for Ophelia Murdock, Camri didn't believe that had happened. Still, she had felt that speaking with the young woman was important enough to risk her own safety.

She drew a deep breath and knocked. She waited, listening for the sound of someone coming to the door or at least calling out from the other side. When no one came, she raised her hand to knock again just as the door swung back and a broad-shouldered man filled the opening. He wore his reddish-brown hair a little longer than was fashionable and had a well-trimmed beard and mustache. His blue eyes seemed to sparkle as a smile broke across his face.

"And to what would I be owin' the pleasure of yer visit?"

She lost herself in the beautiful lilt of his Irish brogue. He just watched her, his smile never waning. "I'm . . . ah . . . I'm Miss Coulter." Her senses began to return. "Caleb Coulter's sister."

The effect was immediate. His smile faded, and a look of concern crossed his face. "Come in." He stepped back.

Camri wasn't sure it was the wise thing to do, but she'd come this far and felt she must see the matter through. She stepped inside and glanced around the room. It wasn't all that large, but it held a kitchen on one side and a sparsely furnished living area on the other. There was no sign of the woman she'd come to see.

She turned back to face the man who had let her in. "I . . . I'd hoped to speak with Miss Ophelia Murdock."

"I'd be her brother, Patrick," he said, extending his hand.

Camri shook his hand and forced a smile. "Is she at home?"

"Aye. She is that. Let me fetch her." He started for a door across the room, then stopped. "Can I ask ye why ye've come?"

"I'm trying to find my brother. We've heard nothing from him in over three months, and my parents sent me to San Francisco to look for him."

He shook his head. "That wasn't their wisest decision."

Camri bristled. "Why not? My brother is missing, and someone has to find him. Caleb and I are very close, and I know he wouldn't just disappear and say nothing."

"Aye, I can believe that. Caleb is most considerate." Murdock leaned back against the wall and studied her for a moment. "But I doubt he'd want his sister risking her life to find him."

"Why do you say it that way? Do you know something that suggests it's a risk to search for him?"

He folded his arms across his chest. "'Twould seem only reasonable that risk is involved, no? Logic suggests that a responsible man doesn't just disappear without there being the threat of trouble."

Camri had reached the limit of her patience. Her fear was replaced by anger. "Are you going to let me speak to your sister or not?"

"Ophelia can't help ye. I'd be more use to ye than she would, but I'll call her."

He watched her for a moment longer, then pushed off the wall and went to the door at the back of the room. He didn't knock or bother to call out, instead disappearing inside. Camri heard muffled talk, and then the big man returned.

"She'll be pleased to meet ye in a few minutes. Why don't ye sit down, and I'll make ye a cup of tea."

"No, that's all right. I don't need tea. I just need to find my brother." Camri drew a deep breath to steady her nerves. "What, if anything, do you know about his disappearance, Mr. Murdock?"

"Call me Patrick." He motioned for her to take a seat at the small table.

She knew she'd already put him on his guard, so rather than argue, she did as he asked. "Very well, Patrick. Please call me Camri. It's short for Camrianne."

He smiled and pulled out a chair for her. "An unusual name for an unusual lass."

Camri took her seat, not knowing whether he was complimenting or making fun of her, and a minute later a petite young woman came to join them. She was thin and pale—obviously sick. Her reddish-blond hair hung limp and disheveled. Patrick quickly went to her side and helped her to a chair.

"I'm Ophelia," she said with a smile. She clutched a large shawl close. "Patrick tells me ye'd be Caleb's sister."

"Yes. My name is Camri."

"How pretty." Ophelia smiled, but her pale blue eyes held none of the joy that her lips suggested. "Patrick said ye're here to find Caleb."

"That's right. He hasn't been in touch with me for over three months. Our parents are extremely worried. They would have come themselves, but they're both ill and weak."

"Aye, I know how that is." Ophelia shook her head. "But I don't know why ye'd be comin' to me to find Caleb."

"Well, in one of my conversations with Caleb's employer, Mr. Ambrewster, he suggested that Caleb might have eloped."

"Eloped?" Patrick asked before Ophelia could respond. "And just who would he be runnin' off with?"

"Your sister, Ophelia."

He roared with laughter. "Ambrewster said that, did he?"

"Well, at first." She didn't like Patrick laughing at her but reminded herself that taking offense wouldn't help her find Caleb. "He said Caleb was interested in Ophelia—in helping her and . . . well, I don't really remember what all was said."

"Your brother is dear to me," Ophelia replied. "I fancied myself in love with him, but it was all on my part. He never knew, or if he did, he was gracious enough to overlook my silliness. He's just a good friend, lendin' a hand when one was needed."

"That sounds like Caleb."

Patrick picked up the conversation. "My sister is sick, as ye can probably see for yourself. Caleb was good to bring doctors around, and when I was in jail, he looked after her."

"I heard about your being falsely accused of murder. I'm glad my brother was able to help you." Camri kept her focus on the business at hand. "I don't want to pry, but I need to know anything you can tell me that might help find him."

Patrick shook his head. "There isn't much to tell. I owe him my life, and that's why I've been lookin' for him."

Camri's eyes widened. "You've been looking for him?"

"Aye. He's a good friend."

She nodded, eager for him to continue. "Have you found anything that might point us to where he is . . . to what happened?"

"I'm sorry, no." His expression darkened. "But I'm fearin' the outcome won't be good. Your brother upset a great many powerful men by defending me."

"But why? Can you tell me exactly what happened to put you in jail and why Caleb would be in danger because of it?" Camri knew what Ambrewster had told her, but since the lawyer seemed to have several stories, she needed to hear it from someone else.

Patrick leaned back against the wall. "Aye, I'll tell ye. How far back do ye want me to go?"

"Ah . . . I understand you and your father worked together. Why don't you start there?"

Patrick gave her a stern nod. "We had a construction business—mostly commercial. A very successful one, for a couple of Irishmen. We were good at what we did, and there was no cuttin' of corners to save a few pennies. We had men we trusted workin' for us, and we put in long hours to meet our deadlines."

Camri nodded. She wasn't sure why he felt the need to convince her of their worth, but apparently it was important.

"We were to be puttin' up a large buildin' downtown—a new

hotel. The man who wanted it was from New York City. He had made all the proper arrangements with those in charge—Ruef and his bullies."

"The papers say there are accusations against Ruef and the mayor."

"Aye, and we pray God that they are made to account for their deeds." Patrick nodded toward the small stove in the kitchen. "Are ye sure ye won't be takin' a cup of tea?"

"No. Please just continue."

"Our da was a proud man. He feared no one and did the work he was paid to do. I followed in his footsteps, and he taught me to be a man of integrity. The trouble started when some fellas came to us, tellin' us that they'd make it worth our while to revisit our original plans and reduce the cost by usin' less costly materials. Da said he would only use the best available to him, because he had made a name doin' so. These fellas came callin' more than once, and each time things got a little more heated. I tried to step in and make it clear to them that we weren't goin' to be pushed around. It wasn't so long after that when Da was killed."

"He fell from a high place at the construction site?"

Patrick scowled. "He didn't fall. He was pushed. It was murder, and I was determined to prove it, but I ruffled the feathers of Ruef and his men. I was pretty certain who was responsible for the actual deed and made no bones about sayin' so. Next thing I knew, the man turned up dead, and the police came to arrest me for it."

"But for sure Patrick was innocent," Ophelia added. "He could never hurt a lamb." She smiled at him as if he had hung the moon and stars.

Camri felt a kinship with the younger woman. Her own regard for Caleb was much the same. "My brother believed that too, or he would never have defended him."

Ophelia nodded. "He did. They were good friends after that."

"Aye. We are good friends."

Camri turned to Patrick. His blue eyes seemed to peer deep into her soul. "I appreciate that you speak of him as being alive. I'm sure he must be. I think I'd know if he were dead. It may sound silly, but we're very close."

Patrick nodded. "He said as much."

For a moment no one spoke, and despite the setting, Camri found herself feeling safe and in the presence of friends. It surprised her to find such comfort with strangers.

Then Patrick broke the silence. "I believe he's alive. I don't know where, but I feel that he is. Otherwise I wouldn't be lookin' for him."

"But you've found nothing?"

"Not yet. But I won't give up."

Camri nodded. "Neither will I." She looked at Ophelia and smiled. "I know we'll find him, and who knows, maybe one day he'll return your feelings, Ophelia." She was surprised to find that she didn't mind the idea of her brother falling in love with the impoverished Irish girl.

"Nay, it will never be," Ophelia said with great resignation.

"You don't know that," Camri countered. She gave Ophelia's hand a gentle pat. "You're a beautiful young woman with a sweet spirit."

"But a spirit that will soon be taken up to God." Ophelia squeezed Camri's hand.

Camri shook her head. "What?" No other words would come.

Ophelia gave her a sad smile. "I'm dyin'. The doctor said I haven't long."

The words struck Camri like a slap across the face. Surely the doctors were wrong. There must be something they could do. She looked at Patrick, who had already turned away. The truth was apparently as hard for him to accept as it was for Camri.

CHAPTER 9

*A*fter church on Sunday, Camri cornered Micah Fisher to thank him for the Murdocks' address.

"Mr. Wong took me, and I met with Ophelia and her brother, Patrick."

The handsome doctor beamed at her. "They're good people. I'm glad you didn't go alone, however. The poorer neighborhoods can be dangerous. A hungry man will do most anything to get food, especially if he needs to feed a family."

Camri nodded, but the risk was the least of her concerns. "Ophelia . . . she says she's dying."

Micah's smile faded. "Yes. She has tuberculosis."

"But she seemed to breathe just fine and didn't cough even once while I was there."

"Hers is what we call 'extra-pulmonary.' It affects other parts of her body. Even so, her lungs have been compromised from the disease."

"And is there truly no hope? Can't something be done?"

"Every attempt was made. She's been sick for some time, but the added stress of losing her father and then her brother being jailed . . . well, it took its toll. They lost everything, and while Patrick was in jail there was no money for doctors and treatments. When Caleb found out she wasn't getting proper care, he stepped in and started taking her to her appointments and getting her medicine, but it was too late."

Camri felt a deep sorrow. "She's such a sweet woman—and so young."

Micah nodded. "I wish I could offer some glimmer of hope, but I haven't got one. The poor in this town suffer many woes, and disease is just a daily part of their lives."

"Caleb said there were troubles with bubonic plague in the last few years."

"We have ongoing cases. We've done what we can to quarantine people and clean up their living conditions, but so many reside in situations that can't be improved. And disease comes to port with every ship."

"I do understand that. Chicago also has its share of the poor, and while we don't have an ocean, we do have Lake Michigan, which is vast. I'm sure the two cities have more in common than we might think."

"No doubt. But tell me, were you able to get any news regarding Caleb from Patrick and Ophelia?"

Camri shook her head, doing her best not to sound as hopeless as she felt. "Patrick did say that he's been trying to find Caleb on his own."

"That doesn't surprise me. Caleb saved his life. If he'd been convicted of murder, he would have surely been sentenced to die." Micah lightly touched her arm. "Don't forget, I'm looking into this as well. I've talked to many people and will continue to do so."

"Thank you. It's a relief to know that. Mr. Ambrewster assured me that he's looking into the matter as well. I don't feel I can truly trust him, however."

"It's good to be cautious. This is a town of lies and liars."

On their walk home, Camri told Judith and Kenzie all that she'd discussed with Micah. She couldn't shake the sadness she felt over Ophelia's condition.

"I wish I could do something for her."

"Be her friend," Judith suggested. "Friends are always needed at times like these."

Kenzie agreed. "I'm sure it's hard to be so weak you can't leave the house. You would grow very weary of being confined. Perhaps you can visit her—take her some books to read."

"I don't even know if she can read. I wouldn't want to make her feel worse." Camri shook her head. "I just wish I knew what might comfort her."

"Why don't you ask him?" Kenzie said, pointing to the front steps that led up to their home.

Seeing Patrick sitting there caused Camri to misstep. Judith righted her just before she completely lost her balance.

"Thank you. That would have been embarrassing." Camri straightened, noting that Patrick had jumped to his feet at her near accident.

"G'day to ye, ladies," he said, tipping his hat. "I hope ye'll be forgivin' the intrusion."

Camri looked at Judith and then Kenzie. "This is Mr. Patrick Murdock."

Kenzie nodded. "I recognized you from Camri's description. I'm Miss Gifford."

"Ye look to be a fine Irish lass," he replied, taking off his hat and giving a bow.

"Scottish," Kenzie countered.

"Ah, then we're all but cousins." He looked at Judith. "And who might ye be?"

She laughed. "I'm Judith Gladstone, and I love the way you talk. Are you from Ireland?"

"I was born here in America, but me da and ma were both

Irish and came to this country when they were young. We've always lived among folks from the old country, and it just seemed natural to speak as they do."

For a moment no one said anything else, and Camri took that opportunity to speak up. "I'm sure you came today with a purpose, Mr. Murdock."

"Ye agreed to be callin' me Patrick," he reprimanded.

Camri couldn't help but smile. He could irritate her, but also amuse. "Patrick, would you care to stay for lunch? I know the girls and I are famished, and Mrs. Wong promised us a nice roast." He looked hesitant, and Camri quickly added, "I know there will be more than enough. So much, in fact, that I will send some home with you for Ophelia." She knew the size of the roast might not be quite as big as she boasted, but she would see to it that he had something to take to his sister, even if she sent her own share. "Speaking of which, you should have brought her."

"She could never have made the walk, but thank ye for your kindness. For sure, I will join ye."

They made their way inside with Patrick bringing up the rear. Camri introduced him to Mrs. Wong and then asked the housekeeper to set another place at the table.

At first Camri worried about how comfortable Patrick might be seated at their dining table, given his living conditions, but then she remembered that the Murdocks were once better off. Perhaps not rich, but certainly capable of furnishing a decent house.

Patrick appeared completely at ease, and Kenzie and Judith did as well. They posed a variety of questions about his Irish roots and parents, and Patrick seemed more than happy to answer them.

"I've never been to Ireland, but I had plans to go," he said after loading his plate with food. "Me ma was quite homesick.

She had family there, as did Da, and she longed for a visit. When the construction business started doing well, Da decided to take us back for a trip. But it didn't happen."

"Why?" Judith asked.

"Our ma took sick. She was never all that well. She died before Da could take her home."

"How sad," Kenzie murmured.

"Aye. It was a sad day indeed. Never a day goes by that I don't think of her and miss her laughter." Patrick glanced around the table. "I'm supposin' we say grace at this table?"

Camri gave a nod. "I'll pray." She bowed her head. "Father, we thank You for the bounty You've provided as well as the company. We ask Your blessings on Patrick and his sister, Ophelia. We ask for guidance as we seek to find my brother, and wisdom for our daily living. Amen."

"Amen," Judith and Kenzie murmured. Patrick said nothing and instead began to eat.

The conversation covered the sermon and the pleasant but chilly day. Camri wondered why Patrick had come. He said very little as they ate but seemed to enjoy the discussion. When they had finished eating, Judith and Kenzie dismissed themselves and left Camri and Patrick to make their way to the front sitting room, where Mr. Wong had prepared the fireplace. The warmth from the fire welcomed them like a friend.

Camri wasted no time. "Have a seat and tell me why you came."

He grinned. "You're right to the point. Are ye in a rush to be rid of me?"

She shrugged. "It seems you must have come with a reason, and since you didn't reveal it at lunch, I thought perhaps you desired for us to be alone."

He chuckled. "Aye, I can't deny that desire."

Camri was momentarily taken aback by his tone. Was he

actually insinuating his interest in her, or was he simply playing on her words? She started to sit in her brother's chair, then instead offered it to Patrick.

"I'm sure this chair would be to your liking. It's Caleb's favorite."

Patrick sat and smiled as he gripped the leather arms. "And for certain it's a fine chair. Fit for a large man."

Camri took a seat on the sofa. Her corset was tight and made relaxing impossible, so she maintained her perch on the edge of the cushioned seat. "I spoke with Dr. Fisher today at church. He told me your sister has tuberculosis." Patrick looked at her blankly, so she added, "You might call it consumption."

He frowned. "I know full well what tuberculosis is. It took our ma's life."

"I'm sorry. I realize your circumstances probably didn't allow for you to have an extended education, so I was just trying to simplify."

He leaned back. "I see. From where I'm sittin', it sounded more like ye were puttin' on airs."

Camri stiffened. "It's not putting on airs to support education. I know from your stories at dinner that your family spent a great many years in poverty. You said that your education ended before graduating high school. So many young men have been forced to do exactly that, while young women aren't encouraged to attend school for any other reason than to find a husband."

"And ye disapprove of husbands?"

"Of course not." She knew her tone betrayed her irritation. "But I do disapprove of them being the reason girls stop attending school. Education is important, Mr. Murdock—Patrick." Hopefully using his first name would stave off his belief that she was putting on airs. "I've fought long and hard to see women better themselves."

"Better themselves according to your standards of better?"

The conversation had taken a turn Camri hadn't anticipated. She knew he had come here for a reason other than this debate, and after all, what could she expect from him? His background hardly gave him reason to appreciate the benefits of an education.

"I believe we've gotten off onto a rocky path." She forced a smile. "You didn't come here to hear my support of education."

"No, but now that we're discussin' it, ye might be givin' me a chance to speak my thoughts."

Camri folded her hands and kept her gaze fixed on them. "If you wish to discuss education, I am more than happy to comply. However, I would rather ask after your sister and how she's feeling."

Patrick was silent for so long that Camri glanced up. She found him watching her with a stoic expression on his face. She wasn't sure what he was thinking, nor could she figure out his mood. It made her uncomfortable. She was usually astute at reading people.

"Ophelia enjoyed your visit," Patrick finally said. "She takes to her bed more and more these days, and havin' someone near to her own age to pay a call cheered her day. I had come in part to thank ye for that, and to ask ye to come again soon."

Camri nodded, hoping they could put aside the previous irritations. "It was my pleasure, and I'd be happy to come again. I was just discussing my desire to do something for your sister on our walk home from church. Can I bring her something?"

"Yourself would be enough. She hasn't many needs this world can accommodate."

"What about sweets? I could bring her some chocolate. I work at one of the factories."

"Truly? That hardly seems the place for a college-educated woman." His tone dripped with sarcasm.

She tried not to reveal the needling effect his words had on her.

"A wise person does whatever she must in order to accomplish her goal. I came here to search for Caleb. This requires money, and while our parents are comfortably settled and I had a good savings set aside from teaching, this town is expensive. Besides, I agreed to help Judith and Kenzie with their own searches."

"Well, at least you're not too proud to help a friend."

Her anger returned, and she found it impossible to remain silent. "I'm not proud, but if I were, there is nothing wrong with taking pride in knowledge. God encourages knowledge and wisdom."

"He also makes it clear that pride goeth before a fall. Ye might do well to be rememberin' that and to realize that some folks have knowledge and wisdom that don't come from book learnin'. Ophelia, for example. She has a heart of gold and has more Scripture memorized than most clergy. She knows a lot about usin' herbs for cookin' and healin'. Is that somethin' you're an authority on?"

He didn't wait for her reply but continued. "There's a whole world of folk, Miss Coulter, who haven't the opportunities in life that ye've had yourself. It wasn't for a lack of desire, but for the place the good Lord put them in life. Maybe ye should be instructin' God as to what ye think best rather than telling it to me."

Camri found words failed her. She had never been taken to task in such a manner. Patrick's words struck a chord, however, and she regretted how she'd treated him. She had been presumptuous and condescending.

But rather than give her time to apologize, Patrick got to his feet. "I'll be goin'. It's not good to leave Ophelia for too long, despite our neighbors bein' good to look in on her."

He headed for the front door, and Camri could do nothing but follow him. She started to speak while he donned his coat, but she wasn't at all sure of herself. Should she apologize? Should she try to explain further?

Patrick opened the front door with one hand while pushing his hat onto his head with the other. He stepped out onto the portico and turned. "I'll keep lookin' for Caleb unless ye feel I'm too uneducated for the task."

He left Camri standing at the door, still unable to speak her mind. She watched him walk down the street until he disappeared around a corner. It was only then that guilt began to wash over her in undulating waves.

"Lord, I don't know what got into me. I'm sorry for my prideful behavior." She sighed. Father had always told them that just as it was wrong to look down on others for their circumstances and limitations, it was wrong to be prideful of your accomplishments and see yourself as their better. She was ashamed for the way she'd acted and knew that her mother and father would have been too.

She closed the door and leaned against it. There was nothing she could do to take back her words or attitude, but that didn't remove the necessity of giving Patrick Murdock an apology. She owed him that much.

CHAPTER

10

I told you! I told you! Someone is out to ruin me," George Lake declared as he ran in circles around his ransacked office. He pulled off his wire-rimmed glasses and wiped them with his handkerchief while sweat ran down his face. "It's an utter disaster. Who knows where they have their spies?"

Camri looked at the mess of papers and overturned furniture. Even the filing cabinets had been opened and emptied. It seemed George Lake had good reason for his anxiety and suspicions.

Kenzie was already on the floor, picking up papers. "Cousin George, do you have any idea who would want to see you ruined?"

This caused him to halt. He replaced his glasses, nodding. "Of course. It must be Ghirardelli or Guittard's people. I've told you that at least a dozen times before. It's why I must be cautious about who I allow to work for me. There must be a spy—but who?"

Camri started to point out that with as small an operation as George Lake ran, he could hardly be much of a threat. She doubted his yearly profits were even a tenth of what the larger companies realized. But seeing how upset he was, she decided to keep that thought to herself.

Judith pointed at the broken window. "This must be how they got into the office."

Mr. Lake nodded. "They were after my recipes, but they didn't get them." He pointed to his head. "I have them all up here and in a bank box. No one is going to steal my secrets."

"Did you call the police?" Camri asked.

"I did. They came and made their notes and left again. They said it looked like nothing more than a random burglary. Apparently other businesses in the area were also burgled. Probably in an effort to disguise their attack on me."

Camri righted one of the small tables. "You can't know that for certain."

"You sound like the police," Mr. Lake countered in exasperation. "I'm telling you, the other factories want to put an end to my work. I'm a clear threat to their success. No doubt they've learned about the new products I've been creating."

"The new fillings for the boxed candies?" Kenzie asked.

"Yes." Mr. Lake began to pace again. "I knew it would come to this. I'll have to hire some guards. Oh, but who can be trusted?"

He continued ranting, but Camri found her thoughts on other matters. "I suppose," she interrupted, "it would be wise if we got to work. After all, you have many orders that need to be filled before the close of day."

"Yes. Yes." He waved at her. "Go on. Get to work. This mess is mine to set straight."

Kenzie got to her feet with her stack of papers. "Don't worry, Cousin George. I'll come during my lunch break and straighten up. You have other things to tend to."

He looked at her for a moment, then nodded. "You are kindness itself. I must write to your mother and tell her how grateful I am for sending you to me."

Kenzie ignored the compliment and put the order forms and invoices on his desk.

"Now, ladies, we must get to work. Christmas is soon upon us!"

The girls made their way to the processing room, where newly made chocolates waited to be boxed. Camri's thoughts kept returning to Patrick and his reprimand. She didn't understand why he had so completely upset her. If she was wise, she'd avoid him altogether, but his help could prove invaluable in finding Caleb. And then there was the issue of his sister. Patrick had encouraged Camri to visit Ophelia, and who could deny a dying woman?

"I love the smell of chocolate," Judith said, pulling Camri from her introspection. "When I was a little girl, I remember begging my mother to buy me some when we were in town. We so seldom went to town that I was already beyond excited, but when we passed the candy store, I thought I was in a dream. I pressed my nose against the glass to better see the candy. My mother finally agreed to go inside, and I can still remember the smell of the chocolate. It reminds me of her now."

"You must miss her a great deal," Kenzie said, tying ribbon around a finished box.

"I do. She and my father were the only family I had. How I longed for brothers and sisters." She frowned. "I don't know why Mother told me there was no one left. I wish I'd known about her sister sooner. I suppose, however, if she had wanted me to know, she would have said something." Judith pushed a box of candy toward Kenzie.

"Well, before you know it, we will have found Caleb, and then we can locate your aunt." Camri got up to fetch additional boxes of loose chocolates. She glanced down the table. "Where are the strawberry creams?"

"Right here," Judith replied, pointing to the box closest to Kenzie. "And the lemon is next to those."

Camri carefully removed the nearly empty boxes and replaced them with the full ones. She put the last pieces of candy from the old boxes atop the new and moved down the line to do the same for the other varieties.

And so the morning passed. When lunchtime came, Kenzie disappeared into her cousin's office and worked on the mess. Camri had considered offering her assistance, but she and Judith had already promised Mrs. Wong that they would pick up some groceries. It would be far easier to get them now than after work.

By the time Camri and Judith did their shopping and returned, Kenzie had managed to put her cousin's office in good order. There were still stacks of papers to sort through, but Kenzie had managed to get a head start on that as well.

Camri unbuttoned her coat. "You have a talent for organization."

"That's exactly what I told her," Mr. Lake declared, coming in behind them. "I've never had such order to my office."

"I did work at a library," Kenzie offered. "I know a bit about organizing files."

"That's exactly why I'm taking you off chocolate work and putting you in charge of my office. The way you handled taking those orders a few minutes ago, as well as all that you've done here, makes me realize I'm wasting your talents."

"You're going to work in the office now?" Judith asked.

Camri frowned but lowered her head so no one would see. If anyone should have been placed in the office, it should have been her. She was the one who had an education and experience in running offices. She ran an entire department back at the women's college in Chicago.

Kenzie was saying something, but Camri missed it. She tried not to allow her feelings of jealousy but wasn't able to squash them. She hated boxing chocolates, and had she known Mr.

Lake was contemplating having someone take over his office, she would have volunteered.

Why am I thinking this way? I'm only working this job to support the household until I find Caleb. There's no sense in being jealous. Kenzie will remain here in San Francisco once I've accomplished what I came here to do. It isn't like I'm staying. And even if I were, I wouldn't work at the chocolate factory.

She went back to work with Judith and tried to improve her spirits. Mr. Lake brought them one of the boys from the factory who'd helped them when they first arrived. He took over keeping them supplied with chocolates as well as securing the ribbons on the finished boxes. He was twice as fast as Kenzie. He tried to make small talk with the girls, but while Judith enjoyed this, Camri did not.

By the end of the workday, Camri was wearier of her envy and petty thinking than she was of the physical labor. She had prayed at least a dozen times for God's help, only to find herself wallowing in self-pity once more. In Chicago, she had been esteemed—highly regarded and all but put on a pedestal to be admired by all. Was that what this was about? She was glad no one could read her thoughts.

The trio gathered their things to leave, but before they made it to the door, Mr. Lake appeared. His spirits were considerably lighter than they had been earlier that day. "Girls, I nearly forgot. I have something to give you." He pulled some slips of paper from his pocket. "These are three tickets to a play that shows tonight. I'm certain you'll enjoy the diversion."

Camri looked at the ticket he handed her. "*The College Widow*. I've heard of it but haven't seen it."

"Neither have I," Kenzie admitted.

"I've never been to a play," Judith said with such a look of delight that Camri knew they'd have to go.

"I was given the tickets," Mr. Lake admitted with a rare smile. "I hope you'll go and enjoy yourselves."

"Thank you, Mr. Lake," Camri said. "I'm glad to see that you're in better spirits."

"I am. I am. I got word from a good friend of four strong young men he can send to work for me starting tomorrow. They're lads he trusts with his life, and therefore I can trust them with my candy. Two shall stand guard at night, and the other two will help with production. Now we can go about our business with less concern." He motioned to the tickets. "Now, go have fun."

"Oh, do say we can go," Judith interjected, looking at Camri and Kenzie.

"Of course. We'll go and have a very nice time," Kenzie answered before Camri had a chance. "But we'd best be on our way, or we'll have very little time to change our clothes, have dinner, and still make the curtain rising."

"I'm so excited. Thank you, Mr. Lake!" Judith surprised them all by hugging the small man. Her action rendered Lake speechless for the first time since they'd met him.

The ladies rushed to catch their trolley. If sheer desire could have hurried their journey, Camri knew they would have made it in record time. All the way home, Judith chattered about the play and what she would wear. Her enthusiasm helped Camri forget her sour mood and smile. By the time they'd finished dinner, Camri was nearly as excited as Judith. A play was probably just the thing she needed.

At the end of the second act, Camri excused herself and made her way to the ladies' room. She had enjoyed the comical antics of the players very much. The story was funny, and the enthusiasm of the audience had taken her mind off her troubles.

Of course, it was impossible not to think of Caleb. He loved a good play and had taken her to several during their summer visit. Many times that evening, Camri had felt guilty for enjoying herself when Caleb's condition was still unknown. He was her reason for being here—not plays.

As she headed back to her seat, Camri startled at hearing her name called. She turned to find Mr. Ambrewster and another gentleman making their way toward her. They were dressed impeccably in stylish suits, looking for all the world as if they'd just stepped from their tailor's shop.

Camri smiled as they drew near. "I'm surprised to see you, Mr. Ambrewster."

He smiled. "I could say the same. I was afraid you weren't allowing yourself any pleasures at all. I know your brother would be delighted that you were taking a bit of time away from worrying about him."

"I admit to feeling guilty, but I know you're right. Caleb would be the first to applaud my actions."

Henry turned to his friend. "Miss Coulter, may I present Frederick Johnston? His brother is married to my sister, so you might say we're family."

She looked up at the distinguished man. Everything from the cut of his suit to the highly polished leather of his shoes suggested this was a man of means. "Mr. Johnston."

"I told Fred about our search for Caleb, and he's agreed to help. He has many connections in parts of the city with which I'm unfamiliar."

Camri wondered if Mr. Johnston might be able to get to the bottom of her brother's disappearance. There was a look of intelligence about him and, as she'd already surmised, one of money. Still, he had no reason to care about finding Caleb.

"Mr. Johnston, I'm very grateful. Our parents are heartsick with worry over my brother's disappearance." She hesitated a moment. "I hope you won't be offended by my outspoken nature, but I must add that I cannot afford to pay much for a search."

He studied her for a moment, then gave a slight smile. "You don't offend in the least, Miss Coulter. I find it refreshing that a young woman would be so direct and yet . . . gracious. Let me put your mind at ease. I neither require your money nor expect it. I am happy to lend my aid. Henry tells me you've heard nothing in three months."

She breathed a sigh of relief at his reply. "It's now nearly four. He was always faithful to write each month, and our last letter was in August. Henry and my brother's friends pinpoint his disappearance at the end of August. His house servants confirm this as well."

"And you have no idea what might have happened?" Johnston asked, his gaze never leaving her face.

"None. There was no mention in his letters of any trouble or pleasures that might cause him to forget himself and his duties. I know my brother has not willingly left his home and employment."

Johnston nodded. "I am sorry, Miss Coulter. I'll do whatever I can to find answers for you. However, you must allow that after all this time, those answers may not be what you want to hear."

Camri frowned. "I realize that, but his disappearance was not what I wanted to hear either. I would rather know the truth, whatever it might be, than continue in ignorance."

Johnston reached into his pocket, took out a card, and extended it to Camri. "Take this. Should you need to reach me and Henry is not available, you may call my secretary. He will see that I get your message in a timely fashion. Again, I am sorry. I know this must be difficult for you. I will do my best to find out what I can."

Camri accepted the card, and as she did, Henry took her

gloved hand and patted it. "Camri, I assure you that together we will leave no stone unturned. Caleb may have found his way into trouble, but Fred is a powerful ally, and you can trust him to be a man of his word."

Camri pulled back her hand, careful not to lose the card. "I appreciate your concerns and the help you've both offered. Now, however, I must get back to my friends before the third act begins."

She hurried back to her seat with a mixed sense of gratitude and uneasiness. Mr. Johnston appeared to be sincere in his offer, but she still didn't trust Henry Ambrewster. He had lied to her, even if it was to keep her from worrying. Lies of any kind didn't sit well with her. Trust had always been an important issue to Camri, and maybe the most important element of any relationship.

"Ye need to be honest with her," Ophelia told her brother. "Ye know that it never serves ye well to lie."

"I haven't lied. I just haven't told her everything. There's no dishonesty in that." But even as Patrick spoke, he felt guilt well up inside.

Ophelia pulled her shawl closer as they sat near the stove, discussing Caleb and Camri. "There are sins of omission, ye know. Ye should just tell her everythin' and trust the good Lord to take care of the rest."

"And for sure ye'd be doin' it that way, but me and the good Lord are having a bit of a donnybrook."

She giggled at this. "You're not makin' out very well, are ye?"

Patrick rolled his eyes. "Leave off with it."

"I won't. Ye can't blame me for wantin' ye to make peace with God. After all, I'm soon to join Him, and it would break my heart if ye weren't goin' to follow."

Patrick felt his anger drain. He could see the dark halo around her eyes. Every day she slipped a little closer to the grave. "I'm sorry, Ophelia. My mood is not one for company."

"I know you're frettin' about Caleb, but more's to be accomplished in prayer than worry."

"I remember Ma sayin' that." He smiled and put his arm around her.

"'Tis true," Ophelia said, smiling up at him. "You're a good man and brother, Paddy, but ye need to make right with God. He's not to be blamed for our troubles. That'd be on the devil himself."

"Aye. But God allowed for it. Ye can't be sayin' He's all powerful and not accept that."

Ophelia looked back to the stove. "God is all powerful, but the devil and man are always interferin'. The world is full of sin, Paddy, but ye don't have to be addin' to it. Tell Camri the truth of what ye did and what ye know. Tell her lest someone else do it."

"I'll tell her when the time is right, and not until." He got up and stretched. "I'm thinkin' it's time for bed. I've got work tomorrow, helpin' Mr. Flannery muck out stables down south of the city. I'll be headin' out early and back late. Folks'll be checkin' in on ye through the day and bringin' ye somethin' to eat as well."

"I'm happy to call it a day," she said. "I've housekeepin' and cookin' to do on the morrow. Maybe even a little dancin' in the evening."

Patrick picked her up and hugged her close. "You're a treasure, Ophelia. Ye always make me smile. I wish ye could be well enough to tend to all those things—especially the dancin'."

She kissed his cheek. "I will be soon enough. And don't ye be frettin' for me. I know ye'll miss me just like we miss Ma and Da, but once ye let go of yer anger with God, ye'll be confident of seein' us again in heaven. And I'll be a dancin' there for sure."

"Aye," he murmured, feeling tears dampen his eyes. He didn't want to think about losing Ophelia, and yet even now, holding her skeletal body in his arms, he knew he could do nothing to stop it.

She's all I have left, Lord, but You're goin' to take her anyway. Ye might be all powerful, but Ye don't seem all that kind. How am I to make peace with Ye when Ye seem only to want to hurt me?

That night Patrick tossed and turned in his sleep. He dreamed of his father's death and the anger he'd taken on, knowing that someone had murdered him. He dreamed too of Caleb and his disappearance. Then, against his will, he dreamed of Camri Coulter. He saw them arm in arm, walking along a rocky shore. She was laughing, happy to be with him, and in his dream, he knew they were in love. But then everything went terribly wrong, and Camri was ripped from his arms and taken away, while some of the men he'd blamed for his father's death began to beat him. They demanded he forget about the Coulters, then left him battered and bleeding, facedown in the sand.

Patrick gave up on sleep just before dawn. There was no sense staying abed, enduring nightmares and thrashing about, while his dying sister slept just feet away. At least his noise hadn't seemed to bother her, and for that he was grateful. The last thing he wanted to do was rob Ophelia of peace.

In the kitchen, Patrick put on the kettle for tea and then made a small pot of oatmeal. He'd eat his portion and leave the rest for Ophelia. Hopefully she'd feel like eating something. Mrs. Ryan, the landlady, had promised to come first thing that morning. She would see the cereal and try to entice Ophelia to have some. Patrick didn't imagine Mrs. Ryan would have much success.

The kettle began to whistle, and Patrick took it from the burner. He felt swallowed up in sorrow. The doctor had told them Ophelia wouldn't last out the year, and the end of December was only a few weeks away. How could he say good-bye to her? She was all that was left to him of Ma and Da. He heaved a sigh. He felt so helpless.

Glancing heavenward, Patrick shook his head. "Lord, I know I've been a bitter man, but if Ye could just see Yer way to helpin' Ophelia, I'd be grateful. If keepin' her from pain means takin' her, then I'm willin' to let her go. I wouldn't see her suffer."

He ran his fingers through his unruly hair and sighed. "I'm tryin' to let go my anger, but Lord, Ye know all the wrong that's been done to my family. I don't understand why Ye let it happen this way, and it troubles me deep in my spirit. You're supposed to be lovin' and full of justice and mercy, but I don't see any of that. Please help me. Let our name be vindicated. Let me reclaim the company our Da built."

Thoughts of Camri came to mind. She was a feisty one to be sure—just like his ma. He had felt the attraction between them, but he also knew it was impossible for anything to ever come of it.

"Help me keep my heart guarded. I don't want to make problems where none exist. Give me strength to do what I must do. And Lord, let me find Caleb . . . alive."

CHAPTER

11

The next morning at breakfast, Camri shared with Judith and Kenzie about her encounter with Ambrewster and Johnston.

"Mr. Johnston seems to be a moneyed and influential individual, to hear Mr. Ambrewster tell it. I've never heard of him myself." Camri shrugged and helped herself to some scrambled eggs and a couple pieces of bacon. She placed her napkin in her lap and continued to tell Judith and Kenzie her thoughts on the matter. "Mr. Johnston seemed quite willing to help— Mr. Ambrewster, too. Of course, I have no way of knowing if they're being honest with me." She began to butter a piece of toast. "I'd like to believe Mr. Ambrewster, but he's already lied to me, and once my trust is lost, it's difficult to regain."

"I understand that," Kenzie said. She smiled at Mrs. Wong, who had just poured her a cup of tea. "Thank you." She waited until the housekeeper had left the room to continue. "If you can't have trust in a relationship, there is no need to have that relationship."

"But sometimes people lie for good reasons," Judith threw out. "Don't they? I mean, my mother lied to me about there being no other family alive. There must have been a good reason for that, don't you think?"

Camri stiffened. "I don't think lies are ever justified. Inevitably they cause pain or misunderstanding. The Bible says Satan is the Father of Lies. If they are his work, they can't be good."

"I suppose not," Judith said with a sigh. "I just don't like to think of my mother being a bad person." She picked up her fork and began to eat.

"It's possible your mother lied because any remaining family was bad and might harm you." Kenzie seemed far more interested in Judith's situation than the ongoing issue of Caleb. "I've seen families that way. Most were pure evil, while one or two were loving and trustworthy. Maybe that's why your mother lied to you."

Camri realized she'd made Judith feel bad and quickly agreed. "Kenzie is right. Some parents make it a goal to shield their children from the past."

"But that isn't how it sounded in the letter I found," Judith said, putting her fork down again.

Camri considered this for a moment. "You keep mentioning a letter. Do you have it? Can you share it with us?"

Judith nodded. "I keep it close because . . . well, it's all I have to go on. It puzzles and intrigues me at the same time."

"Please share it with us," Kenzie encouraged. "After all, we want to help you locate this missing aunt. There's nothing that says we can't be watchful and investigative while looking for Camri's brother."

Judith pulled the letter from her skirt pocket. "I found it in my mother's things. After she died, I knew that everything would have to be sold. There were debts," she said, lowering her gaze in shame.

"People often have debts these days," Kenzie countered. "Frankly, I blame the banking system. The eastern banks kept lending rates low for their own people and charged outrageous interest for farmers and ranchers in the West. If it weren't for the ability to renegotiate mortgage rates every year, many would lose everything to debt."

Camri couldn't keep the surprise from her voice. "You certainly know a great deal about banking practices."

Kenzie frowned. "My former fiancé was very informative." She looked at Judith. "Please continue."

Judith stared at the letter in her hands rather than at her friends. "We were never wealthy. In fact, we mostly just got by. Not really in poverty, but . . ." She shook her head and finally glanced up. "We did all right, but we were so alone. My parents always kept to themselves. I suppose it was partly because we lived so far from town. My mother schooled me at home, so I never made friends either. In fact, I can honestly say that you two are my only friends in the world."

"Didn't you go to church?" Camri asked before realizing her question might stir up trouble.

"No. My parents weren't churchgoers, but we did say grace." Judith gave the hint of a smile. "And we celebrated Christmas. After all, we were Christians."

Camri refrained from pointing out that celebrating Christmas didn't make one a Christian. There would be time enough to speak to Judith about the gospel of Jesus and how one could be truly saved.

"When it was certain my mother would die, her creditors came calling. It was heartless, but they were determined to get their money or fair share of what little we had in possessions. I didn't want Mother upset further, so I told them there would be an auction after her funeral and bid them wait until that time."

"And they were willing?" Kenzie asked.

Judith nodded. "I think they realized there was precious little to be had save the actual land and house. We didn't have any animals save one ancient horse that did well to carry me to town to get Mother's medicine. Anyway, with Mother sleeping more, I began sorting through our meager possessions. However, I couldn't bring myself to go through her personal things until after the funeral. That's when I found the letter."

Camri tried not to sound impatient. "Why don't you share it with us?"

Judith unfolded the letter. "It starts, 'Dear Edith.'" She paused and looked up. "The name Edith Whitley was written on the envelope, but there was no address."

"Well, at least you have that much," Kenzie offered.

Judith cleared her throat and began to read. "'I know you must be surprised to receive word from me after all these years, but I learned that I am dying and felt I needed to make an appeal for your forgiveness. I know that what I did was unforgivable, but I hope you might find some way to manage a small bit of understanding and forgiveness for your sister.'"

She stopped and looked at Camri. "See, she makes it clear that this Edith is her sister, but Mother never said anything about having a sister. Not once in all my memory can I ever think of a time when she or my father mentioned this woman Edith."

Judith went back to the letter. "'My actions were done out of desperation. You know my reasons. I know I deserve only your reproach and bitter avoidance, but I hope that the years might have eased the rift between us.'" Judith glanced up. "Here's where she mentions me. 'Before I die, I long only to tell you that I am sorry, and yet those simple words are not enough to convey my deep regret for what I did. For Judith's sake, I hope you will forgive me and perhaps try to help her. After all, she is blameless in this matter.'" Judith paused. "That implies Edith knew about me. She knows she has a niece."

"But what did your mother do to need forgiveness?" Kenzie asked. "Does she ever say?"

Judith shook her head. "No, not really. She mentions some money being taken. I presume that Mother stole it from her sister, but then she goes on to acknowledge that the money isn't important. The rest of the letter is much the same. My mother apologizes and begs forgiveness, then clearly states that she knows such forgiveness is impossible. She ends the letter like this." Judith looked back down at the missive. "'Knowing the pain I caused you and the situation itself, I never came home. Leaving as I did was wrong, but returning seemed even worse. I don't know if you're still in San Francisco, but I pray you are and that this letter will reach you.'"

She stopped again. "Mother clearly didn't keep in touch with her family. She didn't even know if they were still in this city."

"Well, if something terrible happened—something so terrible your mother felt it was unpardonable—then it makes sense that she wouldn't have corresponded with her family." Camri nibbled her toast.

"Perhaps your mother stole your aunt's beau," Kenzie murmured. "Perhaps your aunt was engaged to be married—even preparing for her wedding—and your mother ran off with her fiancé."

Judith frowned. "That would be really bad."

Kenzie's pained expression suggested it would be the worst of sins. Camri's thoughts ran in a different direction, however.

"What if your mother ruined your aunt's reputation with lies? Or perhaps she said something about your aunt, either truth or lie, that was humiliating and should never have been shared. Or what if your mother did something, then let the blame fall on her sister?"

"That would be truly terrible—heartless even," Judith replied.

Kenzie's eyes narrowed. "She could have stolen your aunt's jewelry—maybe family jewelry."

"But Mother and Father were so poor," Judith countered.

"Yes, they were poor, but that doesn't mean your mother's family was poor. She mentions that money wasn't important. It's been my experience that only people with plenty of it feel that way. Do you know if your aunt was the elder of the two?"

"No. I know nothing save what's in this letter. I looked through every remaining scrap of paper in the house after finding it, but there wasn't another bit of evidence to support the existence of my aunt."

"Any number of things might have happened," Camri soothed. "It's even possible that whatever happened wasn't nearly the horrific sin your mother believed it to be."

"What do you mean?"

Camri shrugged. "I once invaded my brother's room as a child. He kept a porcelain owl in his window, a gift from an aging relative. For some reason I was fascinated with it and decided to investigate it. Unfortunately, I dropped it, and it shattered into a hundred pieces. I felt horrible and quickly hid what I'd done because I didn't want Caleb to hate me. In the days that followed, my guilt grew, and my self-condemnation threatened to eat me alive. I decided I had no choice but to confess my sin. When I did, Caleb laughed it off. He'd hated that owl but knew he was obligated to keep it. He actually thanked me for what I'd done. So you see, it might be possible that your mother did something wrong but not as terrible as she thought. Since she felt bad enough to run away from the situation, she had no way of knowing if forgiveness was ever given."

"Camri makes a good point," Kenzie said. She took a sip from her teacup. "When people refuse to face the truth and instead run away, it only makes matters worse."

Camri knew Kenzie was speaking of her own situation. "Did your fiancé never offer any explanation?"

Kenzie shook her head. "I never saw him again. My family knew my embarrassment was more than I could bear and sent me to stay with an aunt. My aunt let it slip that someone came to the house, and perhaps it was Arthur, but I'll never know for certain. If it was Arthur and he came to offer an explanation, I had no interest in hearing it. The damage was done, and I was a broken woman."

"You mustn't let a man have that kind of power over you." Camri pointed at Kenzie. "You alone have the power to control your heart and mind. Letting your former fiancé devastate you in this manner only gives him that power."

Kenzie looked at her as if she'd lost her mind. "You've never been in love, have you, Camri?"

Camri felt her cheeks flush. "Well . . . no. I haven't."

"Then you really don't know what you're talking about, and all the university and college classes in the world will not be able to explain it." Kenzie got up from the table. "There are matters of the heart both good and bad that are impossible to understand without personal experience, let alone teach."

She left the room, and Camri wallowed in her regret. "I've put my foot in my mouth once again."

"You didn't mean to," Judith consoled. She folded her letter and put it back in her pocket. "You've lived a different life than Kenzie and I. It doesn't make your life wrong or right. And it doesn't make ours bad or good. It's simply the way it is, and our different experiences should be seen as beneficial rather than something to be condemned."

Camri was humbled by Judith's words. "You're right. I often think myself so knowledgeable, yet I can see I have so much to learn."

Judith beamed. "Well, you're the one who says learning is important. We shall all keep learning what we can, and hopefully it will better us."

115

Camri gathered her things for work. She wanted to apologize to Kenzie. With each passing day, Camri was more and more aware of how different her thoughts and beliefs were from Kenzie's and Judith's. Camri had grown up in a family of intellectuals who valued education above everything else. Her parents and grandparents all had college educations. Camri had always known their attitudes were progressive, but being with Kenzie and Judith had driven that point home.

"Of course, there are things I know little about despite my education," she murmured to herself. "Love is definitely at the top of that list."

She'd never given herself time to fall in love. There had been brief encounters of interest. She'd even attended a handful of events on the arm of a would-be suitor, but nothing had ever come from it. Mostly because Camri hadn't allowed it. She wanted to be a woman of independent means and have a career that gave her the freedom most women lacked. Her family encouraged this as well, although her mother had said on more than one occasion that she hoped Camri might find a young man who shared her values and interests, just as her sister Catherine had done.

Camri gazed upward. "Lord, I need to repent of my pride once again. Please help me better understand people who don't believe as I do—who aren't inclined toward education as I am. I want to be a good friend to Kenzie and Judith." She sighed. She had never managed to make any real friends in life until now. Bosom companions required time and effort, and Camri had given her all to education and to her family. Now that she actually had friends, she found she enjoyed their company. She found their differences fascinating—even useful—most of the time.

"Help me apologize to Kenzie. I know she's hurting."

Camri checked her reflection before heading downstairs. She was still murmuring her prayer when she remembered she hadn't yet paid the Wongs. With Christmas fast approaching, she wanted to make sure their needs were taken care of, as well as those of the household.

She went to Caleb's office and opened one of his lower desk drawers. From there she took out a ledger and lockbox. Together with Judith and Kenzie, Camri had carefully calculated what they could afford to spend out of their pay for groceries, cable-car rides, and personal needs. Each of the women had agreed that their money should also be used to pay the Wongs. After the regular expenses were met, anything extra was allotted to aid the search for Caleb. Thankfully, everyone had been willing to help, which left them with a little cushion of money should an emergency arise.

Camri left the office and placed her things on a table near the door as Kenzie and Judith made their way downstairs.

"I'm going to pay the Wongs and give them the grocery money," she told them. "I'll be right back."

"It's raining, so I'm certainly in no hurry," Judith replied.

Kenzie said nothing, leaving Camri all the more certain that she should apologize. Perhaps later at work she would have a moment.

Camri made her way down the back servants' stairs. She heard the Wongs talking and remembered what Judith had said about how suspicious they were when she'd interrupted a previous discussion. At the sound of her brother's name, Camri stopped to listen.

"Mr. Caleb would not blame us," Mr. Wong said.

Camri frowned. What were they talking about? What would her brother not blame them for?

"But maybe he be here now if . . ." Mrs. Wong's words faded into a muffled sob.

So they did know something about Caleb's disappearance. But why were they not willing to tell her? Why, if they cared so much about him, didn't they share what they knew? After all, they were aware she had come solely to search for her brother. They surely realized that any information they had might be useful.

For a moment Camri wasn't certain what to do. She wanted to storm the room and demand they tell her what they knew, but even as she started to take a step, she stopped. The Wongs were extremely private. They would make some excuse for the situation—tell her it was a misunderstanding. And maybe it was. Camri had no right to jump to conclusions, but given the situation, wasn't she entitled to know what the Wongs knew about her brother's disappearance?

She drew a deep breath. She would simply go to them. Given that Mrs. Wong was crying, she would have an excuse to inquire what was wrong.

Camri took the few remaining steps with more confidence than she felt. She entered the kitchen, calling out to the Wongs. "Oh, you're right here. I've brought your pay and some money for the groceries and household."

She looked at the couple, whose eyes had widened at her appearance, but otherwise their expressions bore no other emotion.

Camri smiled and put the money on the table. "Is there anything you need from me before I go to work?"

The couple exchanged a glance, but Mrs. Wong shook her head. "We need nothing. You have good day. It raining, so you need umbrella."

Camri hid her disappointment and nodded. "Thank you. I'll be sure to take one."

She hesitated only a moment, hoping that one of them might suddenly offer up their information. When that didn't happen, she turned and made a hurried exit. Her mind was a flurry of thoughts and accusations. What did they know? Why weren't they being honest with her?

She rushed to join the others at the front door. "They know something," she said, pulling on her coat.

"What?" Judith asked.

Camri didn't bother to do up the buttons but instead grabbed her hat. She glanced over her shoulder. "The Wongs. You were right. They know something, but they aren't saying what."

Kenzie frowned but said nothing, while Judith nodded. "I knew it. They acted so strange that day I overheard them."

"Well, guilt will make you do that." Camri secured her hat, then took up the umbrella Judith offered her. "Now I just need to figure out how to get them to tell me what they know."

CHAPTER

12

*T*hroughout the workday, Camri's mind was consumed by her suspicions and doubts. She couldn't focus on the tasks at hand, and more than once Mr. Lake had reprimanded her to pay closer attention.

A few minutes before the close of their day, Mr. Lake called Camri into his office and excused Kenzie.

"Please sit down," he instructed.

Camri took a seat and glanced at the clock. She had no doubt Mr. Lake intended to reprimand her again. She only hoped he would do it quickly so she could catch the trolley home with Kenzie and Judith.

"Miss Coulter, I don't know what's come over you." He peered down his nose at her. "We have only days before Christmas arrives, and the orders must be filled and delivered. I need your mind to be on your work."

"I know, and I am sorry, Mr. Lake."

Camri tried her best to look contrite. She *was* sorry, but at the moment all she wanted was to go home. That would mean facing the Wongs, however, and the thought of that left a sour taste in her mouth. Why couldn't they just tell her what was going on? They knew something, and she had to find out what it was. But how?

". . . and it isn't a desire of mine to terminate you, but my reputation is of the utmost importance."

Camri realized she hadn't been listening. "I am sorry, Mr. Lake, but you must admit that until today, I was handling my responsibilities quite well. I can't see that one day of mistakes merits termination."

He began to pace in his customary fashion. "Which is why I am not firing you. However, if this lack of attention continues, I'll have no other choice. I find females to be flighty, which is why I haven't been willing to hire them until now. Would that all women could be as sensible and staid as my dear cousin."

Irritation threatened to work its way into rage, but Camri forced herself to remain silent. She had no spare energy to devote to a battle of women's rights with Mr. Lake. He felt no different than most men.

"Again, I apologize, Mr. Lake. I'll be quite competent on the morrow, I assure you." She got to her feet. "Thank you for bringing this matter to my attention." She had often used this phrase to conclude other meetings in her life. It tended to leave the other person at a loss as to how they could continue. She moved toward the door as the clock struck the hour. "Good evening, Mr. Lake."

She left the room before he could say anything else and hurried to fetch her coat and hat. Judith and Kenzie were already waiting.

"What was that all about?" Judith asked.

"He just wanted to point out that I did not give him quality work today." Camri pulled on her coat.

"As much as he scolded you throughout the day, I wouldn't think it necessary to point out your mistakes again," Judith said, shaking her head.

"He's just anxious about the orders and his concerns about sabotage," Kenzie said, opening the door for them to exit.

Camri secured her hat. "I deserved his reprimand. I let my thoughts command me today. It wasn't right."

They walked from the building, hurrying to make their cable car. The crowded sidewalks were filled with vendors and pedestrians who all seemed determined to act as obstacles to Camri and her friends. They barely reached their destination in time.

Kenzie and Judith took the only seats available while Camri stood directly in front of them, holding on to the bar to keep from falling.

"I want you both to know that I'm sorry for the way I acted this morning at breakfast. Especially to you, Kenzie. I never meant to cause you pain. I know I'm headstrong and prideful, and I often say things based on the life I've led and the people who have influenced me. I hope you'll forgive me."

Kenzie gave a slight smile. "I do. You didn't intend to harm me."

"No, I didn't. I simply spoke without thinking—which seems to be a growing problem. I never realized just how much I speak my mind without thought to others. And lately, with all that's going on, I seem particularly rude."

"You've got a lot on your mind," Judith threw in. "We all do. I can't help but wonder if any of the people around me might be my aunt. It consumes me sometimes."

The trolley passed Mr. Ambrewster's office, as it did every day. Camri glanced up as the car slowed to let off passengers and forgot all about her apology. Mr. Ambrewster was standing near the corner of the building in deep conversation with Mr. Wong.

"Look!" She pointed toward the two men.

Judith and Kenzie twisted around to see. "It's Mr. Wong." Judith gasped.

"And isn't that Caleb's employer?" Kenzie asked.

"It is." Camri narrowed her eyes as Mr. Wong put something into Mr. Ambrewster's hands. She couldn't see what it was, but a dozen ideas ran through her head. Could it be information about Caleb? Might it be money to pay for some deception? Maybe the Wongs knew exactly where Caleb was and this was the address needed to find him.

"What do you suppose he gave to Mr. Ambrewster?" Judith asked as the cable car moved on down the street.

Camri shook her head. "I don't know. It doesn't make any sense to me that they should be meeting for any purpose."

"Do you think perhaps Mr. Wong owed Mr. Ambrewster money? Maybe because he was your brother's employer, Mr. Wong went to him when Caleb disappeared in order to borrow some," Kenzie suggested. "They would have needed something to live on."

A woman and her five children pushed past in order to squeeze into the newly vacated space opposite Judith and Kenzie. Camri nearly fell into Kenzie's lap when the mother whirled on her heel to count her children. She offered no apology as Camri straightened and steadied herself.

"I think that makes sense. Caleb wouldn't be around to give them their salaries. It's possible Mr. Wong had to borrow money," Judith said. "After all, how else would they survive?"

Camri nodded and tried to speak above the noise of the disgruntled children. Apparently they'd just come from the dentist and some promised treat was yet to be delivered. "I suppose you could be right. I'm afraid my first thoughts ran to more devious ideas. Perhaps when next I see Mr. Ambrewster, I will ask him about it. After all, if the Wongs are repaying a loan due to Caleb's absence, I can help."

"And if it's not a loan?" Kenzie asked.

Camri shook her head. "What do you mean?"

"Simply that if you ask Mr. Ambrewster about it, and it turns out to be something more . . . sinister, then they'll realize you know they're up to something."

It wasn't like Kenzie to come up with such an idea, but Camri knew she might be right. Mr. Ambrewster had lied about Caleb and might be lying still. And the Wongs were clearly involved in some capacity. What if they were all conspiring together? What if they each played some role in Caleb's disappearance?

―――――

That evening after dinner, Camri decided to visit Ophelia. Her trip would serve two purposes, beyond befriending Ophelia. First, she would get Mr. Wong to drive her over, and during their ride, she might find out what he was doing with Mr. Ambrewster. And second, she would have a chance to apologize to Ophelia's brother.

Mr. Wong seemed less than happy to be driving her back to the Irish neighborhood, but Camri promised him they wouldn't stay long. She only wanted to check on Ophelia, since she was so sick. He finally relented, but on the way to the Murdocks' apartment, he said very little.

Ophelia was delighted to see Camri again, but Patrick was nowhere to be found.

"I'm afraid Patrick is still off workin'. He had a chance to help a friend."

"I really came to check on you." Camri saw the look on Ophelia's face. "Well, and to apologize to your brother. I'm afraid I was rather brusque with him." She knew that was an understatement but didn't want to ruin her brief time with Ophelia by explaining her issues of pride.

"I know he'll be sorry to have missed ye."

Camri took a chair beside Ophelia, who sat snuggled up by the stove. "How are you feeling? Is there anything you need?"

Ophelia shook her head. "I have all that I need. Patrick and the good Lord see to that. But I'm wonderin' if maybe I can do somethin' for yerself. Ye seem rather troubled."

Camri didn't want to burden the poor girl with all of her troubles. She shook her head. "It's really nothing. I've just got a lot on my mind."

"Our ma used to say that when a person has a lot on their mind, it has a way of blocking out yer eyes and ears so as to keep ye from hearin' and seein' what the Lord has for ye to know." She smiled. "All of our troubles are made lighter by sharin' the load. I may not be strong enough for physical burdens, but spiritually, I assure ye, I'm quite strong."

"Of course, you are. I didn't mean to imply otherwise. I . . . it's just that . . ." Camri wrung her hands. "I feel like so many people are lying to me or, at best, guarding me from the truth. I don't like it. Not one bit."

Ophelia reached out and stilled her hands. "I can't say as I blame ye. Ye've a great deal of worry about your brother and it doesn't help when ye feel that everyone is settin' up obstacles rather than helpin' ye to uncover the truth."

"Exactly. It's all so exasperating. Even those who claim to be my friend are deceiving me. I've never been able to abide deception."

"Nor should ye." She smiled, but her sunken eyes betrayed her pain. "But just remember, God hates deception as well. Give it to Him, Camri. The truth will win out."

A sense of peace settled on the room, and Camri found her fears ebbing. "Thank you. I needed to hear that. I know the truth of it, but I . . . well, I suppose I'm just weary."

"Aye. There is a weariness that goes deep to the soul, but as the Word says, ye'll reap—if ye faint not. Rest in the Lord, Camri. He'll see ye through this."

Camri nodded and got to her feet. "I've taken up too much of your time, and I assured Mr. Wong I wouldn't be long."

"'Tis no problem. What little time I have, I'm happy to be spendin' with a friend."

"I'll try to come back soon."

"Do."

Camri hesitated to leave but knew there was nothing more to be said. She hurried from the apartment and was heading through the building's outer door when she ran headlong into Patrick Murdock. He smelled of horse manure and sweat.

"Oh, I'm so sorry."

He steadied her for a moment, then quickly dropped his hold. "What are ye doin' here?" His tone sounded almost accusatory.

"I wanted to check on your sister and see how she was feeling." Camri fought back her immediate urge to take offense. "I also wanted to speak to you." She glanced past him to where Mr. Wong sat in the old wagon. "I suppose, however, that now is neither the time nor the place."

He just stared at her for several long moments, leaving Camri uncomfortable. She knew she should apologize for her previous behavior, but somehow the words wouldn't come.

"Well?" he finally said.

"I should go. We can speak another time. I'm sure I'll be back to visit Ophelia soon."

With that, she made a dash for the wagon. Her heart wanted to pound out of her chest, and not for the effort of reaching the wagon. Why did Patrick Murdock leave her feeling so confused—so incapable of speaking a simple apology?

———

Patrick sat opposite his good friend Liam O'Connell. The big man matched Patrick in size and ability when it came to all things physical. Liam had, in fact, once worked for Patrick's father, and their friendship had been solidified over many a contest of brute strength.

"Busy night?" Patrick asked. He'd come to see Liam just as the night shift at the factory ended and suggested they breakfast together.

"Aye, to be sure." Liam rubbed grimy fingers across his brow and yawned. "And what of yerself?"

"I worked some for a friend, then had a strange encounter with Caleb Coulter's sister."

"His sister, ye say?" Liam grinned.

"Oh, get on with yerself. It wasn't like that."

"And what was it like?"

"I can hardly tell ye." Patrick ran his hand back through his thick hair. "She's a puzzle. Prideful and all full of fire. She'll give ye a lashin' with her tongue, but then turn her eyes on ye all soft."

Liam laughed and slapped the table. "Sounds like a fine Irish lass."

"I don't think she's that, but she's got the feistiness of one, to be sure."

"Seems like she's gotten herself under your skin."

Patrick leaned back and crossed his arms. "Hardly that." But even as he said it, he wasn't sure exactly what Camrianne Coulter had done to him.

The waitress appeared with two large mugs of coffee. She placed them on the table, then left again without a word. Just as quickly she came again, this time with a plate of Irish sausages and two bowls of stirabout.

"That'll be four bits," she announced, putting the food on the table.

Patrick reached into his pocket, but Liam handed her some money and waved Patrick off. "'Tis my treat. Ye bought last time."

The waitress went off to take the order of another table while Liam put a generous amount of sugar into his stirabout. The

Irish porridge was thin as soup, but the portion was large and filling—especially the way Liam added to it.

"They make this any thinner, and they'll be serving hot water," Liam said with a grin. He handed Patrick the sugar. "This'll thicken it up."

With a laugh, Patrick took the glass jar and added an ample amount of sugar to his porridge as well. "For certain it cannot hurt."

They settled into eating before getting down to the business at hand. Patrick had asked Liam to keep his ear to the ground for any word about Caleb, but also about the shanghaiing business in general. Given Caleb's complete disappearance, Patrick was almost certain this had become his fate. Now, if he could just prove it and find someone who remembered which ship he'd been put on.

"There's been plenty of activity," Liam offered without prompting. "I've asked around about our friend, but if anyone knows anything, they aren't sayin'."

"For all the time that's passed, it's unlikely anyone will be rememberin' him. Still, I cannot lose hope. Caleb saved my life, and I owe it to him to keep lookin' and maybe even save his. If he were dead, a body would have turned up by now—even if he'd been thrown into the bay." Patrick sliced into his sausage and took a bite before continuing. "Somebody somewhere knows somethin'."

"No doubt they do," Liam replied, "but for sure they ain't talkin' about it. However, I've had a thought on the matter."

"Do tell." Patrick eased back in his chair.

"Ye said that ye tracked him to a place called Daniels' Dance Hall and Drinking. A friend of mine has a brother workin' there. They have a reputation for findin' men to serve aboard ships."

"Ye mean they shanghai them," Patrick said matter-of-factly. His eyes narrowed. "Are they in the habit of takin' men right off the streets? Because Caleb wouldn't be gracin' the Barbary Coast. As I understood him, Caleb intended to be in the neighborhood to meet a potential client. Nothin' more."

"Malcolm Daniels would take a man from his granny's garden," Liam said with a grin. "He's ruthless and has no concern whatsoever about whether a man is from a good neighborhood or a bad. He has quotas to fill, and he's not the only one, as ye well know."

"Aye."

"Better still, it's been rumored amongst seedier folk that he has an agreement with Abraham Ruef to take troublesome folks off his hands."

Patrick leaned forward. "For sure?"

"Aye. It's said that once Daniels was hired to confine the son of a rich man and hold him until his father gave in to Ruef's demands. Another story tells of Daniels being paid to rid the mayor of a particularly annoying opponent. I have it on good authority that the man was drugged and put to sea under a ruthless captain who wasn't at all moved by the promise of reward should he return the man to his family."

Patrick nodded. "If Daniels has that kind of reputation, he could very well have been paid to take Caleb. The whole thing about meetin' a client could have been a ruse. Ruef could have had someone arrange to meet Caleb, only to take him hostage."

Liam smiled. "That was my thinkin' exactly."

"So how would I go about findin' out what he knows? I'd need to get close to him without arousin' his suspicions."

"I've already thought of that. Ye didn't happen to go into Daniels' place, inquirin' about our friend, did ye?"

"No. I had no reason to think anyone there would know anything. Besides, even if they did, they'd not be speakin' to me."

"True and good it is that ye refrained, for they'll not know ye."

"Know me?"

Liam nodded. "My friend with the brother workin' there owes me a debt, and I'm thinkin' I could call it in by having him help ye get a job at Daniels' place."

Patrick shook his head, frowning. "I couldn't be involved in shanghaiin' helpless men."

"I doubt they'd let ye help with that right away. Ye'd have to be provin' yourself first. Still, with my friend's brother workin' for Daniels, he could hopefully clear the way and get ye in."

"And once I'm in, then what?"

"Faith, man! Do I have to be doin' all your thinkin'?" Liam asked in an indignant tone.

Patrick laughed. "Somebody ought to. I'm not doin' such a great job on me own."

Liam's expression was amused. "Well, I won't be takin' it on. I can get ye a job, hopefully, but after that, it'll be up to yerself to figure out what to do with it. Are ye game to try?"

Patrick considered it for a moment. He hated the idea of working in such a place, but this was the best lead he had. "Aye, I'm game. Talk to yer friend. If Caleb was shanghaied, it seems logical that Daniels might have been the one to do the job."

13

*C*amri spied Patrick Murdock sitting on the front steps outside Caleb's house before he saw her. She slowed her pace to study him as she walked. Something about him appealed to her, and yet he was nothing like the men she usually found attractive. Patrick was all muscle and brawn, yet he had such a gentleness about him. There was a roughness to his appearance that betrayed the difficult and physical life he had lived. Most of the men she'd known had been educated and refined. Their hands were smooth, even soft, where Patrick's were calloused.

As if feeling her gaze on him, he slowly turned his head and fixed her with a smile. He jumped to his feet as Camri approached and tipped his hat.

"Top of the day to ye, Miss Coulter."

She nodded and returned the smile. "And to you. How is your sister?"

"That's the reason I've come on this fine Sunday. Ophelia would like to see ye, if ye have the time."

"Of course. I'm sorry I wasn't here sooner."

"Your friends explained that ye were helpin' the parson's wife."

"Yes. I wish you had just come to the church to find me instead of waiting for two hours. I wouldn't have taken lunch with them had I known."

"'Tis no problem. Ophelia's no doubt still sleepin'. She does that more these days. I left her curled up by the stove, and my landlady promised to look in on her."

Camri frowned. "Is Ophelia worse?"

His smile faded. "Aye. The doctor says she won't make the new year."

"But . . ." She had known things were bad, but to hear him say that his sweet sister only had a matter of days left was almost more than Camri could bear. Her emotions ran so high these days, and logic often failed her. "I . . . I'm sorry to hear that."

His stoic expression never wavered. "Aye. 'Tis a sad bit of news, to be sure."

Camri admired his strength. To be able to speak on the matter without giving in to emotion had to be difficult.

"I'll need a moment to let Kenzie and Judith know where I'm going." She started up the steps, then paused. "Have you had any lunch?"

"Aye. Your Mr. Wong brought me a bite."

She nodded, then hurried up the steps. Once inside, she found Judith and Kenzie sitting in the front room, a warm fire blazing in the hearth.

"I'm going with Patrick to see his sister, Ophelia."

"We invited him to come inside," Judith said, looking up from her book, "but he declined. I'm sure I wouldn't have wanted to sit in the damp cold for two hours."

"Nor I," Kenzie said with a shrug. "Are you sure it's safe to go? I remember you talking about how downtrodden the neighborhood was, and Mr. Wong made it clear it wasn't at all safe."

Camri chuckled. "You've seen Patrick Murdock. Do you doubt his ability to keep me from harm?"

Kenzie shrugged again. "Yes, but who will protect you from Mr. Murdock?"

Judith giggled and defended him before Camri could. "Mr. Murdock is a good man. I can tell. Besides, he was friends with Caleb, so he must be trustworthy."

"He was a client of Caleb's," Kenzie corrected. "If they became friends after that, it still wouldn't be the same as, say, his friendship with Dr. Fisher. They're hardly from the same social set."

"Well, I've always considered myself a good judge of character," Camri interjected. "I think, given the various men I've run across since beginning this search, that Patrick is the most trustworthy of the bunch. I haven't any idea when I'll return, but try not to worry. I'm confident that with Mr. Murdock at my side, I'll be safe." Camri headed for the front door.

"You should take your umbrella," Judith called after her. "Mrs. Wong says it's going to rain."

Camri smiled and plucked her umbrella from the stand. Mrs. Wong had an uncanny ability to predict the weather, whether the skies were clear or overcast.

She rejoined Patrick, who waited patiently at the foot of the stairs. "I'm sorry for the delay."

"Ye need not apologize." He held out his arm for her to take. "I'm the one apologizin' for havin' no wagon. 'Tis a long walk."

"Yes, but it's a pleasant enough day." She hooked her arm through his.

He laughed as they headed down the hill. "'Tis cold and threatenin' rain."

She smiled. "This weather is like Chicago in the spring. This time of year, however, San Francisco is far milder. My folks wrote me and said they have quite a bit of snow."

"I loved the snow when I was a lad. That was before we moved to San Francisco, of course. The snow rarely falls on this city."

"Where did you live before here?"

Patrick smiled. "Too many places to count. When me da came to America, he was determined to find a place that reminded him of home, but of course nothing ever suited. He told me that after a time, he realized he wouldn't find his Irish home in America. Instead, he'd be needin' to make a new home, and so he did. When we came here to San Francisco, Da said he felt a settlin' inside that he'd never had before. That made it clear to him this was the place to call home."

"What about you? Do you feel it's home?"

Her question seemed to take him by surprise. "I feel at home wherever my family is. When Ophelia's passed on, I'm not sure how this place will feel."

Camri nodded. "I understand that. My folks are older than some. They had their children late in life, taking time to establish their education and careers first. Worrying over Caleb has sent them both to their beds."

"So ye said they'd written. How are they bearin' up?"

"Mother tries to sound strong. She tells me their health has improved, but I fear she's merely trying to keep me from fretting. Father suffered a bad cold that turned into pneumonia, and he hasn't regained his strength since. Mother, on the other hand, has been troubled by her stomach. She was always a robust, active woman, but over the summer, she began to fail. When Caleb disappeared, she wasn't able to eat at all. The doctor ordered tests just before I came here. I wrote to ask her what the tests revealed, but she didn't answer me."

"And that worries ye?"

Camri looked up. His expression was pure compassion. "Yes," she barely whispered. "I sometimes wonder if both of them are much worse than they're telling me. I'm sure they mean to protect me, but I've written to Catherine for the truth."

"And do ye suppose she'll be givin' it?"

"I sincerely hope so. Truth is important to me—I cannot abide someone keeping it from me, even when they hope to protect me."

"Aye," Patrick murmured.

"I don't know what I'll do once they're gone. I suppose if Caleb remains here, I might join him. I'm not that close to my sister. She's ten years my senior, and we had little in common."

"So ye like city life then?" His tone lightened. "All the blather and ballyhoo?"

She glanced around. They had passed from Caleb's rather refined neighborhood to one that was common—even a bit run-down. Someone who struggled to keep food on the table could hardly be faulted for having no money to spruce up the outside of their home.

"There are definitely aspects I enjoy. The theatre and attending concerts and lectures. Those are some of my favorite ways to pass an afternoon or evening. I suppose I could do without other things, like the crime and constant feeling of rush, and the noise." She smiled.

"Aye, and this city has more than its fair share of all of that. My ma used to say there was no quiet to be had except in her soul."

Camri smiled. There were times she felt the same way. "I've never really known anything else, growing up in Chicago. I suppose, above all, a city of this size offers almost anything a person could want or need. Good schools, doctors, and manufacturers."

They turned a corner, and the gradual descent into poverty began to feel more like a plunge. All around them the signs were clear. Broken windows had been boarded, garbage cans were overflowing. An unpleasant odor from burning trash filled the air.

"Doctors and good schools can be had for sure, if ye have the coin and the right ancestry." Patrick's sober tone seemed prompted by their surroundings. "There's limitations and prejudices aplenty if you're Irish or Mexican. Even worse if you're Chinese, Jewish, or Negro."

Camri nodded. "Yes, unfortunately that is a universal problem." She didn't wish to dwell on that topic and hurriedly moved on. "Where did you live before? I know your business was very successful."

He gave her a smile, but there was a look of regret in his expression. "'Tis true enough. Da and I built a fine house some blocks to the south and west of where your brother's house stands. I was only nineteen, and it pleased me greatly to be able to do such a thing. Our ma was so happy. She used to just walk through the rooms, smilin' and talkin' about how she wished she could show the place to her ma." His voice softened. "The next year she passed on. Ophelia was but ten. Our da was never the same after that."

"I'm so sorry." She wanted to ask whether he had sold the house, or if it, like the business, was taken from them when he went to jail, but she didn't want to further his sorrow.

A few sprinkles of rain fell, but Camri didn't think it merited opening her umbrella. Most of the people on the street had nothing to shield them from the rain, and it felt almost pretentious that she did.

"Just a few more blocks," Patrick offered. "We should pick up our feet."

She smiled at his comment. Despite his being uneducated, she enjoyed his manner of speaking. She remembered her folks had once had an Irish cook. She created the most impressive meals, but she could curse like a sailor, and Camri's mother finally felt it necessary to let her go. Until now, Camri had never wondered about her—where she went or if she found work. A twinge of guilt unsettled her thoughts. Perhaps the cook lived in a place similar to Patrick's. A place like the sad, neglected buildings that lined these streets—tenements where the owners had little desire to make things nice. The people here had so little. No doubt the Jewish and Chinese neighborhoods were even worse.

She realized that they'd stopped talking. Glancing up, she found Patrick's face fixed in a sober expression. It looked as if he too might be considering the plight of his neighbors. Camri chided herself for never having taken much interest in helping the poor. Her causes were always about benefiting women, which she hoped would in turn raise their status of living. However, she had never truly given thought to the impoverished conditions that a good portion of the population faced.

Patrick noticed her watching him. He shrugged and pointed ahead. "There, see now. We're all but home," he said as the rain began to fall more steadily.

Camri hurried to keep step with him. She was glad that current fashions allowed some skirts to be shortened. Her wool skirt was modern, so the hem was just a bit higher than that of her other gowns, allowing her to avoid dragging her skirts in the muck of the streets.

Patrick threw open the door to his ramshackle building and ushered her inside. "I'll build up the fire and see that you dry off," he said as they made their way to his apartment.

An older woman was sweeping the hall just beyond his door. When they arrived, Patrick gave her a wave and spoke in what Camri presumed was Gaelic. Then he smiled down at Camri and introduced the woman.

"This is Mrs. Ryan. She and her husband collect the rents and oversee the building for the owner."

Camri smiled and gave a nod. "It's a pleasure to meet you."

Mrs. Ryan returned the smile, showing she was missing a good number of teeth. "Ye've picked a day of it to come callin', but welcome ye are."

"Thank you."

Patrick opened the door to his apartment and motioned Camri inside. Ophelia sat near the stove, bundled in blankets. She looked up when Camri entered.

"Oh, 'tis good to see ye've come."

"I was happy to do so," Camri said, taking the chair beside her. I apologize that it took so long. I stayed behind at church to help the pastor's wife with some things and then joined them for lunch at their house."

"'Tis no matter, ye're here now." Ophelia's voice was weak, and her face held a grayish cast.

"How have you been feeling?" Camri regretted the question the minute it left her mouth, but she felt at a loss for words. Ophelia was clearly much worse off than she had been when Camri first met her.

"I'm doin' just fine. Don't fret about me." Ophelia sat a little straighter. "Paddy, take Camri's wet coat and hang it on the peg by the stove. Then put on the tea."

Camri stood to put aside her umbrella, then pulled off her damp gloves. She placed her gloves on the small table by the door, then unfastened the buttons of her coat. "It only just now began to rain in earnest. I didn't even have time to use my umbrella."

Patrick helped her with her coat. "Aye, but it was already a chilly day, and the rain made it all the colder." He hung her coat up as Ophelia had directed, then grabbed the kettle.

Camri turned her attention back to Ophelia. "I was glad for the invitation to come see you. I enjoyed our last visit and had hoped to come this afternoon anyway. I was going to see if Mr. Wong, my brother's . . . gardener, could bring me." She felt uncomfortable referencing servants when it was clear Ophelia and Patrick had to do everything for themselves.

"I told my brother that ye had the makings of a good friend."

"I'm glad you think so. Sometimes I'm not so sure." Camri glanced over to where Patrick was putting the kettle on the stove. "I've come to see that I can be quite overbearing and opinionated at times."

"For sure, we can all be that way, but ye have a grace about ye and a sweet spirit," Ophelia countered.

"If ye feel that ye can handle the tea," Patrick said, turning to the ladies, "Mrs. Ryan asked if I might be able to lend a hand in repairin' some steps on the third floor."

"I'm happy to take care of things here," Camri replied with a smile.

He gave her a nod, then went to Ophelia. "I'm thinkin' ye might be more comfortable in bed."

"In a while, perhaps. For now, I want to sit and have a good long visit with Camri."

"Well, she could easily bring a chair to your bedside."

Camri nodded. "Absolutely. I don't want you wearing yourself out on my account."

Ophelia shook her head. "I'll be fine. Go on with ye."

Patrick bent and kissed the top of her head. "I won't be far, if ye need me."

Camri waited until he'd gone before speaking again. "He seems quite attentive."

"He is that. He's a good brother and does far more than he ought to have to do."

"My brother is the same way. He's always looking out for others." Camri didn't add that it was probably the latter that had gotten him in trouble.

"I wanted ye to visit today because I have somethin' to ask ye," Ophelia said.

"I'll do whatever I can." Camri couldn't imagine what the young woman needed from her.

"I know your brother is missin', so I feel bad askin' a favor of ye in regard to my brother." Ophelia paused and drew a rather ragged breath. A shadow of pain darkened her face for a moment and then passed.

Camri was even more curious now that Ophelia had made it clear that her request involved Patrick. "As I said, I'll do whatever I can."

"Paddy is at odds with God. He blames God for the bad things that have happened to our family. At least, he did. I know he's been wrestlin' like Jacob did with God, to understand it all."

"It's hard to lose so much." Camri's murmured words seemed inadequate.

"Aye. 'Tis hard, to be sure. But Paddy knows the truth of things. He can be angry at the good Lord, but it doesn't change the truth. He needs to come around right, and I fear he won't. It frightens me, because I want to know that I'll see him again one day."

"I know nothing about your faith or Patrick's, but I do know that God understands our doubt and fear. They don't come from Him, but He does understand how weak we are. Patrick is angry and hurt because of his fear. After all, it's troubling to realize that God allows Christian folk to face tragedy and injustice."

The teakettle began to whistle, interrupting the conversation. Camri got to her feet and smiled at seeing that Patrick had readied two mugs. The canister of tea and a small sugar bowl sat just beyond. "Do you want sugar in your tea?"

"I don't want any tea, thank ye."

Camri didn't really feel like it either, so she put the kettle aside and reclaimed her seat beside Ophelia. She was surprised when Ophelia reached out to take her hand. The poor girl's fingers were ice-cold despite her blankets and the warmth of the stove.

"I know ye love God and that ye have a strong faith. I felt the good Lord speak this to my heart. When I pass on, Paddy's goin' to need someone like yerself to help him through. If Caleb were here, I know he'd do the job, but until he returns, I'm hopin' ye'll agree to be there for Paddy."

Camri didn't know what to think, much less what to say. How could she be a spiritual encourager to this man she hardly knew? "I . . . well . . . to be honest, I don't know if I can." She looked at Ophelia's hopeful expression. "You must understand, I don't give my word without the full intention of seeing it through. I'm something of a stickler for that."

"I know that honesty is important to ye." Ophelia paused for a moment, and a pained expression replaced her hopeful look. "I want ye to know that I don't ask this lightly. Folks here will do what they can to encourage Paddy, but I just have the feelin' he's goin' to need ye."

With a sigh, Camri resigned herself to doing whatever this dying woman asked of her. "I will endeavor to be there for him in any way I can."

Ophelia seemed to relax, although the pain hadn't yet passed from her face. "There's somethin' else I'd be sayin'. I've been prayin' for Caleb's return every day since he disappeared. I know yer heart is heavy for fear of what's happened to him."

"It is. Sometimes I can keep myself busy enough that it doesn't eat me alive, but his absence and not knowing what's happened to him consumes me. I came out here with such confidence that I could get to the bottom of things." Camri paused and shook her head. "False confidence." She drew a heavy breath. "Now I don't know what to do."

Ophelia squeezed her hand. "Aye, and I know you're hard-pressed to know who ye can trust."

The younger woman's astute understanding surprised Camri. "It is hard. I feel there is so much deception going on where

Caleb is concerned. I don't trust the man he used to work for because he lied to me. Then recently I overheard things that make me suspicious of Caleb's house servants." She shook her head as the words poured from her heart. "Trust is vital, and I feel that the people who were closest to Caleb are the very ones who can't be trusted."

"Just remember that sometimes a person might seem deceptive when they're not. Sometimes they seek to protect. Sometimes they fear sharing the truth of the matter will only cause more danger."

"I understand that, but they need to realize that I won't stop looking just because they say one thing or another. If I can't trust Caleb's friends, then I'll find someone I can pay to trust."

"God says we aren't to put our trust in man, but in Him. Ye cannot be misled then. Trust God to show ye the way, Camri. Ye will know deep in yer heart if a person is worthy of yer trust. Just don't jump to conclusions."

Her comment seemed strange, but Camri nodded. "I know you're right. I have to trust that God will guide me. After all, He's the one who brought me here in the first place. I prayed about how to help Caleb, and when my parents suggested I come here to seek the truth, I knew it was my answer. God wanted me here."

Ophelia's expression brightened. "Aye. Ye're in the right place, to be sure."

CHAPTER 14

*P*atrick finished nailing down the loose steps and returned to his apartment. It had taken almost an hour to see to all that Mrs. Ryan needed, and he hoped Camri wouldn't be put out by his long absence.

"Would ye have me pay ye, Patrick, or put it against your rent?" Mrs. Ryan asked him.

"On the rent, if ye please." He dusted off the front of his shirt. The amount the owner would allow her to credit him for rent was much greater than what she could pay in cash.

"The owner is comin' by on Thursday for an inspection. I've made a list of all the problems ye told me about. Do ye have anything else to add?"

"No. That list is long enough already. I doubt he'll be wanting to spend much money as it is."

"Aye, but knowin' that ye'll do most of the work in return for rent should loosen his purse strings a bit."

"Let's hope so." Patrick smiled. "Now, I've neglected our company long enough. Ye have a g'day, Mrs. Ryan."

He made his way back to the apartment, hoping that Camri and Ophelia had gotten along. He heard laughter coming from inside and smiled. Ophelia had so few joys and almost no friends close to her own age. The friends she'd made in their old neighborhood had turned away from her when Patrick had been accused of murder.

He opened the door. "Sounds like ye're havin' a grand time."

"We are," Camri admitted, "but I do believe I've worn your sister out."

Patrick nodded. "I'll be puttin' ye to bed, Ophelia, whether ye like it or not, and then I'll be walkin' Miss Coulter home."

"Camri."

He looked at Camri and nodded. "Aye. Camri." Saying her name made him feel like an awkward schoolboy with his first crush. There was definitely something about this woman that left him off-balance.

"Thank ye again for comin' today," Ophelia said, smiling at Camri.

To Patrick's surprise, Camri leaned over and encircled Ophelia in her arms. The two women hugged, and Camri whispered something to his sister. She kissed Ophelia's cheek, then rose. "I hope I have the chance to come again soon."

Patrick carried Ophelia to her bed. The room felt damp and chilly. How he wished they had a proper heating system.

"Ye look worried," she said as he tucked her in.

"Just tired." It wasn't exactly a lie. "And I don't like how cold this room is. I'm going to put more coal in the stove and leave this door open.

Ophelia smiled. "Well, don't ye be worrying about me. I'm fine. These blankets will keep me warm enough. Go enjoy your walk with Camri. She's a good friend, and I know ye care for her."

"She's Caleb's sister. Of course I care."

Ophelia shook her head. "Ye know better than to try to hide yer feelings from me."

Patrick was confused enough already and didn't want to start up a conversation about his conflicting interest in Camri. "I wouldn't dream of it." He gave her a grin. "Now behave yerself, and I'll be home soon."

The rain had abated, but the streets were still wet as they made their way back to Caleb's house. Here and there, the puddles were large enough to be difficult to traverse.

Patrick offered his arm to help Camri over the worst of them. "Sorry things are such a mess. We've had so much rain that it doesn't run off as well as it should."

"As hilly as this town is, you'd think it would just all run off into the bay." Camri's lighthearted tone made him smile.

"Aye, 'tis true. The sewer system needs a lot of work. I've seen it flood the lower areas when the rains get bad."

He found it easy enough to converse with Camri about their surroundings. It was only when she spoke of education being necessary to better a person that he felt uncomfortable. But truth be told, he felt that way because he knew she made a good point. He'd once overheard some upper-class men talking about the need to keep the Chinese and Mexicans out of the schools. One of the men had clearly remarked that educating them would only make them discontent with their place in life.

"I really like your sister. She's a very smart young woman," Camri said.

"Aye. She is that. She went through high school, ye know."

"I do. She told me. She said your mother wanted it for both of you."

"Aye." He wasn't about to get off on that conversation again and quickly refocused on Ophelia. "I appreciate ye spendin' time with her. It means a lot to me. She hasn't any friends to speak of."

"Well, she has me as a friend."

"I could tell ye'd hit it off by the laughter and whispers." He still wondered what Camri had said to his sister before their departure.

She seemed to understand his curiosity and shrugged. "Girls must have their secrets."

As the neighborhood around them improved, there were fewer issues with standing water and broken walkways. Patrick relaxed a bit, no longer concerned about Camri's ability to navigate. She was a sensible woman. He had to give her that much. Not only that, but she reminded him a lot of his mother. They would have been in perfect agreement about education. His mother had fought a hard battle to keep him in school and wasn't happy to have lost out, even to his father.

Still, he didn't regret the choice. He'd had those years working day in and day out with the man he most admired in the world. He'd learned a great deal from his father. No university degree could have topped the experience and wisdom he had gained at his father's side.

When they were only a block or two away from Caleb's house, Camri interrupted his thoughts. "Patrick, I want to say something—need to say something." She stopped and waited until he did also.

He looked at her oddly. "And for sure we've been talkin' all this time. Say what ye will."

She smiled. "That's true enough, but I suppose I've avoided what I most want to say."

"Which is what?"

"That I'm sorry."

"Sorry for what?"

She looked away as if embarrassed. When she lifted her face again, he could see tears glistening in her dark brown eyes.

"I'm sorry about Ophelia. I wish I could spend more time with her. I didn't realize just how bad things were. I mean, I know what you said, but . . . well, the idea of one so young dying is hard to take in."

"Aye. 'Tis no easy matter to watch her die. But ye shouldn't be so hard on yerself. Ye have yer brother to worry about and yer job at the candy factory."

"I know, but I realized today just how lonely Ophelia is. I know she has you, but I know too that you often have to be gone. You have to work and see to other matters."

Patrick wanted to hug her for her concern but knew it would be completely improper. "Ye have a good heart, Camri. Don't be frettin' over this. Ophelia is wise beyond her years. She's got a way of understandin' things that go beyond anythin' I can know."

"She does. I know that for myself." Camri squared her shoulders, and Patrick started to walk again. "Wait, there's another matter I want to discuss," she called out.

He turned back with a shrug. "Go on, then."

"I realize I've said some things about education and learning that were harsh. I've always been opinionated, but until now I hadn't often been in the company of people who didn't share my opinion." She twisted the umbrella in her hands. "I mean . . . well, I'm used to speaking to crowds of people who disagree or challenge my beliefs, but generally the people I'm close to—those whose opinions matter—have been in agreement with me." She sighed. "I'm saying this all wrong, but I'm sorry for the snobbish way I've acted."

Patrick wasn't sure he heard anything past her comment about the people she felt close to. The ones whose opinions mattered. It seemed to him that she was implying he was part of that group.

"I hope you'll forgive me. I want us to be friends."

Her words surprised him but touched him deeply. "There's nothin' to be forgivin'. Ye're not wrong to hold dear yer beliefs."

"I know, but how I share or portray my beliefs can be changed. I don't mean to look down on people who have little or no education—it's just that I have seen how important it is. Education is the only way people will better themselves and rise above poverty." She stopped and shook her head. "There I go again. I'm sorry."

Patrick couldn't help but chuckle. "But I'm agreein' with that. Education *is* important, but there are all sorts of ways to be educated. Colleges and universities are but one way. I've a great deal of knowledge, but it wasn't learned inside a school."

She seemed to consider this and then nodded slowly. "You are so right. I'm sure you probably know a great deal more than I do."

"It's not a competition, Camri." He barely whispered her name. Their nearness was starting to overwhelm him.

"No, of course not." She smiled and gave a casual shrug. "But I'm sure you could teach me all sorts of things that I didn't learn in school."

Her comment caught him off guard. Embarrassed at the things that immediately came to mind, he cleared his throat and looked away. She had no idea the effect her words and appearance had on him, and he intended to keep it that way. "I should be gettin' back to Ophelia."

They started once again for Caleb's, and as they rounded the corner, Patrick spied an automobile parked outside the house. Camri noticed it at the same time.

"Oh dear. That would be Mr. Ambrewster's car. I have no desire to see him." She glanced up at Patrick.

"Neither do I. I don't trust him." Patrick stopped, forcing Camri to do so as well. "I don't know if Caleb did or not, but he . . ." He stopped, realizing he'd nearly said too much. "I don't know that ye can trust him either."

Camri's eyes widened. "I don't." She paused to cast a quick

glance down the street and then looked back at Patrick. "Do you think he knows more about Caleb's disappearance than he's letting on?"

"For sure I wouldn't be knowin'." Patrick didn't want to say anything more, lest he reveal that he was keeping things from Camri himself. "If ye don't mind, I'll be sayin' good-bye right here."

Camri looked at him with a puzzled expression but nodded. "Thank you again for coming to get me. I hope we can do this again . . . if you find you have the time."

Patrick lost himself for a moment in her dark eyes. Without knowing it, she was quickly laying claim to his heart. He couldn't let that happen. It would only add more pain to his life.

"Aye, if I find the time."

He turned and quickly retraced his steps home. His thoughts swirled with images of Caleb and Camri, Ophelia and the men who had risen up against his father. Men who had tried to see him hanged for a crime he didn't commit. He would find Caleb, and he would avenge his father and restore their good name. He couldn't keep Ophelia from dying, nor ever hope to share a life with someone like Camri Coulter, but he could see to it that the men who'd wronged him were held accountable.

"That's where I must keep my focus and my heart." He determined then and there that he would put aside all thoughts of Camri.

Well, almost all thoughts.

CHAPTER

15

"Mr. Ambrewster, we weren't expecting a visit from you today," Camri said as she entered the front sitting room.

The lawyer got to his feet, while Judith and Kenzie remained seated on the sofa. Camri handed Mrs. Wong her coat and gloves. "If I'd known you were planning to come, I would have made arrangements."

"Nonsense." Ambrewster smiled. "This was a surprise."

"He brought us a Christmas tree," Judith declared before Henry could continue.

Mrs. Wong stepped forward, still holding Camri's coat and gloves. "Decorations are packed in basement. You come and I show you."

Judith jumped up. "We'll fetch them, Camri." She turned to Kenzie. "Won't we?"

The redhead reluctantly got to her feet. "So much for resting on the Sabbath."

"You really don't have to do that," Camri said, unpinning her hat. She turned back to Henry Ambrewster. "You shouldn't have bothered. We had no plans to decorate for Christmas." She placed her hat on the table just inside the room, then gave her hair a pat with her hand to make sure it wasn't too out of order.

"Again, I must say, nonsense." Henry took her arm and led her to the sofa. "It's Christmas, and Caleb would be appalled to see you ignore it. He was quite the celebrator when it came to this holiday."

The memory of her brother's enthusiasm for the day made her smile. "I'm sure you're right. However, we made an agreement among the three of us that we wouldn't spend money on frivolity and gifts."

Henry frowned. "If money is a problem . . ."

"No." Camri held up her hand. "It isn't that. We are merely trying to be frugal. Each of us came to San Francisco with a specific goal in mind, and as you know, this is an expensive town."

"Yes, but Caleb would want me to assist you in any way. I am happy to help with the financial aspects. I've been covering Caleb's mortgage and electricity. To help with other things would be easy enough."

Camri hadn't considered that Caleb had bought the house on credit. She felt some of the wind go out of her sails. "I didn't realize. We're doing our best to be self-sufficient."

He gave her a fatherly smile. "But, my dear, you needn't do without a few joys at Christmas."

"We won't. We intend to have a nice Christmas dinner, and that's enough."

For a moment it seemed he might argue with her, but then he gave a nod. "Well, now you have a tree. I think the merriment will do you good, given the circumstances." He sat in Caleb's chair and fixed Camri with a look of admiration. "I must say, Camrianne, you grow lovelier each time I see you."

Camri stiffened. The last thing she wanted was words of wooing from this man she didn't even trust. "Mr.—ah, Henry, have you had any word from Mr. Johnston?"

He nodded. "Yes. That's the other reason for my visit. Fred is good at getting matters resolved. I'm not sure why it didn't occur to me to ask for his help earlier. But that aside, he has heard talk about Caleb causing problems for the current mayoral administration. That is enough to put him in jeopardy. Fred learned this through his spies who work with Abraham Ruef."

"The man who's known to be the power behind Mayor Schmitz?" Camri asked, pretending it was all news to her.

"Yes. Ruef is as corrupt as they come, I'm afraid. He supposedly gets paid for legal consulting to the tune of hundreds of thousands of dollars. However, no one so far has been able to prove either the legality *or* the illegality of it. He has most of the judges and labor politicians in his pocket and pays them well to stay there. Nothing happens in this town—nothing gets built or torn down—without Ruef's involvement."

"But what does this have to do with Caleb?"

"Fred believes that the Murdock Construction Company was approached by Ruef's men. Ruef was slighted when the man who hired Murdock to build his hotel bypassed Ruef's suggestions and directions."

"Suggestions and directions for what?"

Henry leaned back and crossed his legs. "Well, that's not entirely known. From what I've seen in Caleb's notes and Fred's understanding of the situation, Ruef had a construction team ready for this man to use. It was an unwritten condition upon which the legal permits were issued."

"Who is this man—the one who wanted the hotel?"

Henry shrugged. "Grayson Springer. He's actually from New York but wanted a stake in San Francisco. In return, he was helping Ruef make some investments in New York. But I digress. Ruef had laid out who was to build the hotel. He has a dozen contractors willing to do his bidding, and in turn Ruef makes a tidy profit and sees to it that they get extra work."

"But how?" Camri was having trouble understanding all these twisted political machinations.

"It's fairly simple. Someone decides they want to erect a building in San Francisco. They need land, permits, and approval of their plans. The mayor's office and the Board of Supervisors, under Ruef's control, are the ones who give those permissions. In order to make anything happen, Ruef must be paid. Generally speaking, he receives a large amount of money for legal consulting and arranging for quality contracting companies to take on the project, most of which, it is rumored, he owns or has a stake in. The consulting fees are pure graft. Ruef keeps at least half, if not more, then passes the remainder to the mayor, who then takes his portion. After that, the Board of Supervisors receive their cut, along with the complete understanding that anything needed for the building project is to be put through posthaste. It has served all of them well. They've made a great deal of money and will no doubt go on making a great deal until someone finds the ways and means to stand up to them."

"But how does my brother figure in on this?"

"I don't know exactly, but given the money I found and Patrick Murdock's quick verdict of innocent, I'm afraid that Caleb may have taken money from Ruef."

"But that makes no sense. If Ruef was upset with Mr. Springer for not using his appointed contractor, and if he owns the courts as you suggest, why would he allow Patrick to be found innocent?"

Henry's eyes narrowed as a frown formed on his lips. "We can't know for certain, at least not just yet, but Fred believes that when Springer chose to give Murdock the contract, Ruef decided to punish Springer. Patrick Murdock attested to the fact that men approached his father and first offered money if he would use substandard product in the building. He wanted

Murdock to build a shoddy hotel. Murdock refused, according to Patrick, and then threats were made which resulted—"

"In his death," Camri interjected. "Patrick believes his father was pushed from the building, while the official report said he fell—that it was nothing more than an accident."

"Right. No one expected Patrick to create a fuss, and when he did, Ruef sent his men to put the fear of God into him and get him to cease his protests. Instead, it only made Patrick more determined to prove his case. So Ruef sacrificed one of his men—the one Patrick accused of pushing his father to his death. The man turned up dead with circumstantial evidence pointing to Patrick as the culprit."

Camri heard laughter coming from downstairs and knew it wouldn't be long until the decorations were located and the girls returned to join them. "Henry, does Mr. Johnston think that because Caleb defended Patrick, Mr. Ruef decided to cause him harm?"

"Quite the contrary. At least in the beginning, Fred believes that Caleb was offered a bribe."

"But a bribe for what?"

"His guess is that at first it was offered to entice Caleb to resign from being Patrick Murdock's counsel. Believe me when I say this wasn't the first time the firm has been approached by Ruef and his men. I'm sorry to say that I've often given in— short of purposefully breaking the law or allowing an innocent man to be condemned," he said, as if that excused his behavior.

She shook her head. None of this made sense. "But Patrick was found innocent. You said yourself that Ruef had the judges and other officials under his control. I have to believe it would have been easy enough to pay members of a jury as well, so it surely wouldn't matter if Caleb represented Patrick or not. If Ruef is so powerful, why didn't the jury just find Patrick guilty?"

"Fred's sources suggest that when Caleb wouldn't resign,

another deal was offered. Perhaps your brother convinced Ruef that it would be in his best interest to see that Patrick was declared innocent. Perhaps Caleb had found something on Ruef. You know there are men in the city working to see Ruef's empire toppled."

"No doubt you're right, but surely Caleb wasn't one of them."

Henry shrugged. "I cannot say. The notes found and rumors unearthed suggest that Caleb was somehow involved. It's even possible that Ruef offered to ensure Patrick Murdock would be found innocent if Caleb would agree to come to work for him."

Camri twisted her hands together. "But he would never do that. Caleb is a man of great conviction."

"I know." Henry's reply was one of resignation. "However, I wouldn't put it past Caleb to pretend to accept in order to get Patrick set free. It would account for the ten thousand dollars I found, as well as the notes suggesting Caleb's involvement with Ruef."

"So you think my brother took the money and then turned on Ruef after Patrick was found innocent?"

"If he did, then it most certainly would bring about retribution. There's something else. As I mentioned, Caleb kept a book of notes, and in them, it appears that he hired Patrick Murdock after he was set free."

"To do what?" Patrick had said nothing of this. What if he knew a great deal more than he was admitting? What if he, too, was lying to her?

"It would seem that Patrick was helping him gather information."

"Information about what?"

Henry shook his head. "I can't be sure, Camri. The notes are in a sort of code. I haven't been able to completely decipher them."

This news troubled her as nothing else had. In all the time she and Patrick had spent together, he'd never said anything about actually working for Caleb. What was he hiding?

". . . but then I would have expected him to say something."

Camri shook her head, trying to clear her mind. "I'm sorry, I didn't hear you."

Henry looked momentarily annoyed. "I asked if you had discussed with Patrick his thoughts on where your brother might be."

"Some. He's been trying to find Caleb since he disappeared."

"But he clearly said nothing about working with Caleb." He shook his head and *tsk*ed. "If he had nothing to do with Caleb's disappearance, then why not admit working with Caleb?" He didn't wait for her response. "Oh, well. Perhaps I should have a meeting with Mr. Murdock and see if he can tell me the extent of his employment with your brother. Perhaps he even understands your brother's code. If Caleb was as virtuous as we both believe him to be, I fear he may have gotten in over his head. If he resolved to take on Ruef and his political machine alone, then he most certainly would have been in danger."

Camri could hear the girls returning. Judith was even singing a Christmas song at the top of her lungs.

"I don't want to discuss this in front of the others," she said. "Just tell me this—does Mr. Johnston know what happened to Caleb?"

"No. Not yet. He's doing his best to find out."

A cold shiver ran down Camri's spine. "Does he believe my brother is dead?"

Henry glanced away. "If he crossed Ruef . . ."

He left the rest unsaid as Judith and Kenzie burst into the room with armfuls of decorations.

"Look what we found!" Judith had a wrapped bundle in

her arms, and she opened it to carefully spill the contents onto the sofa. Gold and red-ribboned ornaments clattered onto the cushion beside Camri.

"Be careful, silly," Kenzie chided. On her arm hung a basket. "Those are glass, you know."

"I'm sorry," Judith said, kneeling beside the sofa to make certain the ornaments had survived. "I'm just so excited. I love Christmas, and decorating is one of my favorite things to do."

Kenzie shrugged and held up her basket. "I have strands and strands of glass beads and tins for the candles."

"And I suggested we could string cranberries for added color," Judith announced.

Camri barely heard her, however. Henry's news hadn't been at all encouraging. No matter what choice Caleb had made, it seemed almost certain that the decision had resulted in his disappearance. Possibly his death. But if that was the case, then how did the Wongs figure in? And why hadn't Patrick been honest with her about working for Caleb?

"Come on, Camri. Come help us decorate the tree."

Camri cast a glance at Henry. His expression was sympathetic. She shook her head. "I'm afraid I'm not feeling up to it, Judith." She got to her feet. "You'll have to excuse me. I'm going to my room to rest."

She heard their protests as she hurried upstairs. But instead of going directly to her room, Camri went to Caleb's instead. She closed the heavy door behind her and stood for a time in the dark. Tears spilled onto her cheeks as she thought of Caleb lying dead somewhere without a proper burial. For all that she had feared for him, Camri had never really allowed herself to dwell on the possibility that he was dead—that he would never be found. How would she ever bear it if this was true? How would their poor parents and sister take the news?

She turned on the bedroom light, then crossed the room to

pull down the shades. She wanted to shut out everything that wasn't related to her brother.

"They could all be wrong," she whispered as she glanced around the room. "Mr. Johnston, Henry . . . they might not know anything at all and simply be telling me this because it seems reasonable."

Camri shivered and hugged her body to ward off the chill. She longed to throw herself into comforting arms that would embrace her and hold her close. She longed to hear words of encouragement that would reassure her that all was not lost.

She longed for Patrick Murdock.

But even as she allowed that thought to take form, she pushed it away. It was absurd. She didn't even know if she could trust Patrick. He and Caleb had apparently been working together on something other than Patrick's murder trial, yet Patrick had never revealed this to her. What if Patrick knew more than he was saying? What if he knew something more about the money and the choices Caleb had made before he disappeared? What if he'd betrayed Caleb to Ruef and his men? Maybe that was where the deal truly had been made. Maybe Ruef promised Patrick freedom if he helped him capture Caleb. But why would Ruef want her brother? Nothing made sense.

Camri glanced at the ceiling. "I have no answers, only more questions. I don't know what's happened to Caleb, and I certainly don't know who I can trust."

Ophelia's words came back to her. "*Ye will know deep in yer heart if a person is worthy of yer trust. Just don't jump to conclusions.*"

"But those conclusions seem to jump at me."

Going to her brother's dresser, Camri picked up his folded handkerchief and breathed in the fading scent. There were so many puzzles to solve, and as soon as she managed to make headway with one, a dozen more presented themselves. It was like a series of Herculean tasks that she could never hope to master. But if she didn't master them, the truth about Caleb might never be known.

She clutched the handkerchief to her breast. "And I cannot let that happen."

CHAPTER 16

I'm glad you agreed to see me," Henry said, showing Patrick Murdock into his office. "Have a seat, and I'll get right to the point." He reached over and turned on his desk lamp.

Patrick did as Henry instructed, unbuttoning his coat as he took a seat. "For sure I wish ye would. My sister isn't well, and I don't like leavin' her to the care of others." His tone was curt, and it was clear he didn't want to be here.

"It's about the work you were doing for Caleb." Henry could see Patrick's eyes widen just a bit as his right brow raised. Henry held up the book from Caleb's desk. "I found this ledger. It's filled with notes, most of them in code, but others not. I surmised from what I read here that Caleb hired you to help him investigate something to do with Abraham Ruef."

For a moment, Henry wasn't sure Patrick would admit his involvement, but then the large Irishman shrugged. "Half the honest men in San Francisco are doing that. 'Tis no secret Ruef needs to be taken to task for what he's done."

"True, but why the secrecy?"

"Well, protesting Ruef's actions in public only served to have

163

me thrown in jail for a murder I didn't commit. Caleb and I agreed secrecy was the way to go about it."

"To what end?"

Patrick fixed his gaze on a spot somewhere over Henry's head. "I don't suppose it could hurt anythin' to tell ye that much. Caleb promised to help me reclaim my family business and home by provin' Ruef had my father murdered."

Henry leaned back in his leather chair. "So it was a personal matter?"

"Aye."

"And that's all there was to it?"

Patrick's expression suggested he was carefully considering his reply. Henry didn't know why he should be hesitant unless he was intending to lie.

"The truth, Mr. Murdock. You owe that much to Caleb."

The large Irishman's expression changed from passive to angry. His eyes narrowed. "Don't be tellin' me what I owe Caleb Coulter. I know full well what I'm owin' him. But yerself, on the other hand, I do not owe. In fact, I don't even know but what ye were part of Caleb goin' missin'."

"How dare you accuse me? I had nothing to do with Caleb's disappearance. I cared for him like a son." Henry yanked open a drawer and pulled out a set of papers that had been carefully folded together. "I had this drawn up just before Caleb went missing." He threw the papers at Patrick and waited until he'd opened them. "I made Caleb a legal partner in this practice."

Patrick scanned the pages, then refolded them and handed them back to Henry. "I meant no offense, but ye have to admit that everyone is suspect. I know ye look at me in the same way, but I'm tellin' ye I'm not to blame. I suppose now I must be allowin' that ye're not to blame either."

"Well, that's good of you to offer me that much." Henry

threw the papers back in his open drawer, then slammed it shut. "Now, will you please tell me what you know?"

Patrick scratched his bearded chin. "Aye. Helpin' me was the start of things, but the more we dug for proof, the more incriminatin' evidence we uncovered."

"Incriminating evidence of what?"

"Of the underhanded devilry bein' done by Ruef. Caleb started talking to folks who were sufferin' because of Ruef. Then he and I made records of everything we had, but I haven't any idea where those records are now."

"Well, as I said, I found a ledger of notes."

"But there was a stack of papers with proof of bribes and fees paid to Ruef. I know, because I stole them from his residence."

"You stole them?" Henry was surprised at the casual way Patrick admitted to this.

"Aye. 'Tis no shame to steal from the devil."

"And now those papers are gone?"

Patrick shook his head. "I don't know what's happened to them. Caleb had them, and I figured him to have them hidden in a safe place. But ye haven't found 'em here, I'm guessin', and Camri hasn't found them at Caleb's house. Caleb's study at the house was ransacked. It could be those papers were found and retaken."

"It's possible." Henry rubbed his chin. "What of the ten thousand dollars?"

"Money Ruef gave Caleb."

"For what?" Henry leaned forward so quickly that he sent several pens flying off his desk.

Patrick retrieved the pens and handed them back to Henry. He settled back in his chair, acting almost as if he hadn't heard the question.

"Well?" Henry pressed.

"Ruef wanted Caleb to work for him. Not to leave yer place here, but just help on the side. He gave him the money just after the trial concluded. See, before the trial, Caleb had a talkin' with Ruef about me and the charges. Somewhere in the conversation, Caleb mentioned powerful allies he had made back east, men in the government and such, and apparently in the tellin' of it, Ruef decided it'd be to his advantage to get Caleb on his side. After that, things began changin', and next thing I know, I've been found innocent.

"Of course, Ruef made it clear that this had happened by his good graces. He told Caleb that he would see to it that I was thrown back in jail if he refused to help Ruef. Caleb pointed out that I'd been found innocent and couldn't be standin' trial again for the murder, but Ruef said that wasn't any trouble. He'd simply have me charged with a new murder. Caleb agreed to take the money and consider the proposition. Ruef told him he had a few days to decide. When those days were up, he came to Caleb for his answer."

"And Caleb agreed to work for him?"

"In a fashion. Caleb and I discussed it and figured it would be one way to get evidence that would clear my name once and for all. Caleb never intended to keep the money, but rather use it as proof of Ruef's bribery. He said Ruef had handled the money himself and had left his fingerprints on it. Caleb said the court didn't allow fingerprints as evidence against folks yet, but the day was comin', and he intended to hurry it along if possible by usin' it to see Ruef imprisoned."

Henry sighed. "I feared it might be something like that. I've had someone looking into the matter, and he told me there was some evidence pointing to Caleb working for Ruef."

"He would never have worked for the man in the sense of helpin' him do his dirty deeds," Patrick threw out. "He was only seekin' to help me, and now he may well be dead."

"Do you understand the code he wrote in his ledgers?"

"No. I cannot help ye with that."

"Very well. I have only one more question. What do you think happened to Caleb?"

Patrick looked toward the ceiling. "For sure it can't be good. I haven't been able to find out anythin', and I have friends in all the places that might prove helpful."

"Camrianne said you were continuing to look for Caleb. That you would help her with her search."

"And so I will. I've got my suspicions, but nothin' yet to be talkin' about. When I know somethin' more, I'll be tellin' her."

"Perhaps it would be better to just tell me. She's already very upset."

"Aye, and well she should be, but I'm not completely sure I can trust ye, even if ye were meanin' to make Caleb a partner."

Henry felt his anger rise. "What do you mean by that?"

"I've told ye what I have because ye already knew that I'd been workin' for Caleb. But I don't know ye well enough to trust ye with everythin'."

"If you know more—more that will aid in locating Caleb—then you must tell me." Henry slapped his hands on the desk, sending the same pens skittering to the floor.

This time Patrick didn't bother to retrieve them and instead got to his feet. "I don't feel obligated to ye, Mr. Ambrewster. My loyalty is to Caleb and then to his sister. I'll be biddin' ye good-night." He headed for the door, then turned. "I don't mean to be tellin' ye your business, but I'd be puttin' that ledger somewhere safe where no one else could be gettin' to it. Could be someone will come lookin' for it."

With that he left, and Henry could only sit, staring at the door. He'd never anticipated Murdock's distrust. After all, it was his office that had taken care of all their business dealings. It was by his willingness that Caleb had represented Patrick in court. How could Murdock doubt that Henry was just as eager to find Caleb as he was?

Henry picked up the ledger and turned it over and over. Murdock made a good point regarding the book, however. He needed to make sure it remained safe. He got up, thinking to put it in his wall safe where he'd put the ten thousand dollars, then changed his mind. He walked to the bookcase and moved a bookend that held his prized first edition commentaries by Blackstone. The set had been a gift from his wife a decade earlier. The ledger was about the same size and very nearly the same outer binding as the other volumes. At a glance, no one would notice the book wasn't a part of the set.

He put the ledger between the commentaries, then re-secured the bookend. He stood back to survey the shelf. It looked good enough to fool most prying eyes.

He'd no sooner done this and returned to his desk, however, than he heard someone enter the outer office. Perhaps Murdock had come back to apologize.

But when the door opened, it wasn't Murdock. Instead a seedy-looking character entered with a revolver pointed at Henry's midsection.

"I've come to get the goods Coulter had on the boss," the man growled.

Henry shook his head. "I don't know what you're talking about. What boss? What goods? Do I represent his company?" He gave the pretense of checking his appointment book. "I don't have anything in my book that suggests we were to meet this evening."

The man crossed the distance from the door to the desk in three long strides. He leaned across the desk and pressed the gun into Henry's chest. "Don't play dumb with me. Boss Ruef says your boy Coulter was looking to ruin him. Your boy has some sort of evidence, and the boss wants it back."

"If my employee took something from Mr. Ruef, how should I know about it? Coulter's been missing since the end of August. It's now December. Whatever papers Mr. Ruef is seeking are most likely with Mr. Coulter. And I have no clue where he might be."

The man grunted and without warning hit Henry against the temple with his gun. The pain was intense, and for a moment Henry saw stars.

"The boss said to tell you that if you don't hand the papers over, along with his money, then I can kill you."

Henry found himself hoping Patrick Murdock might return for some reason. The big Irishman was intimidating and would no doubt strike a bit of fear into the smaller thug.

"Where is it?" the man demanded.

"I don't know." Henry put his hand to his head and pulled it away sticky with blood. He stared at his hand for a moment. Would this man really kill him? "Tell me something." Henry pulled a handkerchief from his pocket and wiped his hand. "Did your boss kill Caleb Coulter?"

The thug grinned and shrugged. "He ain't telling me if he did. But then, I know better than to stick my nose into business what ain't mine. What *is* my business, is that you give me what I came for."

"But I don't have it. Look around my office if you don't believe me." Henry remembered what Patrick had said about Caleb's office being ransacked. "Tear it to pieces like you did Coulter's study at home."

The man's eyes narrowed. "I'll give it a good going-over after I give one to you." He came around the desk and yanked Henry to his feet.

Dizzy from the blow to his head, Henry fought to remain upright. "You can do what you will, but I honestly do not know where your boss's papers are. I've never seen them and didn't even know they existed until tonight."

The hoodlum punched Henry in the stomach. The blow knocked the wind out of him, and Henry's knees buckled. For the oddest reason, he found himself thinking of a conversation he'd had with Caleb shortly after he'd come to work for him. Henry had found Caleb reading his Bible over lunch and asked him why.

"Because I want to know God," Caleb had said, smiling. *"That way, when I go to meet Him, there won't be any doubt in my mind as to who He is. And in the meantime, I'll be able to tell other folks about Him so they can know Him too."*

Caleb's faith had helped Henry come back from his dark despair over losing his wife. It had helped put Henry back on a more positive path. He'd returned to church not long after that and from time to time shared Caleb's noontime Bible study.

Henry looked up to find the man once again pointing his revolver. "This is your last chance, old man. Give me those papers and the money."

Strangely enough, a peace washed over Henry, and a smile came to his lips. "I can't give you what I don't have."

———

Patrick arrived home to find Liam sitting by the door of his apartment. "And why would ye be waitin' out here?"

Liam got to his feet and dusted off his threadbare pants. "Your landlady said Ophelia was sleepin'. I didn't want to bother her, knowin' that she's sick."

Patrick nodded. "'Twas considerate of ye, but come on inside." He unlocked the door and ushered Liam in. "Just let me go check on her, and I'll be back."

He tossed aside his hat and coat and made his way to the bedroom. Someone had lit the bedside lamp and turned it low. Patrick could see his sister's pale face in the glow. For a moment he feared she was gone, but her ragged breathing told him otherwise. He turned from the room, leaving the door open in case she called to him.

Liam stood beside the window, looking out into the night. "Were ye workin' late?"

"No. I was called to a meetin' with Caleb Coulter's employer. 'Twas rather strange, to be sure. I've never really known if I could trust him."

"'Tis a hard thing to know who can be trusted in this town."

"Aye." Patrick eyed his friend. "But for sure ye didn't come all this way to be talkin' about that."

Liam chuckled. "No, for sure I didn't. Ye need to go see Malcolm Daniels at his dance hall. My friend's brother, Sean Gallagher, will introduce ye. Daniels is looking for a few strong-armed men to keep his customers in line. Sean's brother Bert said there was a ruckus that ended with a couple of Daniels' trusted men being killed, so he's lookin' to replace 'em."

"When am I supposed to go around?"

"Tonight wouldn't hurt none."

Patrick glanced at the clock. "'Tis nearly eight o'clock. I suppose I could go. I hate leavin' Ophelia again, but I know she'll understand. She wants Caleb to be found as much as I do."

"I'll walk ye part of the way," Liam offered. "It's on me way home."

"Let me go speak to Ophelia first, and then we can go."

Patrick went back to the bedroom and pulled up a chair he kept for just such talks. "Ophelia, darlin', wake up."

She stirred but didn't open her eyes.

Patrick put his hand on her shoulder and gave a gentle shake. "Ophelia."

This time she opened her eyes, and when she realized who called to her, she smiled. "Paddy, 'tis good to see ye." Her voice was but a whisper.

"I have to go again, but I wanted to talk with ye first. I have to check somethin' out, and I don't know how long I'll be gone."

"Is it about Caleb?"

"Aye. I've had some word from Liam. He's got me a possible job at the place where Caleb was last known to go."

Ophelia nodded. "Then ye must be about it. I'll wait up for ye."

"No, ye need to sleep."

She smiled and reached out to touch Patrick's hand. "I'll not be needin' it much longer. Now go on with ye and find our Caleb."

Patrick covered her hand with his. He didn't want to leave her. The doctor had already said she could go at any time. Her heart was weak and her lungs congested. She didn't even have the strength to cough, and the pain that coursed through her body was evident in her pale blue eyes.

"I'll be back as soon as I can." He lifted her hand to his cheek.

"I'll be here," she said, her voice barely audible.

"See that ye are." He let go of her hand and tucked her arm back under the covers.

Sorrow threatened to hold him in place, but Patrick knew he had to leave—had to see Daniels. He hated the very idea of working in such a vile place, but if there was even a remote chance of finding Caleb, then he had to try.

CHAPTER 17

The walk to Daniels' Dance Hall was damp and chilly. Patrick pulled up the collar to his coat and wished he'd thought to bring along the scarf Ophelia had knitted him last year. Once Liam parted ways for the warmth of his house, Patrick couldn't stop thinking about how cold he was and how much he longed to be home . . . or sitting by a fire with Camri.

He hurried his steps once he turned onto Pacific Street and made his way deeper into the seediest and vilest part of San Francisco. It was here, in what was called the Barbary Coast, that a man could pay and receive most anything he might dream up. Posters were plastered on the walls, advertising a variety of entertaining acts. Some were such that audience participation was even encouraged. All were of a perverted nature.

As he continued toward Daniels' place, the crowds thickened. Men from various walks of life seemed anxious to spend their money and piled into one place or another. Music spilled out into the street from the various dance halls where women known as "pretty waiter girls" enticed men to drink and dance until the wee hours of the morning.

Patrick averted his eyes as he passed by dance halls and sa-loons where scantily clad soiled doves called out with crude invitations. He could remember his mother's warnings about such forms of sin.

"Paddy, ye ne'er wanna be found in such places, doin' such deeds. 'Tis a sorrow to yer Heavenly Father's heart to see His creation so sadly used. Just remember, it could be yer own sister forced to live such a life. Those poor souls are someone's daughters and sisters. Ye treat them with respect, and if I ever catch wind that ye went to those places for so much as a drink of whiskey, I'll wear off your backside with a switch."

He smiled. She would have done it too, even though at eigh-teen he was a man full-grown and towered over her petite frame by at least twelve inches.

Red lights lit up the sign that beckoned entry to Daniels' Dance Hall. Patrick made his way to the door and the ham-fisted man who stood outside with two women who looked far older than their years. One of them immediately opened her robe to reveal herself to Patrick.

He quickly looked at the bouncer. "I'm lookin' for Malcolm Daniels or Sean Gallagher."

"And who might ye be, friend?"

"Name's Patrick Murdock. I've come for a job."

The man looked him up and down, then nodded. "Aye, ye'll do nicely." He extended his hand. "I'm Sean Gallagher."

Patrick returned Gallagher's firm handshake and waited for him to make the next move. It didn't take long.

Gallagher gave the girls a nod. "Won't be but a second. Don't be givin' too many favors for free."

He headed inside the dance hall, where a tinny piano and four-piece brass band fought to outdo the drummer, who pounded out a beat as if leading troops to war. The room was filled with smoke and the odor of unwashed bodies and whiskey.

A few tables were set up against the wall opposite the bar, but most of the crowd was on the dance floor.

Gallagher led Patrick through the room at a quick pace, but not quick enough. Patrick was appalled at the way the women were dressed and equally disgusted by the way their dance partners groped them. With such displays given so casually, he could only imagine what happened behind closed doors. How could he possibly work in a place like this, knowing what was going on?

"It's just this way," Gallagher said, pushing open a door. Patrick's eyes adjusted to a dimly lit hallway just as Gallagher opened another door farther down the corridor.

"Mr. Daniels, here's the man I told you about. Patrick Murdock."

Patrick met the older man's gaze. Malcolm Daniels was no stranger to a hard life. His face bore scars from previous battles, and his large nose looked to have been broken on more than one occasion.

"Get on back to work, Sean. Murdock, take a seat." Daniels motioned to the well-worn leather chair that sat in front of his desk.

Patrick said nothing and did as he was told. He kept a keen eye on Daniels, however, even as he pretended to glance around the small room.

"Sean tells me you're looking for work," Daniels began.

"Aye." Patrick saw no need to add to his reply and said nothing more. He did fix Daniels with a stern gaze, however.

The older man's eyes narrowed. "Why did you come to me?"

"A friend knows Sean's brother and told me ye might be lookin' to hire a man or two."

"I might. Can you fight?"

This actually made Patrick smile. "Aye. I used to do it for money. And before ye ask, yes—I won. Ne'er lost a single bout."

"Never?"

Patrick shook his head. "Never."

"So why'd you quit? Seems you could be making money doing that."

Patrick stood. "Seems that would be my business. If ye're not lookin' to hire, then I won't be takin' up yer time."

"Sit down, Mr. Murdock. I'm still looking to hire, but it's my business to know your business. I need a man who can handle himself in a crowd of drunken sailors and riffraff. The men who come in here can be real brutes, and I won't have them hurting my girls." He laughed and added, "Not unless they pay extra."

"So what is it ye'd be wantin' me to do?"

"Keep the peace and break up the fights. If a fellow gets out of hand, it'll be your job to straighten him out. I need someone on the dance floor at all times. Do a good job, and you might find some bonus work sent your way."

"Bonus work? What kind of bonus work?"

"Right now, that's not important. Do your job, and we'll talk about it again."

"So does that mean ye'll be hirin' me?" Patrick rubbed his sweaty palms against his pants. He hadn't realized until that moment just how nervous he was about this encounter.

"I'm willing to give you a try. I'll need you every night from six to six. You can start right away . . . tonight."

"No, I can't."

Daniels looked at him angrily and growled, "What?"

"My sister is dying. She has just hours . . . days, at the most. I cannot come to work for ye until she passes."

The rough man's expression softened. "I am sorry. Of course, you can wait."

Perhaps he had recently lost someone himself. Patrick didn't much care why he'd suddenly struck a sympathetic note with the otherwise heartless man, but he was grateful.

Daniels regained his fierce scowl. "Can you handle a gun?"

"If I have to."

Daniels nodded. "Good. I keep some revolvers here. It doesn't hurt to let the customers know that my peacekeepers are armed." He got up and headed for the door. "I'll show you a few things, then you can go."

Patrick followed him from the room.

Daniels pointed down the hall. "These are rooms for private card games." He led Patrick down the corridor and motioned to his left when they came to the end. "This door goes upstairs to the girls' rooms."

Patrick looked at the closed door. "Does someone stand guard here?"

Daniels shook his head. "Not generally, although on occasion they do. The men have an incentive to behave themselves. They have to leave their wallets with the barkeep until their business is done. The girls are strict timekeepers, and if the men cause problems, they have a buzzer they can ring for help." He turned to the door on his right and opened it. "This goes down to the storage room where we keep the liquor." He turned on the light and started down the steps.

Patrick followed without comment. There didn't seem to be any good reason to speak, so he remained silent. At this point, it was more beneficial to be aware of his surroundings.

"If you're asked to fetch a case of something, you'll come here." Daniels stepped aside and let Patrick survey the large open room. The walls were lined with crates bearing the names of various liquors.

Patrick heard the sound of water lapping but didn't pose the question on his mind. Instead he let Daniels continue the tour.

"We've got a supply of household things back in this room. Towels, bedding, and such. It don't amount to all that much, but we try to run a clean establishment. There's extra glasses and mugs back here too." He opened the second door far enough for Patrick to get a look.

Daniels pulled the door closed and proceeded across the room to another door. "This is our receiving room." For this he pulled out a key and unlocked the door.

Patrick entered the room behind Daniels. The smell of filth and water mingled, and Patrick understood the sounds he'd been hearing. It was often said that many of the Barbary Coast establishments were built over water inlets and creeks that led into the bay. Daniels' place was clearly one of them.

"We get our supplies of liquor through here as well as anything else we need." Daniels smiled. "Send things out this way too."

Patrick tried not to appear very interested, but by his estimate, they were directly under the saloon. He surveyed the docking area at the water's edge and then looked back across the room where bales of hay were spread out. He glanced upward. There were telltale signs overhead of trapdoors. Men like Daniels would have the barkeeper slip something in the drink of a man who looked able-bodied. As the customer began to lose consciousness, a trapdoor could be used to drop the man here. A spring mechanism would quickly pop the door back in place before any of the other drunks even noticed.

Patrick looked back at Daniels, who seemed to be gauging his reaction. Patrick gave a casual nod. "Seems efficient."

Daniels smiled and nodded. "It is."

He led Patrick back out and relocked the door before heading back upstairs. Once there, Daniels took Patrick to the bar and introduced him to the barkeeper.

"This is Nelson. He keeps the bar most of the time, and when he's not able, his brother Albert takes over."

Patrick nodded. "Name's Murdock. Patrick Murdock."

"Say, not that fella who was on trial for murder here a while back."

Patrick hadn't expected this but hid his surprise. "The same."

Daniels seemed to look at him with new respect. "Murder, eh? Must have had a good lawyer to get you out of that trouble."

"He had good friends," Patrick replied in a knowing way.

The two men nodded in understanding. "It helps to have friends," Daniels replied. "Could be we have mutual friends."

"Could be. But if ye don't mind, I'll be takin' my leave," Patrick said, noting the time.

Daniels nodded, though Nelson looked surprised. Patrick offered no explanation but turned and headed for the door.

At the end of the bar, a man was beginning to get familiar with one of the pretty waiter girls. When he reached out, she quickly jumped back, causing the man to rip open the front of her flimsy dress.

"Look what you did! You're going to pay for that," she said.

"Hardly," the young man replied, staggering to his feet. "Come on now and give me a kiss."

Patrick saw this as the perfect opportunity to solidify his position with Daniels. Just as the man tried once more to kiss the girl, Patrick grabbed him by the collar and drew him up close.

"You're causin' a bit o' trouble, mister. I'm thinkin' ye might want to reconsider your situation. Now why don't ye pay the young lady for the damages ye caused and be gone?"

"Get away from me, you mick."

The boy, barely a man, pushed back and broke Patrick's hold. He came at Patrick with his fists doubled and took a swing. Patrick clamped his hand over the drunken man's fist with his right hand and belted him in the gut with his left. The hit left the boy gasping and staggering.

"Pay the young lady."

The young man fished a bill from his coat pocket and threw it on the bar. The girl quickly grabbed it.

Patrick dragged the boy to the door. He turned him toward

the street, then gave him a swift kick out. He glanced back at Daniels to gauge his response.

The surprised look faded from the owner's face as he roared with laughter. "I think you'll do just fine," he said.

———————

Patrick yawned as he let himself into the apartment. He had turned to lock the door when he heard Ophelia's weak voice.

"Paddy?"

"'Tis me." He went into the bedroom and smiled at his sister. "What can I be doin' for ye?"

"Come sit," she barely whispered. He started for the chair, but she touched the side of the bed. "No. Sit here . . . with me."

Patrick did as she asked, but there was hardly room on the narrow mattress despite Ophelia's tiny form. He took her hand.

She strained to breath. "Won't be . . . long now."

He quickly realized what she meant and frowned. "I can send for the doctor."

"No. He cannot help."

Patrick felt his throat tighten. "Can I?"

She nodded. "Hold my hand."

"I can do better than that." He turned and pulled her into his arms, cradling her like he had when she was much younger. His father had done the same when his mother was dying.

Ophelia gave a weak smile. "I don't want . . . ye . . . to fret. Ye know . . . I'm goin' to a . . . better place."

"I do, but I'll be missin' yer company."

She nodded. "Don't forget." She drew in a raspy, shallow breath.

"Forget what?"

"Make yer . . . yer peace with God."

"I've been workin' on it." The words stuck in his throat.

Ophelia's face tensed in pain. She closed her eyes and panted. Patrick had never felt more helpless. He wished he could do something to alleviate her misery, but he knew the end would come soon enough.

They sat in the stillness of the night saying nothing for the longest time. Patrick's back was starting to ache, but he didn't move a muscle. He had no desire to disturb Ophelia in her final minutes or hours. However much time it took, Patrick would sit here and hold her.

Eventually Ophelia whispered, "I love ye so."

"And I love ye more than life itself." His voice broke. "I wish ye wouldn't leave me alone. Ye're the last of my family."

Her lips gave the slightest upturn as she opened her eyes. "Make a new one—with Camri."

Her words took him by surprise. "So now ye're matchmakin'?" At least it helped him to push back his sorrow for just a moment.

She tried to lift her hand to his face but failed. "Ye need her. She needs ye too." She moaned and pressed her hand to her stomach. "It's . . . not . . . good."

"What's not good?"

"To be alone." She closed her eyes. Her chest barely rose as she struggled to breathe her final breaths.

Patrick knew there was nothing to be done, so he just held her and prayed for her release. As much as he wanted to keep her with him, he couldn't bear to think of her in such terrible pain. The minutes ticked by, and neither one said anything. Patrick could feel her slipping away with each shallow breath. She was really going to leave him—just like Ma had left them years before. Just like their da.

He kissed Ophelia's forehead. His voice was barely a whisper. "I remember when ye were just born. Ye were small, but ye had a set of lungs on ye. Screeched like a banshee, ye did. Ma called me to come see ye and put ye in me arms. Ye opened yer eyes and looked at me like ye had somethin' to say."

He smiled at the memory. "I fell in love with ye from the start, even though I was but a lad. Ye were always followin' me around, askin' me questions and demandin' I take ye with me." Patrick's vision blurred from tears. "I wish ye could take me with yerself just now. This world won't be half as nice without ye here to cheer me on."

She didn't reply or even move. Patrick wasn't completely certain she was still breathing. He pulled her closer and rocked her back and forth as he'd done when she was a baby.

"Ye can go on with yerself. Go on to Ma and Da. I give ye leave."

It was as if she'd just been waiting for permission. She drew one more breath and then nothing more. Patrick felt the stillness of her small body and knew her soul had departed.

He buried his head against her hair and wept. He cried for the loss of her life, for the loss of his father and mother, and even for the distance he'd allowed to come between himself and God. Once the tears began, Patrick wasn't at all certain he could ever stop them again.

CHAPTER 18

*P*atrick had never felt more alone in his life than the day he buried Ophelia. It was a rushed burial without fanfare. There'd been no money for anything more than a gathering of neighbors and the local priest. Thankfully, their father had purchased four burial plots when their mother died. Now all but one were filled.

He stood by the grave, staring at the mounded dirt that he'd helped shovel into place. Ophelia had been such a light in their life. Their father had often called her his little sunbeam. Patrick had thought it quite appropriate.

"But now our light is gone," he murmured.

A chilled wind left him with little desire to remain at the cemetery. Daniels had heard about the death and funeral. He sent Patrick a bottle of whiskey and a note telling Patrick not to report for work until the following evening. It was strangely generous for a man who had a reputation as a ruthless shanghai agent and brothel keeper.

Patrick stuffed his hands into his empty pockets and walked the short distance home. He knew the apartment would seem dark and empty, but he had nowhere else to go. For a moment

Camri came to mind, but he pushed the thought aside. She'd be working today, and there was no sense in going to Caleb's house.

He glanced heavenward. It seemed most everyone he held dear was up there now. Or wherever God had put paradise. He'd heard so many arguments about life after death, and it seemed everyone had a different opinion. He thought again of his mother.

"Paddy, I can't know for sure exactly how God has every-thing arranged and planned out. Folks who spend their time worryin' about such details are missin' the point. Where God is takin' us isn't nearly as important as how we get there. Jesus said in the book o' John that He's the only way."

The wind whipped up, and Patrick pulled his coat collar tighter and picked up his pace. He believed what his mother had told him. He'd learned all about God at his mother's knee. The trouble was, he didn't understand how God could be loving and still allow all that had happened to his family. Maybe it didn't matter if he understood. Maybe these trials were simply a part of life rather than an indicator of God's character. He sighed and wondered if he'd ever really know God as Ma and Ophelia had.

At home, he lit the stove and put on the kettle for tea. While the water heated, he went to the chest at the foot of Ophelia's bed. In it were all the possessions she'd managed to keep after they'd been evicted from their home. He'd promised her he'd go through it once she was buried, and there was no reason to put it off.

He opened the chest, and right on top he found a letter ad-dressed to him. He set it aside and picked up the next thing, her Bible. It was tattered and torn—a hand-me-down from their grandmother. It was one of the few things their mother had brought from Ireland. Beneath the Bible were a variety of things. There were a couple of dolls, one a simple cloth creation their mother had made, the other a fine china doll dressed in blue silk that Da had given Ophelia just after their mother died. He'd told her how Ma had always longed for such a doll when she was a small girl. He hoped having it would remind Ophelia of her mother. It did, but not nearly as much as the old rag doll.

There were a few other trinkets. Little bits of the past that Ophelia had managed to keep when everything else was taken. He lifted several pieces of fancy work that Ophelia had sewn. Years after their mother died, the neighborhood ladies, at least those who didn't mind her Irish heritage, had invited Ophelia to come to their homes for teas and sewing circles. They encouraged Ophelia to set up a hope chest and fill it with all the things she'd one day need as a bride. When their father had heard about this, he fashioned a chest for her. The very one Patrick was looking through now.

It wasn't all that long, however, before Ophelia learned she was sick. After that she seemed less inclined to worry about fancy work and instead made things for Patrick and their da. She had told Patrick that she wanted to keep her eyes on the here and now rather than on a future that would never be hers.

Tears came to his eyes. "But it should have been yers, Ophie."

He hadn't called her by her childhood nickname since their mother passed on. It was at Ophelia's request that he'd stopped. She had told him nicknames were for children, and now she was going to be a grown-up and take care of her mother's household. No amount of reasoning with her could change her mind.

Ophelia could be just as stubborn as their mother. Just as stubborn as . . . Camri's image came to mind, and even though tears slid down his cheeks, a smile came to his lips. Ophelia had liked Camri very much—just as he did.

Ignoring the other things in the chest, Patrick took the letter and Bible with him to the front room and sat down at the small table. He placed both in front of him, then lit a lamp. He hesitated only a moment, then unfolded the letter.

Paddy,

If you're reading this, then I've gone on and you're alone. I hate to think of you sitting in the apartment, mourning me. We both knew this day would come, and you know deep in your heart that I'm in a better place. Still, I know you feel the emptiness, just as we both felt it when Ma and Da left this world.

I have only two requests of you. The first is simple. I want you to give Granny's Bible to Camri. I know she loves God with all her heart, and though we just met, I've found a kindred spirit in her. She cares about you, Paddy. More than I think she's allowed herself to admit. She's a stubborn one, just like you.

"Like me, indeed. 'Tis yerself she favors," Patrick mused aloud.

I know you care deeply for her, and I believe you be-long together. Don't let pride or supposed walls come between you. I believe God has brought you two together for more than just finding her brother. Don't let love slip away without putting up a fight, Paddy. You and Camri belong together.

He reread the last two sentences, shaking his head. Ophelia was such a romantic, but she had no idea of the very real wall that stood between Patrick and Camri. Most of that wall had been put into place by others—people who insisted the Irish were lower than dirt. People—supposedly good people—who felt it important to keep social classes separated lest one be tainted by another. What Ophelia suggested would take more strength than he had to give.

Don't mourn too long, Paddy. You once told me after Ma had gone that she wouldn't want me to be sad because her release was one of joy. 'Tis the same for me. The pain I've felt has been far worse than I've let on, because I didn't want you fretting or working yourself to death to find relief for me. I only mention it now because I want you to know that my release—my freedom from this body and the pain—is most welcome. I'm truly happy to be going home . . . except for leaving you. That's why I hope you'll heed my suggestion and put aside your silly ideas that you don't deserve Camri or that she won't have you. I feel confident she will.

Remember that I love you, that I will always love you, but Paddy, God loves you even more. He's there for you now—just as He's always been. He's just waiting for you to come home. And that's my second request. Get out of the pigsty and come home to the Father who's waiting.

Ophelia

He read the letter over and over until the whistling teakettle drew his attention. He folded the letter and put it in his coat pocket, then made himself a cup of tea. He took his mug back to the table and sat there for a long while, looking at his granny's Bible. His sister's romantic notions were farfetched. Camri was a woman of independent means. Not just money, but of intellect and fortitude. She had no need of a poor Irishman's love.

On the other hand, he couldn't ignore Ophelia's heart for him to make things right with God.

Patrick rested his elbows on the table, then hid his face in his hands. The sadness and loneliness threatened to overwhelm him. It seemed he stood at a crossroads. Caleb had told him this day would come—this moment in time when Patrick could no longer ignore what he knew to be the truth.

I'm a dirty rotten sinner, Lord. Ye know that better than anyone. My heart is shattered in a million pieces, but if there be even one piece worth Yer trouble . . . then I give it to Ye. Forgive me, I beg Ye now. Forgive my arrogance and pride. Forgive my doubt and my anger. I've nothin' left, Lord. I'm an empty man who wants to come home.

———

Camri climbed down from the delivery wagon once again. Earlier that day, George Lake had been completely beside himself. A dozen deliveries to some of the wealthier households in San Francisco needed to be made, and he had no one who could take them. The regular deliveryman was already taxed beyond his ability with deliveries to multiple stores around town. Poor Mr. Lake might have gone himself, but he didn't trust the others to be able to take care of the factory should anything break down.

Camri had volunteered to make the deliveries if Mr. Lake would be so good as to loan her his carriage. She assured him she could drive a team quite capably and was able to find her way around the city. Seeing he had no other choice, the little man agreed.

Camri hoisted down a heavy crate of Lake Chocolates. Mr. Lake had been kind enough to put the boxes of chocolates into smaller crates that Camri could manage. They couldn't count on the household staff to help unload the deliveries, Mr. Lake had explained, so this was the best solution.

"Well, this is the last of it."

She counted the boxes in the crate, then checked the number

against the order list she'd been given. Twenty boxes had been ordered, and twenty boxes were ready for delivery. She tucked the list in her pocket and hoisted the crate in her aching arms.

She made her way to the delivery entrance of the lavish Victorian mansion belonging to Rudolph Spreckels. She'd learned on her first stop that even the kindest of butlers had no tolerance for deliveries being brought to the front door. Camri had never thought about such things. She'd always been on the receiving end of deliveries, and only then after the household staff had seen to them first. More surprising was the snobbery and intolerance among many of those who worked in the nicer households. There was an obvious ranking of importance among the servants, and most of them treated her as if she were far beneath them—a lowly delivery girl.

It was something she hadn't expected. Her world had been filled with fashionable and well-educated people before coming to San Francisco. However, she had always congratulated herself on her knowledge of the workingman's plight and believed herself quite understanding of the poorer populace. Her mother had taught her that even the lowliest servant still deserved her respect. The servants in their house were paid well and treated as valued employees rather than lowly laborers. They were encouraged to attend school and better themselves. Her father had even financed the education of two of their staff. If there was a hierarchy and such attitudes of disdain among those who worked for her parents, Camri hadn't experienced it.

She carried the crate to the back door and then shifted it awkwardly in her arms in order to ring the bell. A uniformed woman quickly opened the door. She looked at the crate in Camri's arms, and only after this did she look at Camri.

"I've never had a woman deliver before," she murmured before turning back. "Jason, come see. There's a woman bringing candy to the house."

A robust young man appeared. He looked to be a houseboy, hardly old enough to be out of school. He took the crate from Camri. "I love candy."

"Well, it isn't for the likes of us," the young woman declared.

The houseboy laughed. "One of the boxes could fall and just happen to spill out. The master wouldn't want it then."

"Get those to the kitchen and stop talking nonsense." The woman turned back to Camri and frowned before reaching into her pocket. She drew out a small coin purse. "If he doesn't improve, he'll be fired before Christmas."

Camri thought of a dozen things she might say but declined them all. She took the few coins the woman offered and headed back to the carriage. People were funny. Under different circumstances, she might have come to this house as a guest and been waited upon by the same young woman and boy. There would have been no conversation between them, and certainly no voicing of opinions.

She climbed back into the carriage and put the horse in motion. She couldn't help but dwell on the matter as she made her way along the avenue of the wealthy. While working at the factory, she'd been able to forget about such concerns as social standing. Where a person lived and where they intended to take entertainment for the evening seemed very unimportant in light of struggling to feed a family.

Back in Chicago, Camri had often lectured younger women on the importance of education and securing for themselves the ability to master their own destinies. With God's help, of course. She was never one to believe a person could do anything without divine guidance. Her students, mostly daughters of upper-middle-class working fathers, had received her wisdom with rapt attention. The times were changing, after all, and women would soon have the right to vote. After that, who knew what rights they might be able to secure for themselves?

But what of the poor who had no hope of leaving low-paying jobs in order to attend school? Most employers wouldn't be as generous as her father had been. Most employers had little desire to see their workers educated. An educated man was dangerous. He would get ideas about how to better his situation. An educated man or woman would soon be discontent and demand more.

Camri thought of Patrick and his sister. Had either of them been allowed an extended education, they might not now be living in poverty. Not that there was anything wrong in being a contractor, but a college education might have allowed Patrick the knowledge to protect his holdings.

But he's Irish.

There were a great many people who felt the Irish were worthless and should be forced back to Ireland. There were an equal number who'd been fighting for years to force the Chinese back to China. There was no desire in people in positions of authority to allow these groups to better themselves. She'd often seen signs in Chicago declaring, *Irish and Jews need not apply!*

Patrick and his sister would have had a hard time getting anyone to allow them a better education. If they'd been rich, their heritage might have been overlooked, but as the children of a common contractor, she doubted they would have changed the hearts and minds of very many people.

She tried to keep her mind on the increasing traffic, but thoughts of Patrick and Ophelia wouldn't leave her. She found herself heading in the direction of their neighborhood almost before she realized what she was doing. Judith and Kenzie would think her mad for venturing alone into a place deemed so dangerous, and Mr. Lake would be furious at the delay of her return. Patrick would probably admonish her as well, but none of that deterred her. Let them all have their say and their worries. She wanted to check on Ophelia and see how she was feeling.

After passing through the better parts of town, Camri made her way along the same route she'd walked with Patrick. Although she'd only been there a couple times, the sights were familiar. She'd always been one to note landmarks and oddities, and this time it was to her benefit. By the time she turned onto Patrick's street, she felt pleased with her decision. She'd arrived safely and on her own.

But then she saw the black crepe hanging from the front door of the building where the Murdocks lived.

For a moment Camri wasn't sure she could draw breath. She stopped the horse and set the brake, unsure what to do. She knew without being told that the crepe was there for Ophelia.

Tears came to her eyes at the thought of that sweet, gentle woman passing away. She wondered how long ago it had happened and how Patrick had taken the news. A sob broke from her throat and without a thought as to what the people around her might think, Camri buried her face in her gloved hands and cried.

It was probably foolish. Someone might come along and take advantage of her, but still Camri couldn't help herself. She felt a deep loss for this woman she barely knew. Life seemed suddenly so overwhelming. Ophelia was dead. Caleb was still missing, and she had no more idea of where he was now than when she'd arrived a month ago.

"Camri?"

When she first heard Patrick speak her name, she thought herself imagining it. But when he said it again, she looked up. He stood beside the carriage, looking at her as if she were some ghostly figure. She barely maintained control as she whispered his sister's name.

"Aye."

She burst into tears anew. Patrick climbed into the carriage and pulled her into his arms. Camri sobbed against his well-worn coat. She didn't care that she was making a public display of her grief and familiarity with Patrick. He didn't seem to care either.

He was sympathetic and tender and all the things she needed in that moment. Things she'd convinced herself she didn't need in life. All of her strongholds of self-created strength dwindled, and in the wink of an eye, Camri felt more vulnerable than she'd ever known. Nothing in her education had prepared her for this rush of emotions.

Finally, after a long while, she straightened. "I'm . . . I'm so sorry." She was barely able to speak.

"Aye." His soft Irish brogue very nearly sent her into another fit of tears.

"I . . . wish—I wish you would have sent . . . me word." She drew a deep breath. "When?"

"The night before. We buried her today."

Camri straightened and wiped her eyes with the back of her coat sleeve. Patrick reached inside his pocket and pulled out a handkerchief to hand her.

"Thank you." She dabbed her eyes and wiped her nose. "I don't know what came over me. I suppose the shock of it all." He still had his arm around her shoulders, and Camri didn't even try to move away. "I wanted to stop by and see her. That's why I'm here."

"Ye shouldn't have come alone." There was no real chastisement in his tone, and the look on his face told Camri he was glad she was there.

"I had to make deliveries to Nob Hill for Mr. Lake. This is his carriage, and I'm sure he's half frantic, wondering where I am."

"Why don't I drive ye back?"

She nodded and handed him back his handkerchief. "Please."

He pushed her hand away. "Keep it in case ye need it again." He picked up the reins and freed the brake. "Get on with ye now." He slapped the lines, and the gelding set off.

Camri couldn't begin to think of what she could say to offer comfort. Patrick and his sister had been every bit as close as she and Caleb were. What if it were Caleb who had died instead? What words of comfort would she want to hear?

They rode in silence as Camri pondered the matter. There was really nothing she could say or do that would prove her sadness any more than the tears she'd already shed. To try to say anything flowery or poetic would be a waste, and to offer religious platitudes might even offend.

"Is it silly to say that I loved your sister? I know I only just met her a short time ago, but there was something about the way she touched my heart that leaves me unable to put it any other way."

"'Tis not silly at all. She loved ye too. She even thought of ye like a part of our family."

Camri nodded. "I'm so glad. I would want her to."

The traffic and noise increased around them as they neared the factory. A freight wagon narrowly missed clipping them as it came around from the right and decided to turn left in front of them. Patrick reined back the horse and reached out to keep Camri from flying forward at the same time.

"There goes a man determined to meet his Maker," Patrick muttered.

A young boy hawking papers up and down the sidewalk drew closer. It was only then that Camri made out the words he shouted. "Extra! Extra! Henry Ambrewster murdered!"

She felt a cold sort of electricity start in her toes and flood through her body. She began to shake uncontrollably.

Patrick immediately understood. He pulled the wagon to the curb and motioned to the boy. "Give me a paper." He flipped him a coin.

The boy handed up the paper and went on with his declaration. Patrick scanned the front page.

"It says he was shot in his office." He was quiet for a moment. "I'm thinkin' it would have happened just after our meetin'."

"What?" Camri looked at him and shook her head. "What meeting?"

"He sent me a message to come to his office. I went to see what he wanted."

"And what did he want?"

"To know what I knew about Caleb." Patrick shoved the paper at her and grabbed the reins. He slapped them and glanced over his shoulder as he pulled them into the city traffic.

"I don't understand any of this. How could he be dead? Who would even want him dead?" Camri asked.

Patrick's face had gone pale. He clenched his jaw tight, but she could see a slight tic in his cheek. What was wrong with him? Then it dawned on her. He'd gone to see Ambrewster. Someone might have seen him there.

Without thinking, she put her hand on his arm. "They can't think that you did it."

He shook his head. "They can think what they will."

"But I know you wouldn't hurt anyone."

He glanced at her, still shaking his head. "If anyone saw me there, I doubt it'll matter much what ye're thinkin'."

*C*amri directed Patrick to where he could park the horse and carriage, then allowed him to help her down. Her mind churned like clouds in a summer storm.

"I'll be takin' my leave of ye." Patrick started to walk away.

"Wait." Camri wanted to ask him about Ambrewster and confront him about his work for her brother, but she knew it wasn't the right time. "Come share supper with us tonight . . . please."

He looked as if he might say no, but then finally nodded. "Aye. I'd be glad to."

"Come any time after six." She glanced at the factory entrance. "We should be home by then."

"I'll be there."

She watched him walk down the alleyway. When he disappeared around a corner, she finally headed into the building.

"I'm glad you're back," Kenzie declared as Camri stepped into the office.

"What's wrong?"

"One of the machines went down, and Cousin George is convinced there's a conspiracy against him." Kenzie rolled her eyes. "I honestly don't know how he manages to keep from having a heart attack. He's been ranting and raving almost the entire time you've been gone."

"Is there anything to be done about it?"

Kenzie shook her head. "If there is, I don't know what it would be. He's had to stop production in order to tear the machine apart and see what the trouble is. He's questioning each and every workman to see what they might know." She nodded toward Camri's hand. "Is that today's newspaper?"

Camri glanced down and remembered all that she'd just learned. "It is. Henry Ambrewster has been murdered."

Kenzie paled. "When?"

"Yesterday. Someone went to his office and shot him." Camri tossed the paper atop Kenzie's desk. "Not only that, but I went to see Patrick and Ophelia." She bit her lower lip as tears blurred her vision. She drew a deep breath. "Ophelia died the same day as Mr. Ambrewster."

"Oh, my. I am sorry." Kenzie put her arm around Camri. "Do you need to sit?"

"No." Camri pulled out Patrick's handkerchief and dabbed her eyes. "I don't think it would help. I'm completely stunned by all of this. I was in such a state that Patrick had to drive me back to the factory."

"I'm glad. It's dangerous enough to drive without such an enormous distraction."

Camri ignored her comment. "I invited him to join us for supper. I hope you don't mind."

"Patrick Murdock? No, I don't mind. I think he enjoys our company—especially yours." Kenzie moved away as the office door opened.

Mr. Lake flew into the room like a crazed sparrow seeking refuge. "I'm sure you've heard the news, Miss Coulter. We are at a standstill until the machine can be fixed. My Christmas orders are doomed. I can't possibly hope to fill my orders now. We've been sabotaged once again."

Camri knew that nothing she said would matter. She pulled

off her gloves and stuffed them in her coat pocket, then began to unbutton her coat while Mr. Lake continued with his rant.

"I knew it was too good to be true. I knew the police were wrong about the break-in being nothing more than random thievery." He went to the filing cabinet and opened the top drawer, muttering as he pulled out first one folder and then another. "I am ruined. Plain and simple. I am ruined."

A knock sounded on the office door. Kenzie went to open it and admitted one of the men who worked for her cousin.

"Sir, we've repaired the problem," the workman announced. "It was just a piece that had come loose and detached itself. The safety mechanism stopped the machine before it could do any damage."

Lake tossed down the folder he'd just pulled. "It's fixed? We're up and running again?"

The man nodded. "Yes. Come see for yourself."

Without another word, Lake rushed past them and out the door. The workman looked at Kenzie, gave a quick shake of his head, then followed his boss.

"Well, that's a relief," Camri said, taking off her coat. "I'm glad it wasn't anything serious."

"This time," Kenzie replied. She went to pick up the folder.

"Do you really suppose someone is trying to sabotage your cousin's work?" Camri hung up her coat. "I know we've talked about this before, but it doesn't seem to be an issue that we'll be rid of anytime soon."

"I wrote my mother about it, and she replied that Cousin George has always been this way about most things in life. He's always been certain someone is out to do him in."

"But why?"

Kenzie shrugged. "No one has an answer for that. He had a very quiet upbringing. His father was a farmer, and there was no intrigue to speak of. Mother thinks Cousin George thrives on dramatics for some reason. She says he's mostly harmless in his fears and worries, and she suggested we humor him when we can and ignore him otherwise."

"So his fears of being sabotaged are probably just his imagination running wild?"

"That is Mother's opinion on the matter." Kenzie put all of the folders back in the file cabinet. "And we obviously haven't seen any proof to suggest otherwise."

"Well, I'm glad it was something that could be easily repaired. As for humoring Mr. Lake, I'm not at all certain that's wise. He has his notions, and I've seen things like this before. He'll either spend the rest of his life fretting and looking under every rock to find his spy, or he'll kill himself—or possibly someone else—trying to prove his plight."

"I'm afraid you may be right." Kenzie looked at the door to the factory. "I've tried to reason with him, explain that he's doing quite well for himself and that the factory is in good order. He has reliable workers and a strong clientele, but that only serves to strengthen his resolve that the other chocolatiers will want to see his demise."

Camri fished the delivery list from her coat pocket and took it to Kenzie. "I suppose we shall just have to endure. Things are bound to calm after the holidays pass."

"I can barely believe Christmas is in four days." Kenzie took the list. "Were all the deliveries made?"

"Yes, and everyone seemed happy." Camri wished she could share that feeling. With all that was going on around her, she felt a growing despair. She squared her shoulders. There was nothing to be done about any of it at the moment. "I'd best get back to helping Judith. She's no doubt overwhelmed."

Patrick sat in Caleb's front room, admiring the Christmas tree the girls had decorated, as Judith regaled them with Christmas carols. Camri said the tree had come from Henry Ambrewster, which reminded Patrick of his meeting with the lawyer. Ambrewster had been angry at his lack of trust, but given what had happened, Patrick was glad he'd said very little. He only hoped that Ambrewster had managed to hide Caleb's book of notes before he was attacked.

Attacked alone in his office. Murdered. There were no clues as to who had committed the act, or so the article in the paper said, but Patrick couldn't shake the feeling that Ruef was setting him up again.

When Kenzie moved to sit next to Judith at the piano, Camri came to sit beside him. "Doesn't she play beautifully?"

Judith looked up to smile. "I'd play so much better if you would all sing."

Camri shook her head. "I'm content to listen. Your playing reminds me of my brother."

Judith's expression became sympathetic. "I hope that's a good thing. I can stop, if you like."

"No," Camri said, shaking her head. "It is a good thing. It's almost like having him with us."

Judith smiled and began to play "Silent Night." Patrick did his best to remain stoic. This song had been his mother's favorite as well as Ophelia's.

"I hope supper was to your liking," Camri said.

"It was. Both the company and the food." He remembered Ophelia's Bible and reached into his coat pocket. "I have somethin' for ye. It's from Ophelia."

"Something for me?"

"Aye." Patrick handed her the Bible. "Ophelia wrote to me in a letter that she wanted ye to have it."

Camri opened the front of the Bible, shaking her head. "I'm deeply touched." She gasped. "This is a family Bible."

"Aye. 'Twas our granny's. She gave it to Ma before she left Ireland, and Ma gave it to Ophelia."

Camri closed the book and pressed it back into Patrick's hands. "I can't take your family's Bible."

He pushed the Bible back toward her. "It was Ophelia's final wish that ye have it. I'll not be takin' it back."

"But it's something that should be handed down through your family. There are records here that you'll want to keep."

"I'll be keepin' the records elsewhere, ye needn't worry." He smiled. "I'm glad for ye to have it." He wasn't about to tell her that Ophelia's desire was for them to add to those records by making a family together.

Camri looked at the Bible and gave a slow nod. "I'll take it for a time, but please promise me that you'll let me know if you want it back."

He felt a deep sadness. "Aye. I'll be lettin' ye know."

While Judith played on, Patrick thought of his sister's letter and her comments about not letting love slip away without a fight. Was it possible love could exist between two people from such different walks of life?

He glanced at Camri, who was looking again at the list of family names in his granny's Bible. The soft glow from the electric lights and fire in the hearth created a sort of halo around her head. Her chocolate brown hair seemed to take on a reddish tint, making him smile. Maybe there was a bit of Irish in her blood.

Camri seemed to sense his gaze and looked up. She had a single tear on her cheek, and he couldn't help but reach out to wipe it away.

"Ye shouldn't be cryin'."

"I can't help it. I know it's a time of celebration, but with all that's happened and Caleb still lost to me, I don't feel like celebrating."

"Aye. 'Tis well I understand, but ye cannot bring those souls back to us through tears."

"My mother used to tell me that God keeps all of our tears

in a bottle. It says so in the Bible. I think I've cried more since coming to San Francisco than in all the years prior. I've never been given to great emotion—at least not that I showed."

"Ye kept it in places hidden." Patrick gave a nod. "Just as I do."

"Yes, I suppose that's true." She leaned back. "I've always considered myself so well-educated, but as I sit here, none of that matters. I would gladly trade my knowledge and education to bring my brother back, to have made your sister well . . . even to keep Henry Ambrewster from being murdered. I've come to see myself as a prideful woman who really knows very little, and it shames me greatly."

"But ye've a heart of repentance and"—Patrick hesitated— "love. I've seen yer kindness to yer friends and others. Ye're a good and godly woman, Camrianne Coulter, and 'tis pleased I am to call ye friend."

She met his gaze, and in her eyes, Patrick saw a reflection of his own longing. Maybe Ophelia was right. Maybe they were meant for each other.

Without giving himself a chance to think it through, Patrick took Camri's hand. "I thank ye for makin' this evenin' bearable. I dreaded goin' home to empty rooms. Sittin' here listenin' to Judith play . . ." He glanced up, only to realize that sometime during his conversation with Camri, Judith and Kenzie had left the room. They were now quite alone.

Camri seemed to notice the girls' absence at the same time. "It appears we've been deserted."

"Aye, but I don't mind." He looked deep into her brown eyes.

She shook her head. "I don't either."

The fire popped and crackled as a log shifted in the hearth, but otherwise the room was silent. For all intents and purposes, they might have been on a deserted island. Patrick found he suddenly wanted to tell Camri about his life, about making peace with God, and about his growing feelings for her.

"Yer brother has been a good friend to me. We took to bein' friends even before I was accused of murder. Whenever he'd come to the worksite with papers for Da, he and I would spend time in discussion. Mostly about God."

She smiled. "That sounds like Caleb. Mother was always surprised that he didn't go into the ministry. He did study it, you know."

"He would have been good at it. He always seems to know what a person is thinkin'. I was strugglin' deep in my heart. My ma had taught me to put my trust in the Lord, but her death and Ophelia bein' sick, not to mention the growin' troubles we were havin' with our business . . . well, it caused me doubts and made me angry."

"At God?"

"Aye." He still held her hand, and since she hadn't tried to pull away, he took that as a sign that she approved. "Ophelia likened me to wrestlin' as Jacob did. I suppose 'twas a good way of seein' it. I just couldn't understand how God could allow such sufferin'."

"There's certainly a lot of it," Camri admitted.

"I've seen it all of my life. We always stayed with our own people—livin' in Irish neighborhoods and keepin' Irish ways. I learned to speak the Irish before I could speak English." He smiled. "Ma always said 'twas the language of angels."

Camri smiled. "I'd love to hear you speak it sometime. I've come to enjoy your brogue."

Her radiant expression caused his heart to beat a little faster. "That brogue can get me into trouble, ye know. A great many folks don't hold much appreciation for the Irish."

She sobered. "I know, but as you probably learned from Caleb, those things don't matter much to our family." She turned but still didn't pull her hand away from his. "Patrick, I know I've been prideful regarding my education and opinions on it. I'm sorry if I ever made you feel bad because of it." She lowered her gaze. "I'm ashamed to say that I thought myself so forward in my thinking and attitudes. I thought I understood the world and what was needed, but coming here, I've learned I don't know nearly as much as I thought. God has opened my eyes to a great deal, including the realization that I was putting far more trust and importance in my education than in Him."

He gave her hand a gentle squeeze, causing her to look up again. He smiled. "Seems we've both been wrestlin' with Him."

She bit her lower lip and nodded. She was so close. Her face was only inches away, and Patrick could sense that she wanted him to kiss her as much as he wanted to.

But something held him back, and when Kenzie and Judith entered the room, it was the perfect excuse to get to his feet. Camri set the Bible aside and rose as well.

"Ladies, I thank ye for havin' me to supper. It did my heart good. I hope I didn't put too much of a damper on yer evening."

Kenzie spoke first. "Not at all. You had every reason to be morose, but I didn't find you to be that way at all. I'm glad you agreed to share our company."

Judith stepped closer to add her agreement. "Death of a loved one is never easy. I still miss my mother. There are even times I start to turn and tell her something only to remember she won't be there to hear it."

"Aye. I've had that same experience. But time does ease the pain, and I know I'll be seein' them again in heaven. It's for sure not the same as them bein' with me in the here and now, but 'tis a promise of what's to come. I find a great deal of comfort in that." He looked at Camri and smiled. "But for now I must be takin' my leave. Ye've got work tomorrow, and so do I."

"Would you . . . I mean, tomorrow evening . . ." Camri stammered and looked to Kenzie and Judith for help.

"I think she's trying to ask if you'd like to join us tomorrow for supper," Kenzie interjected. Camri and Judith nodded.

"I thank ye for the offer, but I have a job that's gonna keep me busy in the evenings." He wasn't about to tell them where he'd be working or what he was really trying to do. He still had no idea how the dance hall fit into Caleb's disappearance.

"Well, just know that you're always welcome here," Camri murmured. "I'll get your hat and coat." She quickly left the room.

Patrick nodded to Judith and Kenzie. "If I'm not to be seein' ye before Christmas, I wish ye merry."

"Merry Christmas to you," Kenzie and Judith said in unison, then looked at each other and laughed.

Patrick chuckled at their amusement. "Farewell to ye, ladies."

He followed in the direction Camri had gone and found her waiting with his hat and coat. He took the coat from her and pulled it on. "I'll be glad for this on the walk home."

"I heard someone on the trolley mention snow."

"It won't snow here. It's rare as hen's teeth in these parts."

He finished doing up the buttons, then turned to take his hat. Camri's expression held a look of mixed emotions. He could almost guess that her feelings were as unsettled as his own.

"Thank ye again for havin' me and for bein' a good friend."

She extended the hat, but her gaze never left his. "Thank you for comforting me earlier today. You have proven to be a good friend as well."

He nodded, not daring to speak the thoughts that came to mind. Thoughts that had the potential to put an end to their friendship altogether if Camri's feelings proved to be different from his own.

"*Oíche mhaith agus Dia leat.*"

Camri cocked her head slightly. "Which means?"

"Good night. God bless ye."

She nodded and smiled. "Good night, Patrick. God bless you."

CHAPTER 20

Christmas Eve services on Sunday morning were what Camri expected. Pastor Fisher spoke of the unimportance of worldly gifts—trinkets bought with money that might have been better used to aid the poor and sick. He stressed that the only gifts worth cherishing were the gift God had given in sending His Son to earth, and Christ's gift to mankind by dying on a cross. Pastor Fisher concluded with an encouragement that the congregation share the gift of God's love with each other, as well as giving generously of their money to the benevolence fund.

Camri thought of the poor Irish neighborhood where Patrick lived. Those people suffered greatly because of the attitudes of others, as well as their own lack of education and money. She wanted to do something more to help them, but what?

She thought about talking to Patrick but worried about two things. One, he might feel belittled if she spoke of his neighborhood's poverty. And two, he might realize just how deeply she'd fallen in love with him.

Camri looked at her gloved hands. They were trembling. She had never fallen in love before. Most of her life she had been solely focused on getting an education and teaching others. Teaching had given her a sense of fulfillment. Working in the women's suffrage movement had given her a sense of purpose. But now, neither of those things did a bit to still the longing in her heart.

I'm in love with Patrick Murdock.

There was no use denying it, and yet there was also little she could do about it. Not because Patrick was Irish, as some might have figured. Not even because of his state of poverty and lack of education. No, she couldn't act on her feelings, because Caleb was still missing. How could she possibly put her own desires ahead of finding her brother?

On their walk home from church, Camri continued to ponder the matter. With Henry Ambrewster dead, she had lost not only his help but that of Mr. Johnston. Of course, it was possible she could talk to Mr. Johnston herself and see if he would continue to help her. She had his card, so perhaps it would be acceptable to call. Henry had just died, however, and Mr. Johnston was family, of a sort. She could hardly call on him, requesting his help, when he was in mourning for the loss of his friend.

"Camri, are you even listening?"

She barely caught Kenzie's question. "What? Oh, I'm sorry."

"No doubt thinking about a certain man," Judith said, smiling.

Camri felt her face grow hot. "Well, if you must know, yes. I was wondering who might help me find Caleb now that Henry Ambrewster is dead. Mr. Johnston was supposed to be getting us information, but now I don't know if he'll be inclined to help me. After all, Henry's sister is married to his brother, and the loss of Henry is no doubt great."

Judith's teasing look faded. "I'm sorry for teasing you. I know you're still worried about Caleb."

Camri shook her head. "I don't mean to be dismal about it,

but I'm truly at a loss. Patrick said he's looking for whatever clues he can find, but honestly I don't have much hope anymore. It's been over four months."

"You must always have hope," Judith said, looping her arm through Camri's. "Like the pastor said this morning, Christmas is all about God's gift of hope."

Kenzie had been quiet throughout the morning, but now she nodded in agreement. "We have to have hope, Camri. Life without it isn't worth living."

Camri looked from one woman to the other. "I know you're right. I want to be hopeful. I want to be strong and have no doubts. I'm afraid, however, that I'm weakening in my resolve. How can I hope to find my brother in this huge city? A city rife with murder and corruption of every sort?"

"Well, do you suppose we could just . . . set aside our worry about such matters for Christmas?" Judith asked in a hesitant tone. "Not that your brother isn't important. He is, and I pray for him all the time. But . . . well, it is Christmas and . . ." Her voice trailed off, as if she feared she'd said too much.

Camri knew her negative heart could ruin the holiday for everyone. She resolved to do what she could to make the day merry. "I think it's a good idea to do just that."

"I know," Kenzie said, "why don't we have a Christmas party—a dinner? We can invite my cousin and Patrick. They have no one else to be with, and we wouldn't want them to be alone on Christmas."

Judith looked at Camri. "Could we?"

"I think we should." Camri made a quick determination to put aside all her worries. "Let's send an invitation to Patrick and Mr. Lake right away. The Wongs intend to visit elsewhere, so we'll have to prepare the dinner ourselves."

"Are they spending the day with family?" Judith asked.

"I honestly don't know." Camri shrugged. "Mrs. Wong told

me Caleb always gave them the day off. She said they would leave early in the morning and probably not return before evening."

"That's all right. I can bake quite well," Judith offered. "I can cook other things too, but baking is my specialty."

"I can cook," Kenzie offered. "I've made more than my share of meals. We figured to have ham, so that will spread far enough to include other people. We'll just add another side dish or two."

"I've not had much experience in cooking," Camri admitted. It was yet another reminder that not all education came from a book. "But I am happy to help with arranging the table and cleaning up afterward."

"It sounds like we can manage this quite well," Kenzie replied as they reached the house. "I suggest we get the invitations out right away. Perhaps Mr. Wong would be willing to deliver them for us."

Camri felt her spirits rise at the thought of seeing Patrick again. "I think he might be persuaded."

After all their plans were made and the invitations on their way, Judith and Kenzie retired to their bedrooms while Camri made her way to Caleb's office. She felt almost intrusive being there, even though she knew Caleb would never have kept her from the room. In fact, when she'd last visited, he'd encouraged her to use the study for reading or writing letters.

She sat down at his desk and rubbed her arms. They'd kept the room closed to the rest of the house, so it held a damp chill. She leaned back in the leather chair and gazed around the room. She had put everything in order as best she could remember it, but somehow it just didn't seem right. Of course, the most important thing missing was Caleb.

"Where are you, Caleb?" she asked for what seemed the thousandth time.

She shivered, imagining him beaten so severely that he no

longer knew his own name. It was the only thing she could figure had happened. Otherwise he would have sent word.

Unless, of course, he was dead. Lately she'd had to allow that this was a strong possibility. Just the day before, she had penned a letter to her parents and alluded to that very thing. She knew her parents had been fearing such news since before she departed for San Francisco. They weren't naïve enough to rule out the possibility, no matter how much they wished it untrue. Catherine was even more pragmatic about such matters.

I don't know what I'll do if he's dead. How can I even know for sure unless I see his body?

She pressed her fingers to her temples. She had prayed so hard for answers, for Caleb's safe return. Yet she had no more idea of what had happened to him than when she'd first arrived. There were, in fact, even more questions, and now they had the matter of Henry's death to complicate things.

The hall clock chimed four. In days gone by, days when she and Caleb were still at home, they would have been preparing for a big Christmas Eve party. Her parents held one every year and invited all of their academic friends. It had been the finest of parties, with wonderful gifts and food. Camri had always enjoyed visiting with her parents' friends, but perhaps the most memorable and pleasant moment of all was her father reminding their intellectual guests the true reason for their Christmas gathering.

Just as Pastor Fisher had stressed, Jesus came as a gift to save lost souls. *"It's a gift,"* her father had said every year. *"A gift that we can accept or refuse, but nevertheless a gift. It comes without cost to us, but of considerable price to the giver. A gift more valuable than gold or silver. A gift of immeasurable value."*

After her father shared this, Caleb would play the piano and lead the guests in singing Christmas songs. "Silent Night." "O Little Town of Bethlehem." "Thou Didst Leave Thy Throne."

So many old favorites and a few new songs as well. Caleb always kept an eye out for the latest tunes.

She smiled and picked up one of Caleb's pens. Turning it in her hand, she tried to picture him sitting there at the desk—holding it as he prepared to write her a letter.

"I feel like there's so little I can do. I came here thinking it wouldn't be that difficult to find you, Caleb. I had this strange sense of confidence that it was nothing more than a misunderstanding—that I'd get here and find you, and you'd be safe."

She rolled the pen between her fingers. "Am I doing enough? Is there something I'm missing?" She sighed. Maybe the situation was like that old saying about not being able to see the forest for the trees.

"You must come back to us," she whispered. She fought off a wave of despair. "You will come back to us." She glanced heavenward. "Please bring him back to us."

She heard someone in the hall and got up quickly, losing her grip on the pen. When she bent to retrieve it, she found it had rolled completely under the desk. She thought about leaving it there, then feared the ink might leak out onto the beautiful Aubusson rug she'd helped pick out.

With a sigh, she carefully dropped to her knees and crawled under the desk. She had just reached the pen when she hit her head. She dropped to her stomach and reached up to rub her head, seeing stars.

Looking up, she was puzzled at what she found. There was some sort of box protruding out of the underside of the desk. It wasn't large at all, but long and narrow, and stuck out just enough to become an obstacle to anyone crawling under the desk.

"What in the world is this?" It clearly didn't belong there. Perhaps Caleb had put it there.

She reached up and pulled on the box. It gave a little, but not much. Camri backed out from under the desk and got to her feet. She needed something to pry it from the desk. She spied the thick, silver letter opener. Surely that would be strong enough.

She picked it up and returned beneath the desk. This time she stretched out on her back and reached overhead. Working the letter opener into the small space between the box and desk, she managed to work it loose. When it finally pulled away a bit, Camri gave a yank.

The box dropped into her hand, and inside she found multiple pages of paper rolled tight and tied with string. As quick as she could manage, she wriggled out of the small space and got to her feet. She untied the string and spread the pages atop Caleb's desk.

The first few were lists of names and amounts of money—a bookkeeping page of sorts. She ran her finger down the list, not recognizing many of the names. She turned page after page and came to the conclusion that this was a list of money received by someone. Then she found a page that listed numerous businesses. Again there were amounts of money recorded at the side, but this time there were notes made as well.

Owes $30,000 to Parker, Inc. Agree to pay this in return for assistance with Whitson merger. She frowned. What did it mean?

She came to the final piece of paper and found it was nothing like the others. This was a handbill for a business called Daniels' Dance Hall. The lewd sketches of women nearly made her put it aside, but just as she looked away, she saw the name *Liling* written in Caleb's hand. Beneath this was another name.

"Wong," she whispered. Beside the name was written *Room 210* with a question mark.

Liling? Wong? Did the names go together? Was it someone related to the Wongs, or did Liling mean something else in Chinese? What about the room number? Was it a room at this dance hall, or had this piece of paper just been utilized to jot down a note? Surely it wasn't the kind of place Caleb would venture.

She sat for a long time, staring at the handbill. Something inside told her this was the answer to finding Caleb, but for the life of her, she didn't know how it fit or what it meant. One thing was certain. It was well past time to have a talk with Mr. and Mrs. Wong.

———

Patrick awoke at the sound of knocking on his front door. He was exhausted from his night of manhandling drunks and keeping brawlers from destroying the dance hall and had little desire to crawl out of bed, even if it was just past four o'clock in the afternoon.

"Aye?" he said in a questioning tone as he pulled back the door.

He was surprised to find Mr. Wong outside. Before he could speak, however, the gardener extended a piece of paper. "Miss Coulter send this. You tell me yes or no."

Patrick yawned and forced his eyes to focus on the brief missive. It was an invitation to celebrate Christmas with Camri and her friends.

Please come share Christmas dinner with us at two o'clock tomorrow.

Camri

He couldn't help but smile. "Tell her for sure, I'll be happy to come."

Mr. Wong smiled and bobbed several times before he left. Patrick stood for a moment in the open doorway, staring after

214

the little man. An invitation to spend Christmas with Camri was definitely worth getting up early for.

He closed the door and yawned again. He glanced at the clock and tried to figure out whether to go back to bed or not. Malcolm Daniels intended to throw quite the Christmas Eve gala, and Patrick knew he'd need his mind to be sharp. Working for Daniels didn't preclude pickpockets from trying to steal what little he had, and Patrick had learned rather quickly that Daniels' bartender wasn't the only one slipping things into the drinks. More than one man had tried to kill another by lacing his drink with poison. Of course, Daniels' attitude about the latter was that so long as his workers weren't bothered in the process, anything was allowed.

Seeing as how he'd have to be to work in less than two hours, Patrick decided to stay up. He put some water on to heat, determined to clean up as best he could before reporting to Daniels. Not that it would matter. After only minutes in the smoky, heavily perfumed dance hall, Patrick had no doubt he'd smell just as bad as everyone else.

He glanced in the mirror. It wouldn't hurt to trim his hair and beard a bit. He was starting to look rather scraggly. Since losing their business, Patrick had relied on Ophelia to cut his hair, but now he'd have to tend to the matter himself. There was no extra coin to be paying a barber.

Thoughts of Camri came to mind as he took the scissors in hand. He had thought about her constantly last night as he kept an eye and ear open for anything related to Caleb. It wasn't hard to imagine that she wouldn't approve of his working for Daniels. Patrick wrestled with the idea of telling her about his position—telling her everything about the things he and Caleb had done to regain his business. He wondered how she'd receive the news. Ophelia had told him he owed it to her to be honest, but what if his honesty caused him to lose her good favor? Or what if once she found out he'd kept things from her, Camri decided to end their association altogether?

"Well, I just can't be lettin' that happen," he mused as he gazed in the mirror at his reflection.

He knew that things had changed between them. He couldn't be sure exactly what Camri's thoughts were on the matter, but he knew his own. He loved her, and he intended to see that she loved him in return. He'd woo her in whatever fashion was needed, but the secrets between them created an obstacle that had to be dealt with.

"I have to tell her what I'm doin' . . . what I've done and why." He wrapped a towel around his neck, then picked up the scissors. His pensive reflection only served to feed his fears. "I have to tell her the truth," he repeated in a firm voice.

His eyes narrowed as he tried to strengthen his resolve. "She might not be likin' that I've kept things from her, but it's been for her own good and Caleb's." He paused and frowned, re-membering Henry Ambrewster. What if telling Camri the truth put her in further danger? What if it caused someone to want to kill her?

"The truth is always best," he could hear his mother say.

He let go a heavy sigh and squared his shoulders. "I will tell her. I'll tell her tomorrow after dinner."

But even as he made that pledge, Patrick feared the result. The truth might be best, but it might also end any dreams he had of winning Camri Coulter for his own.

CHAPTER
21

"Thank you for a pleasant Christmas dinner," George Lake said.

For once he actually appeared calm and collected. Camri knew he was pleased. They'd managed to meet all of the Christmas orders and then some. Now perhaps he could relax a bit and ease up on his workers.

"Patrick, the plum pudding was an especially delightful treat," Kenzie said, smiling. "I've never had it before."

"Nor I," Judith admitted. "When you set it on fire, I thought the entire thing would burn up completely. I was happy to be wrong."

"It ne'er burns long, just enough to warm it a bit. Ophelia would be pleased to know ye enjoyed it. She made one every year usin' an old family recipe. She would always start it just after Michaelmas so it would have plenty of time to cure."

Camri had been touched that Patrick had decided to share Ophelia's last plum pudding with them. It made it seem like the young woman was with them in their celebration. Not only that, but it was delicious.

"Maybe you could share the recipe with me," Camri murmured.

Patrick gave her a wink. "I'm thinkin' Ophelia and Ma would approve."

There seemed to be something more implied in his statement, making Camri blush. Perhaps it was her own feelings running away with her, but she couldn't help but believe things were different between them.

"Well, there's a bit left," Kenzie said, lifting the cake plate. "Would you care for another piece, Cousin George?"

Mr. Lake shook his head. "No, my dear. I fear I would burst at the seams. No, I believe I shall retire to my little house and enjoy a Christmas nap."

"Must you go just yet?" Camri asked. "We thought to have Judith entertain us with some music and perhaps play some games."

Mr. Lake shook his head again. "I'm not one for such entertainments." He tapped his ear. "Tone deaf, I fear. I've never really enjoyed music. As for games, I haven't the patience."

"I would never want to impose something unpleasant upon a guest." Camri turned to Patrick, who sat opposite her. "How about you? Would you care to stick around for a little music? Maybe a game?"

Patrick folded his napkin and put it to the side of his plate. "I do enjoy Miss Judith's playing, but in truth, I had hoped for a few minutes alone to discuss a matter."

"Well, I suppose since it is Christmas, I should be willing to grant your wish." Camri smiled.

"I'm going to remember ye said that," he said with another wink.

Camri felt her face flush and hurried to dismiss her audience. "Shall we adjourn, then?"

Patrick got quickly to his feet and came around the table to help her up. He turned then to help Judith, while Mr. Lake assisted Kenzie.

"Ladies, thank you again for having me. I fear I've been less than kind to you at work, but I'm hoping this might help show you my gratitude," Mr. Lake said, reaching into his jacket pocket. He pulled out three crisp fifty-dollar bills and handed one to each of the girls.

Camri couldn't contain her surprise. "Why, thank you. I'm sure I didn't expect such a generous gift."

"Nor I," Judith replied. "I can't say that I've ever had this much money in my life."

Kenzie leaned over and kissed Mr. Lake on the cheek. "Thank you, Cousin George. How very generous."

He held up his hand. "I know I was a bear to work with, and I do apologize for that. The holidays are always stressful, and what with the questionable happenings at the factory, I fear I was a less than ideal employer. I hope this bonus will allow you each to buy some of those fripperies that women so enjoy. Now, if you'll excuse me, I must depart."

Kenzie nodded. "Come, I'll get your coat and hat."

They left the dining room, discussing something that Camri couldn't quite make out. She looked at the money. It would go a long way to helping her keep up with the household expenses. Now that Henry Ambrewster was dead, she had to find out the details of Caleb's mortgage.

Judith came to Camri and held out her fifty dollars. "It was fun to hold such a sum for a few minutes."

Camri shook her head. "Mr. Lake intended that as a gift. You needn't add it to the household monies. He might ask you what you purchased."

Judith's eyes lit up. "Fifty dollars to spend on myself? I've never heard of anything so luxurious."

"Well, you were just saying how you were in need of a new dress and—" Camri remembered the rest of what Judith had need of but felt it wasn't proper to discuss such things in front of Patrick. "You'll be able to get quite a few nice items with that."

"Oh, I'm going to go upstairs and dream on it. Maybe I'll take the newspapers with me and see what's on sale." She all but danced from the room.

Patrick laughed. "Ye made her day for sure."

Camri shook her head. "It doesn't take much to please Judith. She's a sweet girl who has never known much wealth. I'm sure fifty dollars seems like five hundred."

"And what of yerself? What will ye be buyin'?"

Patrick looked at her with a grin, causing Camri's heart to skip a beat. He was so handsome with his hair and beard trimmed in an orderly fashion. She couldn't help but be taken in by his nearness, and stuffed the fifty in her pocket lest he see that her hand was shaking.

"I have no needs, so my money will go for whatever expenses we have."

"'Twas a gift," he reminded her.

"Yes." She looked up and nodded. "And mine to do with as I please. And I please to put it toward the household." She turned and started to gather the plates. "I believe you wanted to speak to me."

"Aye, but not while ye work. Why don't I help ye clear this away, and then we could sit together somewhere private?"

Camri straightened and put the plate back on the table. "The dishes can wait. Why don't you come to my brother's office? I have something to show you anyway."

Patrick seemed momentarily torn between helping her and seeing what it was she had.

"Are you coming?"

He looked at her with an expression that made her cheeks warm again. "Aye, I'm coming."

She was well down the hall by the time he joined her. She

couldn't explain the giddiness she felt, nor the sense of anticipation. These were such new feelings that both confused and
stimulated her thoughts.

She led the way into Caleb's office and closed the door behind
them. She wasn't yet ready to share her information with Judith
and Kenzie and wanted to make certain they weren't overheard.

Patrick gave her a wicked grin. "So, ye wanted me all to
yerself, eh?"

Camri's mouth dropped open, but no words came. She had
heard of women coming under the spell of a man, but always
thought it silly. She always presumed she'd be above such nonsense. Now, however, she could see that she was just as vulnerable.

Patrick's blue eyes seemed to twinkle, and the lines around
them bore evidence of his happy nature. Despite all the troubles
he'd faced, Camri still found him to be lighthearted. He seemed
so capable—so even-tempered, although she'd heard that most
Irishmen were quite hotheaded. Perhaps it was just an old wives'
tale. She knew from the way he'd dealt with his sister and to
some degree with her friends that Patrick was gentle and kind,
even tender. It was his tenderness that sent her thoughts into
dangerous waters.

"I've ne'er had a lass look at me like ye're lookin'," Patrick
said, sobering.

Camri bit her lip to force her attention elsewhere. It was ridiculous to let her thoughts wander in such a manner. "Sorry,"
she murmured. She wasn't sure why she was apologizing, but
nothing else came to mind.

Without another word, she forced herself to walk to the desk.
She opened the top drawer but hesitated. Could she trust him?
Her heart said yes, but her heart was saying yes to an awful lot
where Patrick Murdock was concerned.

"Before ye go showin' me whatever it is," Patrick began, "I

want to be revealin' somethin' m'self. 'Tis the reason I wanted to speak to ye privately."

He looked uncomfortable, hesitant. "Go on," she said.

He came to stand beside the desk. "I haven't been completely open with ye regardin' your brother. Ophelia told me I should have told ye everythin' from the start, but . . . well, frankly I worried it might bring ye harm. Seein' what's happened to Ambrewster, I'm still not convinced it's wise."

Camri met his blue-eyed gaze. "The truth is important to me."

"Aye. I know, and 'tis the same for me." He surprised her by reaching out to take hold of her arm. "I was doin' a piece of work for Caleb before he disappeared. Actually, he was helpin' me, so we were workin' together."

"I know." She barely breathed the words. "Henry Ambrewster told me." He was so close she could scarcely breathe. "I wish you would have told me from the start."

"I know. I'm sorry. Like I said, I feared for ye." He let go of her arm. "I ne'er wanted to keep anythin' from ye . . . just to protect ye."

Camri reached into the drawer and pulled out the roll of papers. "I found these hidden in a box under Caleb's desk." She unrolled the papers. "I'm thinking you might know what this is about?"

Patrick's eyes widened. "Aye. I know very well. They're proof of Ruef's illegal activities. Caleb and I conspired to take them from his house. I feared they'd been taken."

"Is this why my brother is missing?" She looked into his eyes, certain she'd know if he lied to her.

"I can't be knowin' for sure. Caleb was helpin' me get evidence so that I might reclaim my father's business. Then we found other information, and Caleb decided we needed to put Ruef away for all his misdealings. We found a lot more than we ever intended."

"There's something else here. Something I don't understand." Camri pulled the dance hall flyer from the papers. "What do you know about this?"

Patrick took the paper and studied it a moment. "It's the last place I could track Caleb to."

"A dance hall? Why would he go there?"

Patrick looked up. "I don't know. He ne'er went such places as far I knew."

"No, he wouldn't." Camri shook her head. "Do you know who or what Liling is?"

"No. I cannot say I do."

"He wrote it on that bill along with the name of his household servants. You can see that for yourself. There's also a room number."

"Aye. I see it. But ye should be rememberin' Wong is a common name here among the Chinese."

"I don't know what to do about any of this. I intend to question the Wongs, but what with it being Christmas, I wanted to wait. Besides, they're not even here today. They're off visiting friends or family in Chinatown. At least, that's what they told me. They've been very suspicious in their actions of late. I can't help but think they know more about this than they're letting on."

"Camri, I must be tellin' ye somethin' else." He frowned and shook his head. "It's unpleasant to be tellin', but ye need to hear it."

She could see it was serious. "All right then, tell me."

"As ye know, I've been lookin' for Caleb ever since he disappeared. I felt certain it was my fault that he was missin'. The last place I could track him to was this dance hall, so I got a friend to help me get a job there. I just took it up."

"You're working at a place like that?" She couldn't keep the disgust from her voice and made no effort to hide her expression of distaste. "But why?"

Patrick again took hold of her arm. "I think it's the only way to find Caleb. See, Daniels' place is well-known for taking men hostage, shanghaiing them. They get 'em drunk and then slip somethin' in their drinks to knock 'em out. Sometimes they just hit 'em over the head, but they don't want them injured or killed because they can sell 'em to the ship captains as crew. I'm thinkin' maybe that's what happened to Caleb."

Camri had considered the remote possibility on more than one occasion. She preferred thinking Caleb was forced into service on a ship to him being dead at the bottom of the ocean. "Have you been able to find out anything?"

"Not yet. I've only worked there a few days. I'll have to be winnin' their trust before they'll be free with what they say and do in my presence."

"I still don't understand why Caleb would go there in the first place. I don't know what it has to do with the Wongs, but I'm going to learn what they're hiding. They know something, and they blame themselves for some part of it. They were involved with Mr. Ambrewster, and now they're simply going to have to answer to me about it. I've put this off as long as I dare."

"Don't ye think that if they knew something, they'd be tellin' ye?"

"I don't know." She shook her head. "Sometimes I don't think I've done right by Caleb or my family. I should probably be doing a lot more than I am. Mr. Ambrewster introduced me to a man who was helping him find Caleb, so I think tomorrow or the next day I should go speak to him."

Patrick stepped closer and, to Camri's surprise, drew her into his arms. "Ye need to promise me that ye'll leave it alone. I can go see this man, but it's too dangerous to go yerself. I don't want anythin' to happen to ye."

She was so stunned by his actions that she could scarcely think. When he said nothing more, she lifted her face to meet

224

his gaze. His eyes betrayed such longing that she thought her heart might stop beating all together.

"Promise me, Camri. Promise that ye'll leave it to me. I'll find out whatever I can and report back to ye. I'll tell ye the truth, no matter what. But ye need to promise me that ye'll not say or do anythin' more."

His mouth was only inches from hers, and his breath was warm against her face. Camri had never found herself in such an intimate position. She wanted to speak, but more than that, she wanted him to kiss her.

Which he did.

She didn't know what to expect from a man's kiss. Growing up, she had heard girls speak of stolen kisses and palpitating hearts. She'd thought it silly, useless to her ambitions. It didn't seem so now.

Her knees buckled, but Patrick held her fast. She wanted the moment to go on forever. In his arms she felt that the world was finally set right. There was nothing she couldn't face with him at her side. Nothing she wanted but him.

When he ended the kiss, he barely drew his face away from hers. She knew if he asked her to do most anything in that moment, she probably would agree. Thankfully he only asked for one thing.

"Promise me ye'll not go findin' that man," he whispered.

"I promise."

He pressed a kiss to her forehead, then let her go. "I'll be lettin' ye know what I learn."

Then, without another word, he left the room. Camri collapsed into the desk chair. She touched her lips, still stunned to think that Patrick had kissed her. Her gaze fell to the desk and the place where she'd set the papers only moments ago.

They were gone.

CHAPTER

22

*A*re you sure you don't want to come with us?" Judith asked Camri for the third time.

"No. I have some things to tend to. Besides, I've never really cared for roller-skating."

Judith laughed. "I've never been, so I can't say if I care for it or not, but Micah promised to help me. Kenzie did too." She fussed with her bonnet, trying, with no great success, to get her baby-fine blond hair to cooperate.

Kenzie came into the room, pulling on her gloves. "I heard my name mentioned."

"Judith was just saying that you promised to help her learn to roller-skate." Camri picked up her teacup and sipped the tepid tea.

"I am fairly accomplished at skating," Kenzie admitted. "I did quite a bit of it back in Missouri. Ice-skating too."

"I tried ice-skating in Chicago," Camri admitted. "I was even worse at it than roller-skating."

"I'm just excited to try it," Judith interjected, finally satisfied with her hat and hair. "I think it was awfully nice of Micah to invite us to go."

"Given that all of the young people from church are attend-ing," Kenzie said, "I hardly think it was anything personal."

"I don't know," Judith said in a teasing tone, "I think Dr. Micah rather likes you."

Kenzie's face flushed. "I've done nothing to encourage that and would appreciate it if you would also do nothing. If he speaks of me, tell him I'm not at all interested."

"Interested in what?" Judith asked.

"Anything," Kenzie snapped. She frowned. "Maybe I shouldn't go."

"Oh, nonsense." Camri got to her feet. "Go and have fun. It's not like you to back down from a challenge."

"There's nothing challenging about roller-skating." Kenzie headed for the door.

Judith grinned like an impish child. "No, but there might be to keeping your heart guarded."

Kenzie said nothing and headed out the door, which left Judith no choice but to follow, giggling all the way.

Camri thought about Judith's comment. Guarding one's heart wasn't an easy task. She had lost her own battle to hold off her feelings for Patrick. Their Christmas kiss had left her completely flustered, and his absence from her life since that day had caused her no end of worry and frustration.

He'd sent several notes, which at least let her know that he wasn't avoiding her. Although given the way he'd kissed her, Camri was fairly certain avoidance was the last thing on his mind. She had considered asking him to accompany her to Mr. Ambrewster's funeral, but then thought better of it. She was certain he wouldn't have the appropriate clothes for such an elaborate occasion. Not only that, but she had hoped Mr. Johnston would seek her out after the service, and she didn't want him to avoid her because Patrick was at her side.

However, Mr. Johnston hadn't sought her out. The funeral

had been one of the biggest she'd ever attended, and it seemed perfectly understandable that there would be no opportunity to speak on private matters.

Since then, Camri had often wanted to invite Patrick for supper, but knowing he was working at the dance hall, she refrained. He wouldn't be able to slip away, and there was no sense in making him feel bad. Luncheon on Sunday was also difficult because Patrick would have worked all night on Saturday. Perhaps breakfast before church would work. She thought about this for a moment, given it was already Saturday. She could have Mr. Wong take an invitation to Patrick.

Thinking of Mr. Wong led Camri back to her concerns about the handbill. How were the Wongs involved in Caleb's disappearance? What did they blame themselves for? She had promised Patrick she wouldn't go in search of Frederick Johnston, but she hadn't said anything about not questioning the Wongs. Ever since seeing their name on the handbill, she had been trying to figure out how to address the matter with them.

She glanced at the clock. It was nearly two, and the girls would be gone for at least three or four hours. Longer, if everyone decided to eat supper together at a local restaurant. It would give her more than enough time to question the Wongs.

Camri knew the situation would require patience and kindness. The Wongs were extremely private, and she had no doubt her mere appearance in the kitchen would put them on their guard. It seemed praying for guidance was in order as she headed for the stairs.

"Lord, help me handle this matter in a way that will allow the Wongs to speak openly about whatever they know. I had hoped to avoid troubling them at all. Even from the start, I didn't want to upset them, but now I think I must. Especially since Patrick is risking his life to learn the truth."

The Wongs sat at opposite ends of the kitchen table, each

busy with their own tasks, when Camri entered the room. They jumped to their feet despite her insistence they remain seated.

"Please sit. I hoped we might have a little talk."

The husband and wife exchanged a glance, then reclaimed their seats. Camri took a chair on the side, putting Mr. Wong on her left and Mrs. Wong on her right.

"I want to say first how much I appreciate all that you've done to keep Caleb's house running smoothly." She could see there was still great apprehension in the servants' eyes. She supposed there was no hope of easing their worries. "I know Caleb treasures you both, as do I. He has always held you in the highest regard."

She tried to think of what else she could say that might help the couple relax. A thought came to mind.

"Caleb once told me about you inviting him to celebrate Chinese New Year in Chinatown with your friends. He had such a wonderful time. I know it's nearly that time again. Do you have plans?"

Mrs. Wong gave a little nod and resumed peeling the boiled eggs that sat in front of her. "We celebrate with friends."

"I believe someone told me it's the year of the horse."

Again Mrs. Wong nodded. "Fire horse."

"Oh, is there a difference?" Camri hoped the question might inspire the Wongs to relax and speak more openly.

"Yes." Mrs. Wong offered nothing more.

Camri couldn't help but frown. It would seem this wasn't going to work the way she wanted. She decided to take a direct approach.

"I know this has been a difficult time for you. Caleb's disappearance has been hard for all of us, however . . ." She paused and tried to carefully word her thoughts. "I also know it's been harder on you."

"It hard to worry for his safety," Mrs. Wong murmured.

"Especially when you blame yourselves."

Camri let her statement sink in. She didn't miss the exchange of looks between the Wongs.

"I know this is difficult to talk about, but I need to know why you think yourselves to blame for his disappearance."

Mr. Wong had been sharpening knives and stopped. His expression was grim, but he remained silent. Mrs. Wong had tears in her eyes. She folded her hands in her lap and bowed her head.

Camri held back the urge to demand answers. She didn't know what they had done that made them feel so guilty or why they blamed themselves, but they owed it to Caleb to speak up. Their silence may have already cost him his life.

"You clearly know more than you're saying. I overheard you talking, and you said you blamed yourselves. I also found something that Caleb wrote with your name on it." She hesitated only a moment, then decided to drive the point home. "Who is Liling?"

For a long while, no one said another word. Camri was beginning to despair of ever getting an answer. It was obvious the Wongs were set against telling her anything. But then, just as she decided to leave, Mrs. Wong spoke up.

"Liling is our daughter."

Camri tried not to let her excitement get the better of her. "What does she have to do with Daniels' Dance Hall?"

Mrs. Wong looked at her husband. He nodded. "She work there. She forced to work there." The housekeeper's words were filled with pain. "She not grateful child and run away. We not know where she go for long time. Then we come work for Mr. Caleb. He find her and go to get her. Then he not come back."

Camri began to understand. "Caleb found out she was working at the dance hall and went to bring her back to you, but something happened."

Mrs. Wong had tears streaming down her face. "We not

know what. Mr. Ambrewster tell us it might be that men take Mr. Caleb because he make them mad. It might not be for trying to get Liling."

"You were working with Mr. Ambrewster to find her?"

"When Mr. Caleb not come home, we go talk to him. We tell him what happen, and he tell us to say nothing to anyone else. We say nothing . . . until now."

Camri sighed and tried her best to understand. "I wish you would have at least confided in me. You knew I was only here to find Caleb. You even knew I was working with Mr. Ambrewster."

"We know you look for brother with Mr. Ambrewster. Since he know the truth, we didn't need to speak," Mr. Wong finally said.

She knew it would do little good to berate them further. They were in pain from their guilt, but also from their daughter's situation. What parent wouldn't be?

"Patrick is helping me." She decided confiding in them might help the Wongs at least have a bit of relief. "I found a paper in Caleb's office—a handbill for the dance hall. It had Liling's name and a room number written on it. Patrick has that now, and he's taken a job at the dance hall. He's hoping to find out what happened to Caleb, but I'll ask him to also find out about your daughter."

"It too dangerous," Mrs. Wong said, shaking her head. "Mr. Patrick good man, and we not want him to go like Mr. Caleb."

"Nor do I, but I think it more dangerous for him not to have all the facts. Mr. Wong, I'm going to write an invitation for Patrick to join us for breakfast tomorrow. Will you take it to him this afternoon around five? He has to be at work by six, so hopefully he'll still be at home."

The old man said nothing for a moment, and Camri began to fear he'd refuse her. She wondered how dangerous it would be to walk the distance by herself. Surely God would protect her.

Mr. Wong got to his feet and nodded. "I take it."

Camri breathed a sigh of relief. "Thank you. I'll go right now and see to it."

She left the older couple in the kitchen and hurried upstairs. Patrick might not like that she'd been open with the Wongs regarding what she knew, but it was important he know the truth.

———

Kenzie sat on the side of the rink, watching the other skaters enjoy the afternoon. She remembered the first time she'd coaxed Arthur into going skating. He hadn't wanted to try it, but to please her, he'd given it a go and found that his sense of balance and grace made him a natural. They had made quite the skating pair. People actually stopped to watch them and more than once had come to comment afterward about how beautifully they performed.

"I haven't seen you smile like that all day," Micah Fisher said. He took a seat beside her on the bench.

Kenzie stood. "I wasn't aware you were keeping track."

He chuckled and got back to his feet. "You seem determined to keep me at arm's length. You won't skate with me, and you constantly run away from me."

"I'm not running away. I simply have nothing more to say." She fixed him with a stern look. "I'm sorry if that offends you."

"I'm not offended, but I am rather amused."

She couldn't hide her surprise. "Amused?"

"Absolutely."

"I see no reason to be amused by me."

"Perhaps I should enlighten you." He grinned. "I know you're nursing a broken heart, but I don't think you're completely unwilling to notice me."

"It's hard not to notice someone who is so obviously determined to be noticed."

233

To her surprise, he sat back down and stretched his legs out in front of him in a casual manner. "I don't usually have to work so hard at it."

Kenzie knew it would be better to just go and find Judith, but for reasons she couldn't explain even to herself, she sat down. "Why do you feel the need to work at it at all? I've made it quite clear that I'm not looking for a suitor. Why continue to pursue me?"

"Miss Gifford . . . Kenzie," he said, as if trying the name on for size. "Kenzie is such an unusual name. Why did your parents choose it?"

She'd been asked this question so many times. "My father fought in the War Between the States. He named me after his commanding officer, Colonel Merton Kenzie."

"A rather masculine name for a daughter."

"Yes, well, he wanted a son and made no attempt to disguise his disappointment." She chided herself for sharing this intimate detail of her life. No doubt it would only make him all the more curious.

"Men can be fools," Micah replied, "and it would seem you've had your fair share of fools in life."

Kenzie frowned. "Why would you suppose that, Dr. Fisher?"

He fixed her with a serious expression. "Given that your father was disappointed in you and that your fiancé was a complete cad, what other conclusion could I draw?"

One of the young women from the church skated up to them. "Kenzie—oh good, Dr. Fisher, you're here too. Come quick. Judith has taken a fall and hurt her ankle."

Micah got to his feet. "It would seem duty calls."

Kenzie nodded and watched as he followed the young woman across the rink. She felt almost sorry for Micah. He was clearly trying to win her over, but it was hopeless. She would never stop loving Arthur.

Patrick had barely buttoned his shirt when he heard someone knocking on his door. He hoped it wasn't Mrs. Ryan again. Twice she'd come to him just before he needed to leave for work with requests that he help her with one problem or another.

He stuffed his shirttail into his trousers with one hand and opened the door with the other. He found Mr. Wong on the other side. The man bowed and extended a piece of paper.

"Miss send you message."

Patrick took the note and unfolded it.

Patrick,

I must see you. I have information about Caleb and why he was at the dance hall. Please come for breakfast, and I'll explain.

Camri

"You have answer?' Mr. Wong asked as Patrick refolded the paper.

"Tell her I'll be there in the morning."

Mr. Wong nodded and immediately left.

Patrick closed the door and frowned. If she had information, that meant she wasn't staying out of it like she'd promised.

"She's a stubborn woman for sure," he murmured to no one and finished tucking in his shirt. Still, thoughts of Camri brought a grin. He'd wanted more than anything to have a chance to win her over. Now that he knew she felt as strongly about him as he did about her, he wanted more than ever to sort out the past and reclaim his father's business. He couldn't very well ask a woman to marry him, after all, if he didn't have a means of supporting her.

He finished dressing for work, then slipped from the

apartment as quickly as he could to avoid Mrs. Ryan. The sun had set, and with the heavy clouds overhead, it was already growing dark. It seemed these days he saw very little daylight, and it was beginning to wear on his spirit.

Daniels was nowhere in sight when Patrick arrived at the dance hall, but already there were plenty of patrons. Nelson gave him a nod as Patrick approached the bar.

"Gonna be a busy one tonight," Nelson said. He reached below and came up with a pistol. He handed it to Patrick, as was their routine each night.

Patrick slipped the piece inside his coat. "When's it not busy on a Saturday night?"

"True, but tonight promises to be even worse. Three ships came into the bay a while ago, and Daniels sent runners to bring the sailors here to do their drinking."

The runners were men who worked for the sailors' boarding-houses, of which Daniels owned six. It was a tradition that went back well over fifty years. A corrupt, devious trade that benefited ships' captains and boardinghouse owners, but not the sailors. The runners inundated the sailors with free liquor and entice-ments of generous accommodations. Generally, within half an hour of a ship dropping anchor, the runners had managed to remove almost every sailor. But those free enticements quickly disappeared once a man signed a boardinghouse contract.

Daniels was adept at getting all he could. His contracts ap-peared generous on the surface. The sailor was given room and board without any money up front on the promise that when he signed on to his next ship, the amount due would be paid in full. Of course, that usually meant the sailor was left with nothing. Not only that, but he soon learned the accommoda-tions weren't very good and the food was meager at best.

Daniels wasn't a fool. He was a man of greed and ruthless ambition. He didn't care about the men who came to seek entertainment and comfort at his establishments. He didn't care about the girls he used for his business. His only interest was money and plenty of it.

"No doubt there will be competitors seeking to steal away our customers. Probably a few will get heavy-handed," Nelson said as he returned to discreetly watering down the whiskey.

"I'll be on m'guard," Patrick said.

Nelson nodded with a sneer. "Well, that's what you're paid for. 'Course, I never did meet an Irishman who earned his pay."

Patrick didn't like the barkeep but said nothing more. There was no sense starting new problems when he still had so many to resolve.

CHAPTER

23

*S*unday, January seventh, was cold. It had rained most of the night and was continuing to rain that morning, much to Patrick's frustration. The walk from Daniels' place to Caleb's house was considerable, but spending extra money for the trolley wasn't an option. Aside from paying his rent and feeding himself, Patrick was saving all the money he could to buy a proper headstone for Ophelia.

By the time he knocked on the Coulter house door, he was drenched and shivering. Mrs. Wong took one look at him and called to Camri.

"Take him to Caleb's room so he can change his clothes." Camri looked at Patrick and sized him up. "You have a few pounds on Caleb, but I think most of his things will fit you. If not, I know he has a robe you can wear until your clothes dry. Speaking of which, Mrs. Wong, be sure to take Patrick's clothes and hang them in front of the fire."

Patrick smiled. She was ever the practical one. "For sure I'm grateful, but I don't want to be a bother."

Camri shook her head. "On second thought, Mrs. Wong, take him to the bathroom." She looked at him with concern.

"You should have a hot bath to ward off getting sick. Mrs. Wong will bring you a robe, and there are plenty of towels in the bathroom cupboard. Take as long as you like."

"But what about our talk and breakfast?" he asked in a teasing tone. "Or was that all just a tease to see that I got a bath?"

Camri laughed. "I'm sure after spending your time at Daniels', you probably need one, but no, it wasn't a tease. I'll send Kenzie and Judith on to church and wait to take my breakfast with you. Mrs. Wong will see to you. Now go, before you truly do catch your death. I'll lay some clothes out on Caleb's bed for you to put on after your bath."

Patrick didn't argue. It'd been a long time since he'd been able to soak in a tub, and he wasn't about to pass up the opportunity.

It wasn't until an hour later that he emerged wearing a pair of Caleb's gray flannel trousers and a long-sleeved white shirt. His reddish-brown hair was still damp, but Camri didn't seem too concerned. In fact, the look she gave him betrayed her thoughts. She wasn't at all displeased.

He threw her a smile. "Yer brother's clothes fit a bit snug, but not bad. I must say, I like his slippers. Ne'er had a pair like these." He held up his foot to show off the quilted, tassled footwear.

"I hope you feel better now?"

"I felt better the minute I walked into the house." He grinned. "But I'm thinkin' ye already know that." He glanced around. "Did the ladies go ahead to church?"

"Yes. Dr. Fisher—Micah came and picked them up in his automobile. Judith hurt her ankle skating yesterday—nothing serious, just a sprain—so Micah wanted to keep her from too much walking."

"That was kind. He's a good man. Caleb spoke highly of him."

"You've never met him?" Camri asked picking a strand of hair off her bodice.

Patrick thought she looked rather nervous. Perhaps nearly as nervous as he felt. "I met him once, but it was just a brief encounter."

She looked up. "Well, he is very kind and helpful. I think he's interested in Kenzie, but she can't be bothered to give him the time of day."

"For sure, a man can be blind when it comes to love."

She blushed and headed down the hall. "Breakfast is waiting, if you're hungry."

"Starved." He followed her into the dining room and helped her into her seat. "Smells good."

"Ham and eggs," she said as if he'd asked for the menu. "Toast and jam, and of course tea."

"Of course." He smiled and took a seat opposite her.

"I hope you don't mind us serving ourselves. I told Mrs. Wong to just see to your clothes." She picked up the teapot and poured herself a cup, then poured him one as well.

He took several pieces of ham from the platter in front of him before handing it to Camri. "I'm not one to have anyone waitin' on me, as ye probably already know."

She nodded. "I do." She added eggs and toast to her plate and then picked up the jam. As if sensing Patrick's gaze, she looked up and shrugged. "I like this strawberry jam. One of the ladies at the church made it." She slathered a liberal amount onto her toast. "It's delicious."

"Aye. I can see for m'self it must be."

She handed him the jar. "Judith said it was similar to a jam she used to make."

Patrick sampled the jam on his toast. Camri seemed anxious for his opinion. She watched him with such intent that he smiled. He put the toast aside and gave a nod. "'Tis nearly as good as me Ma's, but not quite."

"I'm glad you like it."

For several minutes she focused on her food. Patrick pretended to do the same, all the while studying Camri. She was dressed quite simply in a pale-yellow gown. It wasn't done up with all sorts of ruffles and lace like most women preferred. Fact was, he'd never seen Camri wear much of anything that bore those things. She was sensible, and he liked that about her.

When she finally braved a glance up, Patrick couldn't help but tease her. "Ye commanded me to come for a talk, but ye're silent. Cat must have yer tongue."

"I didn't command you," she said, straightening. A bit of fire came to her eyes. "I asked you to please come."

He laughed. "Well, I'm here, so tell me what ye need to say."

Camri put down her fork. "I talked to the Wongs and learned about Liling."

He looked up from cutting his ham. "I thought we agreed ye were gonna stay out of it." He eyed her like a father chiding his child. "For sure I remember a promise."

"I didn't go outside of the house looking for clues or contact Mr. Johnston about what he knows," Camri defended. "I simply asked the Wongs who Liling was. She's their daughter, and she's trapped at the dance hall. Forced to—to work there." Her cheeks reddened. "Caleb was trying to find her so that he could bring her back to the Wongs."

Patrick frowned. Caleb had said nothing to him about this. "So Caleb went to the dance hall to find their daughter and never returned?"

"Exactly. That's why they blame themselves for his disappearance. The room number written on the handbill—the handbill you stole along with those other papers—was Liling's room."

"Could be."

"You mean you don't know?"

Patrick shrugged. "I haven't had any experience with the rooms. I know there are a few just off the dance hall by Daniels' office, but that's for private card games. I've been in the lower level beneath the dance hall, but never upstairs where most of the . . . entertainin' goes on."

"Have you ever heard anyone talk about Liling?"

"Not that I recall. For sure men sometimes come askin' for a girl by name, but thankfully, I'm not the one who has to handle that matter."

"What . . . exactly do you do there?"

The hesitation in her voice made him smile. "Nothin' ye need to be knowin' about, but to put yer mind at ease, I mostly keep the peace."

She glanced down at her plate. "I didn't mean to pry. I just don't like the idea of you having to be there. I don't like that you're putting your life in danger. I've heard such foul things about those places."

"Ye can't be knowin' the half of it, but I can handle the dangers so long as ye keep yerself out of 'em."

Camri squared her shoulders. "But I came here to find Caleb. My parents entrusted me with that job, and I mean to see it through. Life can be dangerous no matter where you are, but I won't let that keep me from doing my part."

"Well, given what ye've just told me," Patrick said, recognizing the fight in her tone, "I'd say that things have changed, and with it your part has changed too. I figured from the start that Caleb's disappearance was due to our snoopin' and tryin' to see Ruef taken down. Now it would appear that may not be the case. If Caleb went to Daniels and tried to get him to release Liling, Daniels may not have taken to it well. He doesn't like to be threatened."

"What if Ruef knows Daniels and it's all tied together? I've heard that most of the businesses in San Francisco answer to him in some way. Surely the corruption of the Barbary Coast is even more under his control."

"Aye, to be sure."

"Then it's possible, maybe even probable, that Ruef could have paid Daniels to take my brother." Her brows knit together and a frown lined her lips. "Or kill him."

Patrick felt an uncontrollable desire to comfort her, but at the moment he needed to make certain she stayed away from Daniels and his place. "Aye. Daniels doesn't care about anythin' or anyone. He's only on this earth to make money. If the price is right, there's nothin' he won't do."

"Perhaps if I were to make an appointment to see this Mr. Daniels and offer him money, he might give up the truth about what happened to Caleb."

"Most likely he'd put ye to work in one of the upstairs rooms." He hated being so blunt with her, but Patrick knew he had to get his point across. "Daniels has no respect for women. He sees them as good for just one thing."

Her face reddened, and she quickly looked away. She said nothing—did nothing. For a long while it seemed she was lost in her thoughts. Patrick wondered what he could do or say that would give her hope but not entice her to take chances. It was a fine line to walk with someone as independent and headstrong as Camri Coulter.

After a few minutes, she surprised him by picking up the teapot. She poured herself more tea, then looked at him in question. Patrick raised his cup and waited while she filled it.

"Thank ye."

She nodded and put the teapot back on the table. "I suppose there's still Liling to worry about."

"We aren't givin' up lookin' for Caleb."

She met his eyes. "It'll soon be five months since he . . . disappeared." Her voice broke, and tears filled her eyes. "I'm not a fool, Patrick. I know things are looking worse by the minute." Tears slid down her cheeks, and she lowered her face as if ashamed. "I pray. I truly pray and try to have hope, but . . ."

He stood up and moved around the table to where she sat. Without concern for what she might say or do, he pulled her to her feet and wrapped her in his arms. "Hush now. Ye don't need to fret. The good Lord is still hearin' our prayers."

She cried softly, her face buried against his chest.

Patrick lowered his face to breathe in the scent of her hair. It was lavender and something else, maybe mint. He touched his fingers to her hair. She wore it in a no-nonsense bun pinned at the nape of her neck. It would be so easy to free it from its pins so that he could run his fingers through the dark brown strands.

There was no denying his feelings for her. Without thinking, he put his finger beneath her chin and lifted her face. She had only just opened her eyes in question when he pressed his lips against hers.

Camri looped her arms around his neck. He kissed her for a long, passionate moment in which he could see his future. He wanted a future that included Camri and their children. He wanted a good life with a place of their own—a place where they could grow old together. He trailed kisses along her tearstained cheeks, determined to get a confession of feelings from her.

"Ah, Camrianne, ye do somethin' to me. I cannot help m'self when I'm around ye." He pulled away and gazed into her dark eyes. "I know we're from two different worlds, and even if it is the 1900s, there are always goin' to be differences between us."

She shook her head and looked confused. "What are you talking about?"

"About me bein' Irish and uneducated."

"I don't understand what that has to do with anything."

"It has to do with me knowin' that ye come from a higher walk of life than me. That ye have yer college education and friends who share yer love of book learnin', while I don't. I'd most likely be an embarrassment to ye in those circles."

"You'd never be an embarrassment to me, Patrick. You are my friend, and none of those things matter."

"Aye, but would it matter if I were yer husband? For ye see I love ye, Camrianne, and I cannot be denyin' it. If I were to ask ye to marry me, I know you'd give up a considerable lot."

Her mouth was open, but no words came out. Patrick could see he'd stunned her, and for a moment he feared she'd send him packing. It was one thing to steal a kiss or two, and quite another to imply there was something strong enough between them to warrant marriage.

Fearing what she might say, Patrick did the only thing that came to mind and kissed her again. She didn't resist him, and it gave him hope that she might yet confirm his love for her with a declaration of her own.

"Well, I have to say, I never expected to come home and find my good friend kissing my sister."

Patrick and Camri all but jumped away from each other at the sound of Caleb's voice. For a moment, Patrick thought it must be a ghostly vision, but then Caleb began to laugh at their surprise, and he knew it was real.

It was only then that he thought of the shock it must be to Camri. He looked at her ashen face.

"Caleb . . ." she whispered, then fainted dead away.

Patrick caught her before she collapsed to the floor. He hoisted her into his arms and turned back to her brother with a shrug.

"I guess I should have knocked," Caleb said with a grin.

24

*C*amri heard her name being called and fought against the darkness. She wasn't sure where she was or what had happened, but someone seemed very insistent that she open her eyes.

"Come on, love. Open yer eyes."

She forced herself to obey. Patrick looked down at her with a smile. "There ye are."

Camri tried to sit up. "What . . . what happened?"

"Take it slow," he said, helping her to sit. "Don't ye remember?"

Camri pressed her fingers against her temples. The fog was finally lifting. She scanned the room and found what she was looking for. "Caleb."

He stood by the fireplace, warming his hands. "It's about time you woke up." He came to sit beside her on the sofa. "I'm sorry for giving you such a fright."

She reached out to touch his face. Was he truly here? She felt the warmth of his skin, but it still seemed impossible. She hugged him close. "I don't—I don't understand. I thought you were lost to me forever. I thought you might even be dead. You sent no word, nothing."

"I know." Caleb patted her back. "I couldn't. I'm so sorry for the worry I've caused."

"Mother and Father were devastated, and Catherine . . . well, you know Catherine."

"Indeed, I do. As practical as she is I'm sure I've been dead and buried since I disappeared."

Camri straightened and sat back so she could see him. She gripped his hands tightly, though, and didn't let go. "We must let them know."

"I've already handled it. I sent them a wire from Hawaii. It was for you as well." He grinned. "I never figured to find you out here looking for me."

"They sent me. We knew something was wrong. Hawaii?" She felt a wave of dizziness and thought she might faint again. "Could I have a drink of water?"

"I'll fetch it," Patrick said.

Camri leaned back against the sofa. "Where have you been?"

Caleb chuckled. "It's a long story. From what Patrick said, you've figured out where it all began."

"At the dance hall?"

"Exactly right." He squeezed her hands, then got up and walked back to the fireplace just as Patrick returned with a glass of water.

"Here ye are."

Camri took the glass and sipped. She still felt as if she were in a dream, but at least it was a good dream.

"As you learned," Caleb began, "I went to Daniels' place to negotiate Liling's freedom. Daniels wasn't having any of it, however, and when I threatened him with legal action, well, he'd had enough. He gave the pretense of being willing to let me see Liling, but as he led me to her room, one of his men hit me from behind. Next thing I knew, I was on a ship bound for the Orient."

"Shanghaied," Camri whispered.

"Indeed I was."

"But how did you get away?" She looked at Patrick as if he had answers and then back to her brother.

"It wasn't easy. When I woke up, my head hurt like nothing I'd ever known. I wasn't even clearheaded enough to realize I was on a ship. A man treated my wound, then handed me a glass of something and told me to drink it. I thought he was a doctor and did just as he said. Before I knew what had happened, I was unconscious again."

Camri chewed on her thumbnail. She still found it impossible to believe Caleb was here, safe and sound.

He continued. "When I woke up the second time, my leisure was behind me. A burly sailor all but dragged me from my berth. He took me to the captain along with a dozen other men. We were all rather groggy but awake enough to realize what had happened."

Camri could almost see it in her mind. "Were you already at sea?"

"Yes. In fact, we were three days out. They had managed to keep slipping me medication, and that kept me asleep. It's typically what they do with the men they take hostage." Caleb took a seat in his favorite chair. He rubbed the arms and smiled. "I did miss this chair."

This comment brought a smile to her face. She glanced at Patrick. "Of all that he could long for, my brother missed his chair."

"'Tis a most comfortable chair," Patrick replied with a wink.

Caleb laughed. "Well, I missed a lot more than just the chair, but we can discuss that at a later time. I know you want to know what happened next."

"I want to know how you managed to get back here." Camri made no pretense at patience. "Most men don't."

"I know." Caleb sobered. "I saw some of those men die."

She calmed. "I'm sorry. I'm just beside myself."

He gave her a sympathetic nod and ran his hand through his dark brown hair. "I decided cooperation was probably my best choice. After all, we were days at sea with nothing around us and no hope of escape. They had stripped me of my money and watch, but to my benefit, they didn't realize I had gone to Daniels that night prepared for almost anything. I had hidden some money in the cuff of my boot. I had a penknife there as well."

"'Tis a wonder they didn't steal yer boots and sell them," Patrick said. "They're known to strip a man bare and put him in rags."

"I know. I have to believe God blinded them to the quality of my boots, or else they simply figured to get them off me later." Caleb smiled. "Or maybe they didn't have replacements big enough for my feet." He stretched his legs out in front of him to emphasize his point.

"Your feet are no bigger than Patrick's. He's wearing your slippers, and they fit just fine. Now go on and tell me what happened."

Caleb rolled his eyes dramatically. "Always bossing me around. Can't a man tell a story in his own fashion?"

"So long as he gets to the telling of it," Camri snapped back. Her tone suggested annoyance, but she gave a smile to let him know all was well.

"Now I've lost my place. Where was I?" He raised a brow and looked at Camri for help.

"You had decided to be a good sailor. Oh, and you still had your boots."

He laughed. "Well, that alone gave me hope. Most of the

new recruits, as they called the shanghaied men, were nearly out of their wits. They tried at first to figure out a means of escape. A couple of them actually went into the water, thinking to swim their way home, I suppose."

"What happened?" Camri wasn't at all sure she wanted to know, but the question came out of her mouth before she considered the answer.

"They drowned. The captain said it was the more merciful way to go, given that there were sharks in the water." Caleb shook his head. "After that, most of the men realized their lot wasn't going to change at their own hand. So when we were locked in the hold at night, I began to tell them about God's faithfulness. At first, most weren't interested. But the younger ones were desperate for anything that offered hope."

"Poor men." It was a terrible thing to imagine, being taken from all that you knew and cast into a situation where you had no means of escape.

"Little by little, we became friends, and I told them about the power of prayer. I suggested we pray that something would happen to cause us to have to return to America. We started praying together every night before we went to sleep." He smiled at the memory. "It was like nothing I'd ever experienced." He leaned forward, and his entire face lit up. "I've been a Christian for many years, but I'd never really experienced God in such a way until on that ship."

"You sound almost grateful that you were shanghaied."

"I am."

Camri could see that he was absolutely serious. She grew angry. "How can you say such a thing? We were scared to death that you were dead—that we'd never see you again."

"And for that I'm sorry. I never wanted to cause anyone that kind of pain, but you have to understand something, Camri. Ten men came to the Lord because of that experience. How can I not be grateful that God used me in such a way that ten souls were forever changed for Him?"

She felt a flickering of shame, but her anger was far stronger. "Caleb Coulter, I am very glad that souls were saved, but I will never be grateful for you nearly losing your life. I can't be grateful for months of worry and tears. You didn't see what this did to our parents. They were so sick when I left that I feared I might never again see them alive."

Caleb left his chair and knelt in front of her. "Camri, I'm sorry. I'm sorry that you were afraid—that you worried. Truly, I am. But when you put your trust in God, there are no guarantees as to how life is going to go. The important thing is that we willingly go where He leads. I never planned for that to involve being shanghaied, but when it did, I felt it only right to serve Him there just as I would have here."

She was humbled by his words. "You're a good man, Caleb. I know that. I know that you love God, and I'm glad you were able to share His love with the other men."

He took her hands. "If I could have gotten word to you—just to let you know I was alive and well—I would have. I'm sorry that you suffered."

"I know." She felt her anger subside.

"Mr. Patrick clothes dry now," Mrs. Wong said from the entryway. She saw Caleb, and her mouth dropped open.

"Mrs. Wong!" Caleb declared, jumping to his feet. He crossed the room in three long strides and picked her up in an embrace. "I'm home!" He put her down, and Camri could see that Mrs. Wong was crying. Caleb hugged her close. "Now don't go fretting. I'm just fine. I'll come and tell you all about it in a little while."

She nodded, and when Caleb released her, she hurried away. Camri wondered what the old woman would say to her husband. No doubt they would both be greatly relieved.

Patrick had been silent for most of the discussion, but he chose that moment to speak. "I can't be stayin' much longer. I have to report to Daniels for work at six, and I need to sleep."

Caleb looked at him oddly. "You're working for Daniels?"

"Aye. I tracked ye down to that bein' the last place ye'd gone. Then Camri found yer papers under the desk and the handbill with Liling's name and room number. I'd already managed to get a job there in order to find out what, if anything, they knew about yer disappearance." He came and sat beside Camri.

Caleb frowned. "They know plenty. You and I need to talk before you leave. I can finish this story later."

"You aren't leaving me out of this," Camri said, getting to her feet.

Patrick laughed and pulled her back down. "For sure ye've got yer hands full with her."

She wanted to stick out her tongue in defiance, but instead crossed her arms and fixed him with a glare.

Both men laughed, and Caleb shook his finger at her. "I know that for certain. She's very headstrong."

"Aye."

Camri gave an exasperated sigh. "Don't you need to go home, Patrick?"

"I'll finish where I left off, but I'll do it quick so Patrick won't miss out." Caleb reclaimed his seat. "We prayed for God to intercede, and He did. The ship began having one problem after another, and finally things became critical. The captain decided he had no choice but to go to Hawaii for repairs. Of course he knew we shanghaied men would do whatever we could to escape, so he locked us up. He didn't want to risk any of us speaking to anyone who might come on board, so he put us in the deepest, darkest part of the hold. But you recall that I had money in my boot, and I decided the time had come to use it.

"That night when everyone had gone ashore except for the

men left to stand guard, I told the others my plan. When the guard came with our supper, I took him aside and talked to him. I was in good standing with him, and he had no real loyalty to the captain. I told him if he'd help me, he could come with us, and I'd see to it he was amply rewarded. To convince him I had the means to do so, I gave him what money I had, and he agreed to help."

"What did you do?" Camri asked.

Caleb smiled. "The guard, Jimmy, managed to take care of the other guards. Gave them some of the same grog that they'd fed us when we first came on board. They slept like babies. Meanwhile, we managed to slip away. Once we were on shore, I led the way to the local authorities, where we were promptly jailed."

"What!" Camri shook her head. "But why?"

"We told our story to the man in charge, and he didn't believe us. He figured us to be indentured or otherwise paying off a debt. He locked us up and sent for the captain."

"Grief, Caleb, that must have left ye feelin' a bit hopeless after all ye'd managed to do." Patrick shook his head. "I cannot say I would have bided my time in good spirits."

Camri agreed and asked, "Did the captain come?"

Caleb laughed. "He did, and he was clearly angry at what we'd done. He arranged to have us taken back to the ship, but before we were, God caused an amazing thing to happen.

"I had just told the men to keep praying and trusting God, when in walked a collection of government officials. They were touring the islands in order to set up regional offices. They were curious about what was going on, and our jailer explained the situation. They assumed we were reprobates and thought nothing of it, but I told them that we had all been taken from San Francisco against our will. I gave my name and asked that the officials help us."

"And they did," Camri murmured.

"Not at first. The captain and jailer insisted that we were lying. The captain even made up a story about us being thieves. However, one of the men in the group was governor of the territory, and he and I had met before. I reminded him of that event, and suddenly it was as if the scales fell from his eyes. He immediately ordered our release and took us to his home. He gave us all the comforts he could—fed us and let us bathe. I felt like a new man after a proper shave."

Patrick laughed. "There's nothin' improper about a beard." He stroked his own for emphasis.

Caleb smiled. "Maybe, but I know I felt better for its loss."

Camri was still thinking about all that had happened to her brother and the way God had intervened. Her prayers had been answered—just not the way she thought they would be.

"The governor arranged for us to travel back with the government officials. We just got into San Francisco this morning."

"It was a miracle," Camri said, meeting her brother's gaze. "A true miracle of God."

"Indeed, it was. They still happen, you know."

She shook her head in wonder. "I'm so happy to have you back."

"I'm glad to be here, but there's still much to be done. I have a feeling that even though Daniels did what he did because of my threats, Ruef and his men would have done worse."

"And they have. They killed Henry Ambrewster." She saw the pain on her brother's face. "We don't know who did it or why, but Patrick feels certain it all ties to what you were both trying to do."

"Poor Henry. He didn't know anything." Caleb shook his head.

"He had me come talk to him just before he was killed." Patrick scooted to the edge of his seat. "I told him some of what we were doing because he'd found a ledger of yers and that money Ruef gave ye. I told him he'd do well to hide both. I figure his killer came right after I left, so he probably had no time."

Caleb heaved a sigh. "I'm to blame. I should have warned him—let him know what was going on so that he could be on his guard."

Camri reached for her brother's hand. "You couldn't know what would happen. Henry thought highly of you. We had a chance to get to know each other a little, and he always spoke fondly of you. He was trying to help me search for you."

"Well, be that as it may, he might still be alive if I had just leveled with him about what we were doing."

"Which brings me back to that matter," Patrick said. "I haven't any real news about Liling, but I do have Daniels' trust. At least to a point. He's not asked me to be involved in the shanghaiin', but I figure 'tis just a matter of time."

"Have you seen Liling?"

"No, but then I've not had much to do with the upstairs girls. I can't even say for sure she's there, but I have heard tell that Daniels has one very special, very expensive girl in the room next to his. Apparently he's very selective about who he lets visit her. I've never even heard her name given, although one of the boys mentioned her being a princess."

Caleb nodded knowingly. "That's her. Liling is something of a guarded secret. Daniels keeps a close eye on her. I learned this from some of his richer clientele. Generally speaking, Chinese women are not very valued in this city. Most of the best establishments won't have them. Fact is, most places want to have one or more redheads, but most sought after are those of Jewish lineage with red hair. For some reason they're considered lucky, and a man will pay top dollar. But I digress. Daniels figured out a way to get a lot of interest and money for something normally considered to have little or no value."

"How?" Camri asked. It was so strange to be listening to her brother talk about brothel preferences.

"Daniels set Liling up as something exotic—out of reach. Nothing brings about demand as much as telling folks that they can't have it. She's Daniels' only Chinese girl, and he had it whispered about that she was royalty, secreted from her palace far away and sold into his hands by pirates. He made it clear that only a few select customers would be allowed. He keeps it all hush-hush so as not to give away the truth of it, which is that she's just a down-on-her-luck girl born of Chinese-American parents."

"No wonder nobody talks about her," Patrick said, shaking his head.

"What are you going to do?" Camri tried not to think about the horrors Liling might be experiencing.

"We have to find a way to get her out of there," Caleb replied. "Would that I could set them all free from that life. If you want a cause, little sister, there's a good one for you."

Camri knew such a cause required far more than she could manage. It would take God's intercession for sure to see the lives of those women turned around. But Caleb made a good point. What did it benefit women to have the right to vote if they couldn't even exist without degrading themselves in such a fashion?

Patrick got to his feet. "Like I said, I've seen nothin' of her. What if Daniels got rid of her?"

"It's possible but unlikely. She brings in quite a bit of money." Caleb thought a moment. "Patrick, you have to find out if she's still there. I think it will be to everyone's advantage to keep my homecoming a secret. I asked the government officials to say nothing. They weren't remaining here long anyway, but I told them about the corruption and problems we were dealing with, and they agreed they wouldn't give me away. The men I crewed with were also willing to protect me by remaining silent, especially since I plan to help them get decent employment." Caleb rose and reached out to take Patrick's arm. "You have to be my eyes and ears, hands and feet. At least for a time."

"I'll do whatever I can."

Camri got up. "I will too." She raised her hand. "And before you tell me I can't, just remember that I'm stubborn and head-strong and not given to letting either of you boss me around. I care too much about the both of you to do nothing."

They laughed, but it was Patrick she looked to. His casual suggestion of marriage earlier that morning was still fresh on her mind. He might as well know here and now that she didn't intend to be put in a corner.

"Next thing I know, Ophelia will be insisting I let her help as well," Caleb said with a grin.

Camri glanced at Patrick and frowned. "Ah . . . Caleb, you . . . well . . ."

"Ophelia's gone on to the Lord," Patrick said, meeting Caleb's look of confusion. "She died on the nineteenth of December."

Caleb's expression quickly changed. "I am sorry to hear that, my friend. She was a wonderful young woman. I know you must miss her."

"For sure, I do." Patrick looked at Camri. "Yer sister's been a great comfort. She had a chance to get to know Ophelia, as well."

Caleb nodded and smiled. "Well, knowing Ophelia, she'll be putting in a good word for us with the Almighty."

Patrick grinned. "And for certain she'd be doin' exactly that."

*B*ut if God has a plan for each of us, how can we know for sure what it is?" Judith hobbled into the front room, still discussing the church sermon with Kenzie. She stopped abruptly as her gaze immediately went to the young man who stood by the fireplace. He was tall, and his dark hair fell in a lazy manner over one brow. There was a rugged cut to his clean-shaven jaw but a softness in his expression. His dark eyes fell upon her, and a smile broke across his face.

"Would these be the young ladies you were just telling me about?" he asked.

Camri turned. "Yes, this is Judith and Kenzie. Look, ladies, my brother Caleb has returned."

For a moment, neither woman could speak, but finally Kenzie posed the question on Judith's mind. "I'm glad you've returned, Mr. Coulter . . . but where have you been?"

Judith thought she sounded almost accusatory. She wanted to say something in his defense but found the words refused to form. She was overwhelmed by the vision before her. Her heart raced, and her breathing quickened. Was it possible to fall in love at first sight?

Mr. Coulter was speaking now, and Judith tried hard to focus on what he was saying, but her mind ran away with her. This was Camri's brother. The very man they'd been praying for and hoping to find. But he was nothing like she'd expected.

But what did I expect?

". . . and of course that's just a very abbreviated version," Caleb said, then looked to Judith. "If that's Kenzie, then you must be Judith."

She felt as if someone had put a hand to her throat. She could scarcely draw breath, and rather than speak, she gave a brief nod.

Caleb didn't seem to notice her inability to speak. "I'm glad you could both be here to help Camri keep her wits." He noticed the cane Judith was using. "Are you injured?"

Judith could only nod. Caleb surprised her by moving forward and taking her arm. "Then you must sit."

"She sprained her ankle roller-skating," Camri offered.

Caleb gave Judith a sympathetic smile. "Ah, roller-skating. I once sprained something too, but given this is polite company, I won't say what."

Kenzie seemed completely unaffected by Caleb's presence and spoke up again. "Well, I'm grateful that Camri has allowed us to stay with her. Now that you've returned, I suppose Judith and I shall have to arrange other accommodations."

Judith hadn't considered the possibility of being left without a place to stay. Surely Camri wouldn't let her brother turn them out tonight. She still had most of her Christmas money, but it wouldn't go very far if she had to rent a room.

"There's no need for that, Miss Gifford. I have more than enough rooms, and given my sister is here, as well as Mr. and Mrs. Wong, there is nothing inappropriate about the two of you remaining."

"That's quite kind of you, Mr. Coulter."

"Caleb. I want you both to call me Caleb." He smiled, and his gaze fell again to Judith. "You certainly are a quiet one."

"I . . . I'm. . . ." Judith forced herself to focus. "I'm just very surprised to find you've returned."

"No more so than me," Camri said. "I fainted dead away."

"Well, if you'll both excuse me," Caleb said, heading for the entryway, "I want very much to change my clothes before lunch. We can sort through anything else while we eat. I, for one, am starved."

He bounded from the room without so much as a backward glance. Judith knew this, because she hadn't been able to take her eyes off him.

"Well, that certainly is an amazing answer to your prayers," Kenzie declared.

"To *our* prayers," Camri corrected. "I know it was the prayers of all of us together that brought him back." She motioned at Judith. "Don't you want to get out of your coat and hat?"

It was only then that Judith realized she was still clad for the chilly outdoors. She pulled off her gloves. "I supposed I'm just so shocked."

"I know," Camri said, smiling. "But it's the very best of shocks. I don't know when I've ever been happier. I swear I could float."

Judith stood and shrugged out of her coat, grateful that Kenzie took it. She didn't know what to say. For so long, Caleb's disappearance had been the center of conversation. Now he was home, and Judith was quite beside herself. She had never felt this way about anyone.

I'm being silly. Completely ridiculous. It's just the shock of it and the happiness I feel for Camri. That's all this is about. There's no need to be addlepated about it.

But something like this had never happened to Judith. She'd so rarely been around people growing up, and certainly never around handsome young men with dark chocolate brown eyes that seemed to know the innermost thoughts of her heart.

"Do you?"

Judith looked up. Camri seemed to be waiting for some sort of answer. "What? I'm afraid my mind was wandering."

Camri chuckled. "I asked if you planned to wear your hat to the table."

Judith reached up to pull the pin from the large straw skimmer. "Sorry."

"Perhaps it was on too tight," Camri said in a teasing fashion. "Perhaps the band wouldn't allow for proper blood flow, and hence you are unable to concentrate."

"I'll be just fine," Judith promised as Kenzie took the hat.

But that hasty conclusion didn't prove to be true. Sitting at the table with Caleb just to her left made Judith all the more nervous. She found herself both longing to flee to her room and desiring never to be out of Caleb's company again. By the time the meal concluded, she was exhausted.

The next day boded no better. All day at work, she was dropping things. Mr. Lake tried to be patient, noting her injured ankle, but finally he'd had enough. He demanded to know why she was in such a state, but for the life of her, Judith couldn't give him an answer. How did she explain that she couldn't stop thinking about her dear friend's brother? At least Camri wasn't there to witness it, for she surely would have guessed the problem. As it was, Kenzie seemed to watch her with a critical eye. No doubt Judith would have plenty to answer to on their ride home.

"I do hope you're in a better state of mind tomorrow, Miss Gladstone," Mr. Lake said as they concluded the workday. "We have Valentine's Day orders to prepare, and Miss Coulter's absence today, along with your nonsense, has put us behind."

"I am sorry, Mr. Lake. I promise I will be better tomorrow." Judith hoped it was a promise she could keep.

Kenzie wasted no time in getting right to the point as they headed for the cable car. "What in the world has gotten into you?" She held fast to her hat as the wind picked up.

Judith felt desperate to talk to someone. "Can you keep a secret? I mean really keep what I say to yourself and not share it with anyone? Because I would absolutely die of shame if you were to speak of it. I truly would. In fact, never mind. I don't know why I'm even thinking of saying anything. It's foolishness on my part, I suppose."

"If you'll stop talking long enough, I'll pledge to keep your secret," Kenzie said, shaking her head. "Honestly, I've never seen anyone in such a state. What's wrong?"

They had joined several other people waiting for the same car. Judith lowered her voice. "I can't . . . I . . . oh dear. I'm not sure how to say this."

Kenzie looked at her with mild exasperation. "Just say it."

"I can't stop thinking about Caleb Coulter."

"That doesn't seem like a reason to make so many mistakes. Goodness, you dropped three boxes of chocolates today and then proceeded to put other chocolates into the wrong boxes. I know we're all happy that he's returned, but there must be something else."

Judith gripped her cane a little tighter. "I know it sounds silly, but . . . Kenzie, I think I'm in love."

For a moment, she feared Kenzie might laugh at her. The look on her friend's face was one of complete disbelief, but then she smiled. Was she going to make light of Judith's feelings?

Kenzie put her arm around Judith's shoulders. "Oh, my poor dear. I should have guessed. From the first moment we walked into the house and saw him, you looked like someone tied to the tracks with a train bearing down on you. I thought it was just the shock of his sudden appearance, but now I understand. This makes much more sense."

Judith shook her head. "It makes no sense to me. I've never felt this way before. I don't know what to do."

Kenzie gave her a sympathetic nod. "No one ever does."

———

"Murdock, have a seat," Malcolm Daniels said, ushering Patrick into his office.

Patrick did as instructed. He didn't know what Daniels wished to discuss. It had been days since Caleb's return, and while Patrick had tried to discreetly inquire about the girls upstairs, he feared that perhaps he'd given himself away.

"I like what I've seen in your work," Daniels said, pouring himself a drink. He held up the bottle to offer Patrick one as well.

"Thank ye, no." Patrick felt as if his shirt collar had suddenly shrunk. "I'm glad ye're pleased."

Daniels took his drink and sat down behind his desk. "You have a good eye for troublesome men. I've seen you head off many a fight before there was even a problem. I'm impressed, and because you're good at what you do, I've a mind to use you in another area."

"Another area?" Patrick tried to sound relaxed, almost disinterested.

"Yes, well, I know you understand what goes on here," Daniels began. "Most of Frisco has at least a bit of an inkling." He chuckled and drank down the contents of his glass before continuing. "It's no real secret that ship captains are known to seek me out for their crews. After all, I have six boardinghouses that cater to sailors."

Patrick nodded. "'Tis reasonable to expect they'd call on ye."

"It's the way we've done business for decades here. Most sailors don't have the brains of a flea. They can't be trusted to honor their word. I take 'em in, usually penniless, and they sign a pledge—well, a sort of promissory note for room and board. Then when it comes time to pay up, they think they'll somehow get around it. I have no choice but to take matters into my own hands, and that's where you come in."

"How can I help?"

Daniels smiled. "We have a particular arrangement here that works well for us. No questions asked. Nelson or the girls upstairs slip something into the drinks, and then the men are easier to handle. We get them out of the dance hall below and off to their ships. The captains pay me what the men owe, and everyone is happy."

"Well, I'm supposin' that might be debatable."

The older man shrugged. "Me and the captains are happy." He laughed and slapped his hand on the desk. "And that's all I really care about. In fact, I'm not too concerned about pleasin' the captains, except they put coin in my hand."

"I've heard it said that sometimes a man or two is put to work on the ships who had no intention of ever sailing. Men who don't stay at yer boardinghouse."

Daniels didn't seem at all concerned by the question. "It happens from time to time. Does that present a problem?"

"I didn't say it did." Patrick shrugged. "I am hopeful, however, not to have the law breathin' down m' neck."

A look of understanding crossed Daniels' face. "Oh, but we have an arrangement for that as well. I can see why you think it might be a problem, especially since you had an encounter with the legal system once before. However, I assure you it isn't. I have powerful friends. Friends who see things my way."

"For a price?" Patrick asked, pretending to look at his fingernails. "I heard that was the way things were done." He glanced up at Daniels and smiled. "Seems there's nothin' that can't be bought."

Daniels laughed. "That's true enough. All of the Barbary Coast is proof of that."

Patrick leaned back and crossed his legs. "Aye, that's a fact. So what is it that ye'll be needin' from me?"

"Well, up until now, you've not had any dealings upstairs. I always put new men down here, working with the general population. That way I can keep an eye on them."

"And I take it I've passed inspection?"

Daniels grinned. "More than. You've been better than ten men, and I'm giving you a raise in salary to prove my gratitude."

There was no amount of money that would make working for Daniels worth it, but Patrick didn't have a chance to speak even if he'd wanted to.

"In fact, besides the raise I give you, there are bonuses to be made. All I need from you is help getting the men upstairs."

"I'm not sure I understand."

"I realize you know about the trapdoors, but we seldom use those unless we absolutely have to. Too many people can see and cause trouble for us if we start dropping drunks by the dozen from the main room. No, the best way is to get them upstairs with the girls. The girls have plenty of medicated liquor, if you get my meaning."

"I do." Patrick knew from Caleb that Daniels wasn't against knocking a man out by other means either.

"You get the men upstairs, and the girls will do the rest. Then, once the men are unconscious, they'll ring to let us know. When they do, it'll be your job to go upstairs, get their clients, and get them to the cellar, where we can load them up and take them out to the ships."

Patrick gave a nod. He thought it best to sound like any other poor Irishman. "And how is it I make these bonuses?"

Daniels roared with laughter. "Spoken like a man after my own heart. A lot of the men who come here to drink and dance are leery of going upstairs. They know the possible dangers. And although the siren call of a willing woman is powerful, the experienced sailor knows it's safer to go to one of the street cribs. We want them feeling at ease and willing to go. I want you to carry these." He reached into his desk and produced what looked like six or seven photographs. He handed them to Patrick. "Take these and show them to any able-bodied man between the ages of sixteen and forty-five."

Patrick took the photographs and saw they were of women in various stages of undress posing seductively. He tried not to react in disgust and quickly tucked the photos in his coat pocket.

"After I go showin' 'em around, then what?"

"When you show the pictures to one of the men, explain that the woman is upstairs. Tell him she'll show him the best time he's ever had. You can even go so far as to tell him that you can get the cost discounted because you know the girl personally."

"But I've ne'er met the girls."

"That doesn't matter. You'll get to know them well enough in the next few days." He paused as if trying to remember something. "If they seem hesitant, offer them a drink on the house. Nelson will see they get the right stuff. We have to work fast. I have two ships needing crews by Saturday evening. Both captains intend to leave on Sunday, and we have to have the men to them at least in the wee hours of Sunday morning so as not to attract attention."

Patrick considered the matter. This went against everything he believed, even when he wasn't walking close with the Almighty. Still, he and Caleb had talked about the necessity of continuing if they were to have a chance to free Liling.

"So I'll be gettin' a man interested and then send him upstairs. Then ye'll be tellin' me when I need to go up there and fetch the soul. How am I supposed to get him down to the water without anyone seein' him?"

"We'll coordinate that. I'll have the cleaning boy block entry to the hall, and you'll be able to bring them down the stairs and then on down to the cellar."

"What about the gamin' rooms? Who'll keep them from wanderin' out?"

Daniels laughed. "My dealers know the trade. They'll manage it well enough. It's all worked out, so you don't need to concern yourself with it."

Patrick shrugged. "I wasn't concerned. Just need to know what to expect. If I have to be knockin' men out while carrying a body, it's goin' to be costin' ye extra."

This seemed to amuse Daniels to no end. He laughed heartily and reached into his desk again. This time he pulled out a roll of money. He peeled off several large bills and tossed them to Patrick. "We'll just consider this a retainer in case that event comes to pass. We start tonight."

Patrick took the money and stuffed it into the same pocket as he had the pictures. "I'm yer man."

"So tell me about Kenzie and Judith."

Camri looked up from the book she was reading. "What do you mean?"

Caleb strode into the room, wearing a tailored brown suit. The color matched his eyes and made them seem all the more intense. Camri wondered if her brother had chosen the suit just for that purpose.

"I mean, tell me more about them. Where they come from and why they're here." He took a seat in his leather chair and stretched out his legs.

"Well, Kenzie is from Missouri and is nursing a broken heart. She was forsaken at the altar. As I understand it, the young man's family didn't think her good enough, but Kenzie seldom speaks of it. She's the daughter of a merchant who inherited some money. She also worked as a librarian."

"And why has she come to San Francisco?"

"To heal. I think her family thought it would do her good to get as far away from her fiancé and his family as possible. She has a cousin here, the man I told you about."

"George Lake, the candy manufacturer."

"Yes." Camri couldn't help but frown. "He's going to be angry with me for taking these days away from work. However, I couldn't leave you. Not yet. Now that mother and father know you're safe, I don't think I have to rush off. We need to get to the bottom of this corruption with Ruef."

Caleb laughed. "Yes, I'm sure that's the only thing keeping you in San Francisco."

Camri felt her cheeks grow hot. "It's important to defeat a man as corrupt as Ruef. He's caused a lot of harm to—many people." She met her brother's amused gaze. "But of course, that's just one reason to remain."

"You were never good at concealing things, Camri. Don't try to start now. Remember, I walked in on you and Patrick kissing."

She looked at the book in her hands. "I know you did. I won't try to conceal that I care about him. He's a good man."

"That he is."

Camri wanted to talk more about Patrick, but right now didn't seem the time. Kenzie and Judith were due back any minute. They had gone to help clean the church, and that task never took longer than two hours. "Judith is from Colorado. I'm actually hoping you can help her. She's here to find her aunt."

"What's so difficult about finding her aunt?"

She looked at Caleb. "It's a strange situation. Her mother and father always told her there was no other family. She grew up isolated on a poor ranch in Colorado, schooled at home by her mother. Her parents died, and when she was going through her mother's things, she found a letter that her mother had been writing. To her mother's sister."

"But if she has a letter, then surely she must also have an address."

"No. The letter only mentioned that her mother hoped this sister still lived in San Francisco."

"And what was the sister's name?"

"Edith. Edith Whitley."

"Hmmm, there could be hundreds, even thousands, of folks named Whitley. It's not that uncommon of a name."

"I'm hoping that once you're back in public, you could help her. She's a very sweet young woman."

Caleb pulled on his sleeve cuff. "I should like to help her. I'm not sure what the future is going to bring, since Henry's dead, but I have some money saved up, so even if I don't go right to work for someone else, we'll be all right." He grinned. "Perhaps if things go well in helping Judith find her aunt, I'll apply for a job with the Pinkertons."

Camri frowned. "Maybe it'd be better to return to Chicago. It seems that San Francisco is a very dangerous town."

"And you think Chicago isn't?" He shook his head. "Big cities are full of big schemers. Anywhere there is money to be made, you're going to have corruption. San Francisco has more than its fair share, but it's no worse than any other city. However, good men must take a stand against the bribery, scheming, and even murder being done in the name of progress. I can't leave without at least trying to put an end to Ruef and his dealings."

"Yes, but Ruef apparently is trying to put an end to you and your dealings. Henry was killed in his own office. What's to stop them from coming here to kill you?"

"Well, right now they think I'm already dead. That can be used to my advantage."

"But for how long?"

Caleb shrugged. "I suppose for as long as I need. Patrick is more than willing to help me, and as I said, I've got enough money set aside that I can go some time without working. Ruef can't last forever."

Camri straightened in her seat and set her book aside. "Then I want to help, and don't say I can't."

Her brother eyed her for a moment, then began to chuckle. "I wouldn't dream of telling you that you can't do something."

CHAPTER 26

*C*aleb glanced around his study, feeling a peace wash over him. It was so good to be home. Sometimes he could still feel the sway of the ship and smell the filthy bodies of his fellow sailors. They had been stuffed in a room not even half the size of this office. He shook his head, marveling at how God had taken such a wretched situation and turned it around for good. The months away had given him a new perspective on life, of that there was no doubt. It had deepened his walk with God and had given him a better understanding of the downtrodden. It had also given him new determination to see Ruef and his like defeated and put in jail where they belonged. Ruef and his political machine preyed on the weak and took advantage of hard workers, and Caleb prayed God would give him the strength to help effect an end to it all.

He glanced at the clock. It was just six thirty in the morning, and soon he'd be at breakfast with his sister and her friends. That brought a smile to his face. It was completely unexpected to come home and find his sister in residence. Even nicer to find two beautiful young women with her.

He was still smiling when Judith appeared at the door.

She cleared her throat. "I hope I'm not, uh, interrupting."

"Come in, Judith." He got to his feet and crossed to the door. "Camri told me she'd send you to see me, so I was expecting you."

The pretty blonde had twisted her ankle and was still walking with a cane. She took two steps and tripped over her own feet. Caleb easily righted her and took a firm hold on her arm.

"Steady now. You'll do yourself no good at all if you fall again." He guided her toward a chair by the fire.

"I'm so sorry. I . . . well, I'm sorry." She gave him a nervous smile. "My ankle is still sore, but I'm much improved. Dr. Fisher said it wasn't a bad sprain, and tomorrow I can give up this cane."

"I'm glad to hear that." Caleb motioned to the two chairs in front of the fireplace. "It's nice and warm here, so why don't you have a seat? Did you bring your letter?"

"I did."

He let go of her arm, and Judith scooted past him to the nearest chair. She had nearly made it without incident when she knocked against a small side table that held a stack of books. She dropped her cane as her hands flew out to stop the books from falling to the ground, but it was too late.

"Oh, my!" She shook her head. "I'm so sorry."

He came forward to retrieve the books just as Judith bent to do the same. Their heads crashed together hard enough to send them both stumbling backward. Caleb had no trouble regaining his balance, but Judith wasn't so lucky. Falling onto her backside, she groaned and struggled to get back up.

Caleb quickly came to her rescue. "It would seem your excitement to see me has been your undoing."

Judith's face paled, and immediately he worried that something was wrong. "Did you hurt yourself? Perhaps reinjure your ankle?"

She shook her head and barely managed to squeak out her reply. "No. Not really."

He frowned. "You looked upset just now. Are you sure?" He still held her arm. "If you need, I can call Camri or Kenzie."

"No. I'm . . . fine." She looked away. "Just embarrassed."

He smiled. If that was the only pain she suffered, then he could help to easily dismiss it. "Nonsense. You've nothing to be embarrassed by. You're eager to learn the truth about your aunt. There's nothing to be ashamed of there. I can't imagine learning about a family member after years of thinking there were none." He helped her to sit, then retrieved her cane. "Here you are. Now, could I read the letter? Breakfast will come soon, and I know you're heading to work."

"Yes." She wedged the cane between her leg and the arm of the chair. "I'm so glad you're willing to help." She pulled the envelope from her pocket and held it out to him.

Caleb looked at it. "Edith Whitley. That is your aunt?"

"Yes. She addresses this Edith as her sister in the letter."

He pulled out the letter, then sat down and read through it several times. It was very little to go on, just as Camri had warned.

"So you never heard your mother speak of her sister?"

"No. Never. Neither she nor Father ever spoke of family. The few times I asked, they assured me that everyone was dead."

"It's obvious from the letter that something took place between your mother and her sister—something your mother felt was unforgivable. What do you think this might have been?"

Judith looked completely puzzled. "I have no idea. How could I?"

Caleb turned in his chair to better study her. She was such a pretty little thing. She reminded him of a child's china doll—dainty and delicate.

"Well, were your parents, your mother in particular, religious people? Did they live by certain standards?"

275

"They weren't overly religious. We didn't attend church, but we said grace over each meal."

He smiled. "It may seem strange that I would ask a question like this, but sometimes it helps to shed light on why people do what they do. For example, your mother says that what she did was unforgivable. Having had a more intimate relationship with her than almost anyone else, what kind of things do you suppose she would find unforgivable?"

Understanding dawned and Judith's face lit up. "Oh, I see. Of course. That makes a great deal of sense." Her brows knit together as if she were trying hard to remember something. "I know Mother always said we were to forgive each other—that forgiveness was important." She shook her head. "She didn't say why, but I do remember her talking about how hard it was to live with regret." She became rather excited. "In fact, I remember once when Father was upset with one of the hired men and he threatened to—well, as he put it, 'beat the guy bloody,' Mother reminded him that some things once done, couldn't be undone."

"That's good, Judith. It's little things like this that might well help us. Now, I see from the letter that there was some money taken. It doesn't say from whom, but it looks to me like your mother must have taken it from her sister."

"That's what I presumed. It also seemed to me that her sister had plenty of money. After all, Mother says she realizes the money wasn't important."

"Yes. I came to that same conclusion. Judith, do you know if your mother's maiden name was Whitley?"

She shook her head. "I don't know anything about her or her parents. Whenever I asked about my grandparents, she was quick to say they were dead."

Caleb wondered what had driven the young woman's mother to lie.

As if reading his mind, Judith spoke again. "Kenzie wondered if maybe Mother stole her sister's beau or fiancé. That's a subject near to Kenzie's heart, since her fiancé abandoned her. Camri, on the other hand, wondered if maybe Mother had done something to ruin her sister's reputation."

"All of those ideas are plausible, and given the way the human mind works, I could see any of them being thought to be unforgivable."

The clock struck the top of the hour.

Caleb held up the letter. "Do you mind if I hang onto this for a time?"

Judith hesitated. "It's one of the few things I have left of my mother."

He put the letter back in the envelope and handed it to her. "I understand. Perhaps I could look at it again later."

She shook her head, refusing to take it from him. "No. I trust you. Keep it for now."

Caleb could see that the decision hadn't been easy. He smiled. "I appreciate your trust, Judith. I promise to guard it with my life."

Camri looked up from the breakfast table in surprise when Mrs. Wong announced Patrick had come. He looked tired and unkempt, but Camri still felt as if her stomach were full of butterflies. This was only made worse when Patrick threw her a wink and a smile, making her feel like an infatuated schoolgirl.

"I hope you'll pardon the intrusion, but I needed to share some news." he said.

"It's not an intrusion," Caleb declared. "Sit. Have some breakfast and tell us everything."

Patrick took the seat by Camri. The unpleasant aromas of

smoke, whiskey, and cheap perfume still clung to him. She grimaced and turned her attention to her tea.

"I asked Mrs. Wong to be bringin' her husband, so if ye don't mind, we'll wait for them."

"Of course," Caleb replied. "I take it that you found Liling."

"Aye."

The Chinese couple came into the room. They looked at Caleb, who motioned for them to sit. "Patrick tells me he's got news to share with you."

They nodded, and Mr. Wong took a seat at the far end of the table, while Mrs. Wong brought silverware and a plate for Patrick. She hurried to the sideboard and collected a cup and saucer for him as well, then joined her husband.

"Daniels put me to work helpin' to collect men for two ships. Daniels has been druggin' sailors from his boardinghouse, and he's keepin' them until Saturday night. Then there's to be a transfer. I'm supposed to be helpin' with it."

"But what about Liling?" Camri couldn't help but interrupt. She could see the worried expressions of the Wongs and knew they were desperate for answers.

Patrick nodded. "I have to go upstairs now to carry the unconscious souls from the rooms. Daniels has the girls drug the men, and when they're out cold, I come in and take them to the cellar. I wasn't able to talk to Liling, but I was in her room."

"She is alive?" Mr. Wong asked.

"Aye. She's alive. She was well—at least as well as a soul could be in a place like that. It seems Daniels feeds her better and keeps her in more comfort than the others, although. . . ."

"What?" Mrs. Wong asked, her voice breaking. "What although?"

Patrick's jaw clenched and unclenched. Finally he continued. "He has her locked up to keep her from running away."

Mrs. Wong began to sob into her handkerchief while Patrick

continued. "I wasn't able to talk to her alone, but I hope to. My plan is to try to say something to her the next time I go to retrieve a body."

"You will tell her we want her to come home?" Mr. Wong asked. "We not angry anymore."

"Aye. I'll tell her that."

Mr. and Mrs. Wong's sorrow tore at Camri's heart. Caleb had told her the full story of how Liling had caused her parents a great deal of trouble in her teen years. She had wanted more than they could provide and had taken to stealing it or doing whatever else she could to gain it. She had shamed the Wongs by flirting and acting in a rebellious manner. Eventually, she had run off to marry a white man who promised her the moon and stars. At that point, the Wongs had turned their back on Liling. They had declared her dead to them, had mourned their loss, and after that Liling's name was never spoken. At least that was the case until they learned the truth. The man who'd promised their daughter marriage had been no good and refused to marry her. In fact, after using her as he desired for a while, the man sold her to Daniels. When the Wongs learned this, they knew they had to find a way to save their daughter from such a horrific life.

Patrick was speaking again. "We'll make a plan for how I can get her out of there. I don't figure talkin' to Daniels will do any good."

"No, it wouldn't," Caleb said, shaking his head.

Patrick looked at Camri and smiled. "I've been thinkin' on a plan, but I'm goin' to need a bit of help."

"What can we do?" Camri asked.

"I'm hopin', Caleb, that ye might have a friend or two left on the right side of the law. One of those judges or friends on the police force who could help us."

"I'm sure we could get someone," Caleb answered. "What did you have in mind?"

An hour later, Patrick had sated his hunger and laid out his ideas. He hated the look of worry in the eyes of Liling's parents. He'd tried to encourage them, to assure them that Liling was well, but they knew the truth. They knew that their daughter was in an unthinkably vile situation, and even if her own foolishness had lent a hand in putting her there, they loved her. There would be no comfort until she was safely back in their keeping.

Camri's friends had left for work, and Camri had gone to help Caleb make a phone call to his friend Judge Winters. Caleb wasn't willing to let anyone know that he was alive and home—not over the phone. He knew Judge Winters would keep his secret, but he didn't trust his office people to do the same. Camri would place the call for him.

"Judge Winters says he'll come to the house tonight," Camri said, coming back into the room. She paused and gave Patrick a sympathetic look. "You're exhausted. Go home and get some sleep."

He stood and moved toward her. She had told him she intended to join her friends at work as soon as the plans were laid for meeting with the judge.

"I think I should be walkin' ye to the trolley. Then I can go home to sleep."

Camri's face took on a look that he had come to recognize. There seemed to be some question on her mind, yet she was hesitant to ask it.

"Ye might as well go ahead."

She looked at him and shook her head. "Go ahead?"

"Aye. Go ahead and ask whatever question it is ye have in that pretty little head of yers."

She cocked her head to one side. "You think you know me

so well. What if I were to tell you that I didn't have any question on my mind?"

He chuckled. "I'd be callin' ye a liar."

She looked momentarily embarrassed, then gave a shrug. "And you'd be right. I do have a question."

"So be askin' it." He wanted more than anything to pull her into his arms, but given his stench, he didn't want to leave her smelling as badly as he did.

Camri took a step closer, much to his surprise. "Were you serious about wanting to marry me?"

"Now aren't ye a brazen one? Why, you're just as bold as any Irish lass."

"Maybe so, but I've learned in life—especially being a woman—that if I don't ask questions, I don't get answers."

"And what kind of answer would ye be wantin'?"

They were only inches apart, and Patrick could see the love in her eyes. He knew how she felt, because he felt the same way.

"The truth," she whispered.

He nodded. "Then answer me true. Would ye be sayin' yes, if I were to give ye a proper proposal?"

She grew thoughtful. "I never figured to marry. From the time I was quite young, I thought that I would probably be single all of my life. I knew that I wanted an education and then to help other women with their education. I thought a career and women's rights were what I desired, and—"

Patrick pulled her toward him and kissed her with a passion he'd long denied. The feel of her in his arms stirred his blood. The way she responded to his kiss gave him all the encouragement he needed.

Without warning, he pulled back, dropped to one knee, and took her hand. "I love ye, Camrianne Coulter. Will ye be consentin' to marry a poor Irishman?"

She looked down at him, wide-eyed. Her lips were reddened

by the kiss, and her cheeks were flushed. She'd never looked more beautiful to Patrick than in that moment.

"Aye. I'll be marryin' ye, Patrick Murdock," she said, doing her best to imitate his brogue.

He laughed and got to his feet. "I'll make an Irishwoman of ye yet." He started to leave, then turned. "*Tá mo chroí istigh ionat.*"

She shook her head. "Which means what?"

"That I love ye. Maybe a more exact translation is, 'My heart is in ye.'"

CHAPTER
27

*A*fter Patrick headed home, Camri made her way to her brother's office. She found Caleb at his desk, writing furiously on a pad of paper.

"Do you mind if I interrupt you for a moment?" she asked.

He looked up and shook his head. "Not at all. What is it?"

She smiled. "Patrick has asked me to marry him, and I've said yes. I hope that meets with your approval."

"And if it doesn't?" Caleb asked in a somber tone.

Camri blinked. She hadn't really considered that her brother would protest the marriage. "Well . . . I'm not sure. I suppose I will still marry him, because I love him. However, I also suppose I will strive to win you over to my thinking."

Caleb leaned back in his chair. "You do know that a great many folks will look down on you for your choice? Marrying an Irishman isn't going to be widely accepted among the socially elite."

"I know, but I really don't care. Those same socially elite weren't exactly accepting of my attending college and taking up a career. They certainly weren't supportive of women's rights and the suffrage work I did."

"So you've thought this through?"

Camri pulled up a wooden chair and sat down. "I've given it a lot of thought, Caleb. When I first came here to find you, I learned rather quickly that I was a snob."

To her surprise, he laughed. "And how did you surmise that?"

"I was constantly berating the girls for their lack of education and did my best to encourage them to better themselves. I had a run-in with Patrick too. On more than one occasion, I might add."

"I can well imagine. So what happened?"

"Well . . . I suppose God granted me the wisdom I was lacking. I started seeing that Judith and Kenzie had talents and knowledge that I didn't. I saw how capable Patrick was and how much he knew about things that couldn't necessarily be learned in a book. It humbled me and shamed me at the same time." She shook her head. "All of my adult life, I've wanted to help people get a better education so they could rise above their limited situations. It never dawned on me that they could be content in those situations."

"Sometimes we are blinded by our ambitions," Caleb offered.

"It's true. I presumed that education would somehow resolve any and all class difficulties, but I can see now there are things it can't change. You know, for all my work in Chicago, I never really got involved with the ethnic issues. Coming here, I see them all too clearly."

"Yes. San Francisco is rife with tension regarding the various cultures represented here. The last few years we had problems with the plague—especially in the Chinese areas of town. That led people to believe that the Chinese were carriers of the disease and therefore they should be forced out of the country or killed. All of this despite scientific evidence that it is rats that carry the disease. But the people in this town had been looking for a reason to get rid of the Chinese for decades, and this just stirred up everything once again."

"Do you suppose there is something I might do to help?" Camri asked, forgetting she'd come here purely for Caleb's blessing. "I mean, not necessarily with the Chinese, although that would be all right. But I've been to Patrick's neighborhood and seen how bad things are there. Can I put my education and knowledge to good use to better their lives?"

"I don't know. I suppose only time can tell, but the fact that you're willing to try speaks for itself. I'm proud of you, Camri. You've learned to care about more than just the cause at hand. You've come to see the people for themselves."

She hadn't really considered it that way before. Always in the past she had taken up her parents' battle cry of equal rights among the sexes, as well as freedom from oppression for all. She had lectured groups of women to get their education and better themselves, but until Ophelia, she'd never really thought of the individual, nor of their living conditions.

"I suppose I have. I never realized before that I wasn't looking beyond the benefit education had given me. I presumed it would be beneficial to everyone. I still believe education is a good way to better oneself, but I'm starting to understand that there are needs far more immediate. I'm just not sure what I can do."

"Well, perhaps with Patrick at your side, the two of you will find the answer."

She remembered her original reason for coming. "So you don't mind my marrying him?"

Caleb chuckled. "Not at all. That's why I gave him my blessing when he came to tell me his intention."

"And when did he do that?"

"When we were talking alone the other day. Patrick, being rather old-fashioned, came to ask me for your hand, since Father is so far away. I told him I couldn't imagine anyone wanting to take on such a stubborn, headstrong woman for a wife, but I could see that he loved you and that was really all that mattered to me."

"I'm glad you approve. It means a lot to me."

"I'll give you the same caution I gave Patrick, however."

"And what is that?"

"Take your time. You two hardly know each other, and what little time you've had together has been surrounded by sorrows and tragedy. Take time to learn about each other and what you want out of life. Make sure you're a good match."

His words of wisdom made complete sense, and despite her overwhelming feelings of love, she agreed.

Caleb got up and came to her. Camri rose and embraced her brother. After a brief hug, he went back to his chair.

"Now, if you don't mind, I have work to do, and if I'm not mistaken, you need to get to the chocolate factory."

She smiled. "Indeed, I do. We're preparing for Valentine's Day, don't you know, and Mr. Lake is quite certain that spies and sabotage await around every corner. I doubt he'd trust Cupid himself if he showed up at the factory."

———

At work, Camri could scarcely think of anything but Patrick and the danger he was putting himself in. She knew it wasn't exactly her fault that he was working at Daniels', but she couldn't help feeling responsible.

When lunchtime came, Judith and Kenzie suggested they go to the corner café. For so long they'd saved every penny in order to aid their search for Caleb, and now that it wasn't necessary any longer, they decided a little celebration was in order.

"I've wanted to eat there since we first came to work for Mr. Lake," Judith admitted. "Every time we walk past, it smells so inviting."

"I agree." Camri took up her coat. "Besides, I have something to tell you. Something that may come as a surprise."

"You're going to marry Patrick Murdock," Kenzie said matter-of-factly.

Camri's brow knit as she frowned. "How did you know?"

Judith clapped her hands. "We didn't, but we hoped. The two of you are clearly in love."

"We are. I have to admit, I hadn't planned to fall in love."

"No one ever does," Kenzie said, securing her hat.

Camri felt sad for her friend. Kenzie still bore the pain of her loss. The rejection of her fiancé would no doubt haunt her for a very long time.

"I hope you'll let us help you plan the wedding," Judith said. "I don't know much about such things, and sadly have never been to one, but it sounds terribly romantic."

"Of course, you can help." Camri followed them outside.

"When do you plan to marry?" Kenzie asked.

It dawned on Camri that she hadn't even thought about that yet. "I really don't know. I suppose soon. I can't imagine either of us wanting a big wedding."

Kenzie nodded. "It's probably better that way. Less expense and headache should anything go wrong."

Camri linked arms with Kenzie. They exchanged a glance, but Camri said nothing. She knew Kenzie's pain ran deep, and Kenzie knew Camri cared. Nothing needed to be said.

"When had you planned for your wedding, Kenzie?" Judith asked.

"September. The twenty-ninth." She offered nothing more.

Camri gave Kenzie's arm a squeeze. She wished she could say something encouraging, but nothing came to mind. For all her education and knowledge, words simply seemed inadequate.

"Will you get married at our church?" Judith asked.

Camri frowned and looked away lest either woman see. She

realized she had no idea where Patrick went to church or where he'd expect them to marry. He had been raised Catholic, but over the years had fallen away from the church all together. Ophelia had told her that much. Now that Patrick was working to restore his walk with God, would he want to return to the Catholic Church?

"I don't know," she murmured. "I guess I don't know much at all." Caleb's warning came to mind.

Kenzie surprised her by patting her arm. "Sometimes even knowing all that you can doesn't help a bit."

Camri was still pondering her lack of knowledge where Patrick was concerned when Judge Waters' arrival was announced. She stood and smoothed the skirt of her plum-colored gown, then beamed at the white-haired judge as Mrs. Wong showed him into the sitting room.

"You must be Miss Coulter. I think we met when you were here visiting last year. One of our local newspaper owners gave a party. I believe Caleb brought you as his date."

"Yes, I remember. Caleb continues to speak so highly of you." Camri motioned the older man to sit. "It's because of Caleb that I asked you to come tonight."

He frowned. "I don't suppose there's been any word."

"Oh, but there has been," Caleb announced, coming into the room from the hall.

"Caleb! When did you return?" Judge Winters leapt out of his chair and extended his hand. As they shook, he embraced Caleb and patted him on the back. "I don't know when I've been happier to see anyone in my life. I feared Ruef had most likely killed you."

"I'm sure he'd like to," Caleb admitted. The two men stepped away from each other but continued to clasp hands.

"Tell me everything," the judge said. "I want to know it all."

"Well, that's partially why I had Camri call you. You see, only a few trusted souls know I've returned, and it's to our benefit that we keep it that way. Have a seat, and I'll explain."

"And while he does that," Camri interjected, "I'll have Mrs. Wong bring coffee."

She left as her brother began to tell his tale. Instead of ringing the bell, She made her way to the kitchen and found Mrs. Wong already busy with the refreshments.

"You may serve the coffee anytime now, Mrs. Wong."

The housekeeper looked up, and Camri could see she'd been crying. Without thought, Camri went to her and embraced the older woman. Mrs. Wong stiffened but didn't pull away.

Camri realized she was probably causing the other woman further discomfort and stepped back. "Can I do anything?"

"No. You good to care. I just thinking about my Liling. It make my heart sad to think about her."

"But soon, once Caleb and Patrick figure out how to get her out of the dance hall, she'll be back with you, and then the healing can really begin."

Mrs. Wong nodded. "So much bad happen."

"There has been more than our share of bad, that much is certain. But, Mrs. Wong, there has also been good to come out of all of this. I probably wouldn't have said that a month ago, but Caleb has helped me see how God has directed this situation. He has a plan in all of this, and I know we will be better for it."

"My mother and father hear about God when I was very young. They went to hear a man speak, and the things he said made them glad in their spirit."

Camri smiled. "When I was a little girl, I heard a man talk about God, and it made my spirit glad too. I remember hearing him say that even with all the people in the world, Jesus loved me—that He knew me and wanted me to know Him."

Mrs. Wong nodded. "My father worked for the railroad and he gone many days, but my mother took me to church and I hear about God too. I asked how I get God, and Mama tell me to ask Him to come into me. That made me afraid. So many of my friends say there were ghosts who would come instead, but I believed Mama. She loved me and not want me to get hurt. She said God would not let bad ghosts come hurt me. She said God had special Holy Ghost who would protect me."

"I love hearing your story, Mrs. Wong. It blesses me to know how God touched your heart. Do you go to church?"

The older woman nodded. "We go to church for Chinese. We have good pastor who speaks Chinese." She smiled for the first time. "He come from China, where missionary teach him English and about God."

Camri couldn't help herself. She hugged Mrs. Wong again, and this time the housekeeper didn't stiffen. When she thought about the missionary who answered God's call and went to China, and then the people he brought to the Lord, Camri couldn't help but be amazed. All of that came full circle back to America, where one of those people now preached to others. "I am praying for Liling. I feel certain we'll get her home soon."

"I pray too. I prayed for God to bring Mr. Caleb back to us, and He did. Now I keep praying for Him to bring Liling."

Camri nodded. "And He will."

"It won't be easy," Judge Winters told Caleb. "Ruef has a great many men on the police force who do his bidding. However, I know a few we can count on. I'll call them tonight and see what we can work out."

"Patrick said there's a warehouse at the docks where Daniels is keeping the men. He's got someone there who keeps them drugged so they won't try to escape. Late Saturday or early Sunday is when they plan to make the exchange."

"That just gives us Friday and Saturday to coordinate everything. Frankly, I would move heaven and earth in that time just to see Ruef behind bars, but this won't help us to do that."

Caleb shrugged. "Maybe not, but it's a start. We'll put Daniels and his ruffians in jail and send a strong message to Ruef that we're not going to tolerate any more shanghaiing. Say, I know—let's get one of your newspaper friends to come down and report on the matter. With photographs and a big flashy story on the front page, people are going to take notice."

"I agree. That would be helpful, but you know as well as I do that putting Ruef away is going to take time. Some people have been working on this for quite a while. They're making progress, but Ruef is a slippery one."

Caleb nodded. "I know, but we have to make people aware that there really is a force out there willing to fight for them. I think this will help. Seeing other good men willing to make a stand should encourage folks to join in."

Camri arrived with Mrs. Wong behind her, bringing a large silver tray with coffee and cake. She placed the tray on a polished table by the piano. "You want I serve now?"

Caleb shook his head. "We can manage it, Mrs. Wong, but come here. I want you to meet Judge Winters. He's going to help us get Liling back."

Mrs. Wong hurried over to the men and bowed several times to the judge. "I thank you."

"No need to thank me, Mrs. Wong. I'm just sorry something couldn't be done before now."

"Mr. Caleb try hard, and he get taken away. We so sorry such bad things happen to him."

Caleb shook his head and reached out to take hold of Mrs. Wong's arm. "Mrs. Wong, we already spoke about this. There is no reason to be sorry when God clearly had a purpose in everything that happened. I am not sorry for what happened to me, only sorry that I wasn't able to bring Liling home. But I promise you we will have her here very soon."

She smiled at Caleb and bowed again. "You a good man, Mr. Caleb."

Caleb wouldn't go that far, but he said nothing and allowed Mrs. Wong to return to her quarters. Camri was already pouring cups of coffee.

"Judge, would you care for cream or sugar?" she asked.

"I'll take both." He looked at Caleb. "My wife would chide me to leave them out. She said I'm getting fat." He patted his midsection. "But what she doesn't know won't hurt her."

Camri brought him his coffee. "Yes, but it may hurt you. I hope you won't tell her that I aided and abetted you in the act."

The judge winked and took the coffee. "My lips are sealed."

CHAPTER

28

*P*atrick looked at the drugged men sleeping as if they hadn't a care in the world. Rain poured down on them, but they were oblivious to it, just as they were to the plans Daniels had for them. Patrick had just put the last man into the back of Daniels' wagon, wedging him in with the others and fighting back the urge to confront his boss. He had to stick with the plan—had to convince Daniels that he was in full support.

The dark night and storm concealed their actions for the most part. No one seemed to care that Malcolm Daniels was driving his wagon from one boardinghouse to another with lengthy stops in between. No one had any idea what was really happening.

"Help me cover 'em with the tarp, Murdock." Daniels was already throwing a large piece of canvas over the bodies. "If Sean hadn't up and quit me, we'd have more help." He muttered several curses and strained to secure the tarp.

It was nearly one in the morning, and Patrick could only hope Caleb and Judge Winters had been successful in getting enough police officers to carry out their plan. He pulled the canvas over the bodies of the young men, noting that none of them could have been much older than twenty.

Foolish children. They'd not even really lived yet, and because of their choices, they were facing a questionable future.

"Well, that ought to do it." Daniels shoved the canvas down the sides of the wagon, then took out a revolver and tucked it in the front of his pants.

All evening, Patrick had pondered how he was going to overpower Daniels when the time came. The boss was armed, and Patrick had no desire to see any honest policemen take a bullet. He'd prayed for guidance, but short of using the knife in his boot, he wasn't at all sure how he could keep Daniels from taking the lives of innocent men.

"You sit on the back of the wagon in case anyone comes along and gets nosy," Daniels instructed. He reached into his coat and pulled out a second revolver. "Take this. If anyone comes near, you can wave it around."

Patrick checked to see if the gun was loaded. It was. He gave Daniels a nod. "I was just wonderin' how I would be handlin' things if the need arose."

"We shouldn't have too much trouble." Daniels glanced around. "The dock workers won't care, and Ruef's men know to leave us be. Besides, we haven't that far to go, and the rain will discourage honest folk from leaving their homes—especially given the hour."

Patrick took a seat on the back of the wagon and slipped the gun in his waistband. "I'm sure ye know best."

Daniels grunted. "Just the same, I'll be glad when we get this bunch delivered."

"Do we have more to pick up?" Patrick asked.

"I got the rest at the warehouse. The ship captains will have their men there to help load 'em into the boats and out to the ships."

Daniels put the horses in motion and headed through the Barbary Coast neighborhood. Despite the hour and the rain, the place was still a riot of activity, with lights flashing, music, and women calling out to entice customers. The only difference was that due to the rain, the soiled doves stood in the windows and doorways.

From time to time, Patrick spotted a fight on one of the side streets. Liquor and women got these men up in arms faster than anything Patrick had ever seen. And the downpour wasn't stopping anyone, especially not the bookies taking bets on the fights. It was amazing to Patrick how these men would bet on anything, even two drunk boys fighting over the same dancer.

Men in various states of inebriation wandered the drenched streets in search of a good time, and none were quiet about it. If they'd come a day or two earlier, they might have found themselves one of the nameless boys lying unconscious in the warehouse. If they weren't careful now, they might find themselves beaten and robbed—if not killed.

"Sewer's overflowing up the street," someone called out to Daniels as they passed. "You'll have to go around."

They detoured, only to find the problem affecting more than one area. Daniels cursed and headed the horses in another direction.

Dodging floods and sewage made their ten-minute trip stretch to thirty. Patrick's gaze darted from one corner to another. He was certain the judge's men would be nearby, perhaps even following them at a distance. He hadn't been able to get word to Caleb until earlier that morning as to the warehouse location, but it was more than enough time for the men to infiltrate. At least he hoped it was.

They finally pulled up alongside a run-down building. A sign posted on the door stated it was the property of Daniels Distributing. It made no reference to what was being distributed.

A big burly man appeared from the shadows. Patrick didn't recognize him, but Daniels had a lot of men working for him whom Patrick had never seen. This man looked more than able to handle himself, and Patrick knew he'd have to watch out for him once the judge's men made their presence known.

Daniels climbed down from the wagon and pulled a set of keys from his pockets. He nodded at the man. "Sorry we're late. We had to round up a few more." He nodded toward the wagon. "I'm sure your captain will be pleased."

The man said nothing, just watched Daniels carefully. Patrick left the wagon and stood to one side of Daniels as he unlocked the warehouse door. He had just opened the door when the big man reached out and took hold of him.

A dozen policemen appeared from various hiding places on the docks. Two even emerged from the warehouse.

Daniels was indignant. "What in the world is all this about?"

"It's about drugging and shanghaiing men—forcing them to become crew members on ships bound for the Orient and elsewhere," a suit-clad man announced. "I'm with the *San Francisco Call*, and I intend to see that this story is front-page news."

Patrick hadn't seen where he or the others had been hiding, but given that they were just as wet as he was, he figured it hadn't been indoors.

The newspaperman was eager to make his way into the circle. "Can you state your full name for the paper?" he asked Daniels.

By now another policemen had hold of Daniels, and a third had come to take Patrick in hand. The big burly man waved the officer away.

"This one's with us," he told the uniformed policeman.

Patrick had no idea how the man knew. He'd figured, from the way Daniels addressed him, that the big man was a crew member on one of the ships. He breathed out in relief as the officer dropped his hold on Patrick's arm. The last thing he wanted was to go back to jail.

Daniels fixed him with a scowl. "You'll pay for this with your life."

The threat didn't bother Patrick at all. "Better than lettin' these lads pay with theirs."

Patrick went to the warehouse door, where Daniels' keys still dangled. He took the ring and put it in his pocket. He knew the keys would be the answer to getting Liling out of the dance hall. Without waiting to see what would happen to Daniels next, Patrick left the dock. He ran as fast as he could, backtracking their route and praying for guidance. When he came to Daniels' place, he stopped long enough to regain his wind. No sense running in like his clothes were on fire. It would be enough that he'd come back alone, although he'd already thought up a believable story for that.

He walked into the dance hall like he owned the place. There was plenty of music and noise to distract most of Daniels' men. Nelson eyed him from the bar, giving Patrick the distinct feeling he knew something was amiss.

"Where's the boss?" he asked as Patrick casually walked up and struck a pose of disinterest.

"Drinkin' with the ships' captains and celebratin' his bounty." Patrick grinned. "It was a good haul."

Nelson lost his look of suspicion. "That's good. It'll put the boss in good spirits. Since Gallagher up and left, he's been fit to be tied. Now maybe he'll loosen up his tight hold on the purse strings. I could use a decent bonus for all these extra hours."

Patrick nodded. "I could use the same."

"Hey, you're getting water all over my bar." Nelson picked up a towel.

Patrick straightened. "Sorry about that. It's pourin' out there. I'll go get me a towel and see to dryin' off."

"You do that." Nelson was already focused on tidying up the bar.

No one seemed to notice him, which pleased Patrick to no end. He grabbed a towel from one of the cupboards and wiped his face, then glanced down the hall where the private gaming rooms were. At the end, he saw one of Daniels' men guarding the door to the upstairs rooms. This was the routine when Daniels was out of the building. Patrick would have to make some sort of excuse for going up there.

He thought of the gun still tucked in his waistband as he walked down the hall. Maybe he should just hit the guard over the head and leave it at that. But even as he considered it, Patrick knew someone would easily find him.

"Evenin', Murdock," the guard said.

"Evenin', Jude. I need upstairs. Daniels sent me." A thought came to mind. Daniels' living quarters were up there. He held up the keys. "He left his wallet. I'm supposed to fetch it back for him."

Jude laughed. "Just don't be interrupting the customers."

Patrick shrugged. "Wouldn't dream of it."

"Do what ya will. The boss sent you, and I ain't gonna go against him."

"Aye."

Jude stepped aside, and Patrick took the stairs two at a time. At the top, he nearly knocked a man down.

"Pardon me," Patrick said.

The customer was of a higher class than usual and clearly drunk. He held up his hand, pointing an index finger at Patrick. "Watch yourself, young man." He swayed and tried to grab Patrick.

Patrick steadied the customer and pointed him toward the stairs. "Ye want to go this way."

The customer looked down the stairs and nodded. The infraction was already forgotten, and he started down. Patrick glanced toward Liling's. He had no idea if she had a customer or not, but it didn't matter. He had to get her out of here before word got back that Daniels had been arrested.

He went to the door. It was slightly ajar. That was a good sign. Perhaps the man he'd run into was coming from her room.

Patrick pushed open the door and saw the petite Chinese woman sitting on the side of her bed. One ankle was chained to the frame to prevent her from running away. She was Daniels' caged bird.

Liling looked at him with wide eyes. Her black hair was pulled back but messy. "Why have you come?" She no doubt recognized him.

Patrick glanced back at the door. "I've come to set ye free. I'm takin' ye to yer folks."

She shook her head. "No, they hate me. I've dishonored them."

He knelt in front of her and began searching through the keys to find one that would unlock the shackle. After just three tries, he found it. "They don't hate ye at all. They've been half beside themselves tryin' to find ye and get ye home."

She shook her head, still unable to believe him. Patrick tossed the fetter aside. "Come on. We have to figure out how to get ye out of here."

"That ain't gonna happen," Jude said, coming into the room. "I thought you were up to something. Daniels would never forget his wallet."

Jude started to close the distance between them, but Patrick pulled the gun from his waistband. Jude stopped mid-step. He looked at the revolver and then at Patrick.

"You'll never get her through the dance hall. The other men will stop you. They know who she is and what she means to the boss."

Patrick looked back at the scantily clad woman. Her face was painted and her body more than adequately displayed. He'd have to find her other clothes. Clothes that would keep others from questioning who she was.

He looked back at Jude and smiled. "Close the door."

Jude hesitated for a moment, then shrugged. "It's your funeral." He closed the door then looked back at Patrick. His hand moved slowly toward his waistband.

"If I were yourself, I'd not do that," Patrick said. He knew Jude had a billy club tucked into the back of his pants. "Toss the club on the bed." Jude scowled but did as Patrick commanded. "Now take off yer clothes. Everythin' but yer long underwear."

Jude looked at Patrick as if he'd lost his mind. He shook his head, then made a lunge. Patrick was ready for him and hit him square in the face with the pistol. Jude staggered back, then dropped to his knees. He was used to a good fight, but Patrick had managed to stun him—at least for the moment.

Patrick handed the gun to Liling. "Shoot him if he moves." From the look of hatred on her face, he had no doubt she would do just that.

He went to the bed, pulled off the sheet, and ripped it into several strips. He gagged Jude and then tied his hands behind him. It was only after Patrick had hoisted Jude to his feet that he remembered he needed the man's clothes.

Just then, however, a young man pushed open the door and staggered inside. He looked at the situation for a moment, then shrugged. "I must be in the wrong room."

"No, ye're not," Patrick replied, eyeing him for size. He was smaller than Jude and wearing a hat. "Come on in and close the door."

The boy must have been used to seeing all sorts of things and didn't even blink. He did as Patrick directed. Patrick wrapped the chain to Liling's manacle several times around the iron bed frame to shorten it. Then he clamped the manacle on one of Jude's bound wrists.

"That ought to hold ye for a moment."

All the while the boy watched. He seemed intrigued by what was going on. When Patrick came to him, the boy shook his head. "I ain't payin' extra."

"Ye won't be needin' to pay at all. Take off yer clothes."

"I didn't think we could do that. I remember they said downstairs I could only take off my hat."

"Well, I'm tellin' ye different. Take 'em off and do it quick, or I'll be fetchin' my gun." He nodded toward Liling, but the boy still didn't seem to understand.

Knowing that time was running out, Patrick delivered a knockout blow to the young man's chin. "Sorry about the inconvenience," he said as he lowered the boy to the ground.

Patrick quickly stripped the boy of his coat and shirt and tossed them toward Liling. "Put these on." Next he went to work taking the boots and trousers. When he'd accomplished that, Patrick picked up the boy's fallen hat and brought everything to Liling. "Put these on too. They'll all be too big, but we'll figure it out."

Patrick glanced around the room. The boy hadn't been wearing a belt, so he needed another way to help Liling keep the pants up. Nothing seemed useful. He looked down at Jude, who was finally shaking off his daze. Time was getting away from them.

Desperate, Patrick went to the drapes and cut the cord. Liling was just doing up the buttons on the pants, and he wrapped the cord around her waist, then pulled the band of the pants up under it.

He handed the ends of the cord to her. "Tie this around ye as tight as ye can."

Liling cinched the cord around her waist and knotted it. Next Patrick helped her do up the buttons of the coat. When that was done, he handed her the boots. He glanced down at her small feet. "Ye're goin' to have to make due with these."

"I can put stockings in the toes," she suggested and went to the dresser. She pulled out two pairs of stockings and stuffed them down the boots. Then she pulled them on and nodded. "I can walk in them."

By now Jude was starting to make noise. Patrick thought about giving him a good punch to the nose, but decided it would just be a waste of time. Instead, he grabbed up the hat and went to Liling.

"Stuff yer hair up under this and keep yer head down when we go downstairs. I'm gonna drag ye through the place like ye've caused problems. Just keep yer face down, and maybe no one will notice."

She nodded and followed Patrick to the door. He looked down the hall to see if anyone else was there. It was empty, so he pulled Liling out of the room. They had made it down the stairs without incident when Patrick took hold of her arm.

"Now remember, keep yer head down."

She lowered her head, and Patrick pulled her collar up to help hide her face, then grabbed the front of it like he might to evict a customer.

He dragged her down the hall and passed the bar, talking all the while. "We don't allow trouble-makin' here." He glanced at the bar. Nelson was too busy to notice him. That at least was a break. The men left their wallets with the barkeep before heading upstairs, and Nelson would have reminded Patrick of that had he seen what was going on.

Patrick half dragged, half pushed Liling through the dance hall and out the front door. Thankfully, none of Daniels' men guarded the entry. God had cleared their path.

"Come on, we need to hurry."

Patrick pushed her down the walkway, mingling with the

thinning crowd. He rounded the corner and pulled her with him. Only after they were several blocks away did Patrick slow his pace. Liling was panting for air, but said nothing.

"We've a ways to go. Can ye make it?"

"I'll make it," she assured him.

The rain was probably to their benefit, Patrick decided. The weather and flooding discouraged many people from noticing what looked like a man and a boy sneaking along the street.

The hilly city wasn't easy for a healthy man to hurry through, much less a woman who'd been chained to a bed for who knew how long. Liling stumbled more than once, in part due to the oversized pants and boots, but Patrick knew that she wasn't at all strong. Several times he thought of just carrying her, but that would only draw attention.

Feeling sorry for her, Patrick paused a moment. He pulled Liling into the arched doorway of a large building. The cold rain chilled him to the bone, and the entryway didn't provide much relief from the deluge. He could see in the muted street light that Liling was shaking, but whether from fear or cold, he couldn't say. No doubt both played a part.

He heard something. Was it the sound of someone running toward them? Patrick pressed back against the door and pushed Liling behind him. The footsteps grew louder, and he held his breath and tightened his fists. If Jude or one of the other ruffians had managed to follow him, Patrick would have to fight their way out.

The runner was nearly upon them, and Patrick whispered a prayer. He knew God had put him in the position of helping Daniels in order to free Liling and help those poor unconscious boys. Just as he knew God would give him the ability to defend himself now.

CHAPTER

29

Camri paced nervously. It was three in the morning, and still there had been no word from Patrick. They'd all agreed to stay up and keep her company, but even with the nearness of her brother and friends, Camri found it impossible to calm her fears.

She would have liked to talk to Caleb about the details of the plans, but he seemed to have his hands full just trying to keep the Wongs from fretting. He sat in the corner of the large sitting room, speaking to them. His voice was too low for her to hear what was being said, but she imagined he was assuring them of the simplicity of their plan and God's faithfulness to provide.

God's faithfulness wasn't in doubt, but Camri knew that His plan didn't always work out the way she thought it should. "What ifs" danced in her thoughts like rain on the roof.

"Judith, why don't you play the piano?" Kenzie said, nudging the blonde.

With a yawn, Judith got to her feet. "I suppose I could."

"I didn't know you played," Caleb said, standing. He moved toward Judith. "How marvelous. Do you play Chopin?"

Judith suddenly looked flummoxed. "I . . . ah . . . yes." She looked toward the piano.

Caleb smiled and cupped her elbow. "Then play us a nocturne. How about in E-flat major?"

Judith seemed to forget herself. "Opus nine, number two?" She looked up at him as if for approval. "Andante."

"Yes. One of my very favorites," he replied.

Judith sat down at the piano while Caleb went to the bookshelf. He took down a wooden box and opened it. From the top, he picked up the sheet music for the nocturne. He turned to hand it to Judith, but she had already started to play without it. Camri listened to the melodious tones and marveled at the skill Judith displayed. The feeling she put into the music was almost tangible.

Camri began to relax a bit as the music wove a spell over the room. Her breathing slowed, and her thoughts went not to Patrick's absence, but to God's faithfulness.

Thank you, Lord. You are so good to hear my prayers even when I don't know quite what to say. You've given me Patrick to love, and I feel your peace regarding the events of this night.

Exhausted, Camri sat for the first time in hours. Judith played on, and Caleb stood ever faithful at the piano, as if she might need something. For just a moment, Camri closed her eyes. She thought of all the plans she'd once had for her future. Father had even teased that perhaps Camrianne would be the first woman to win a seat in Congress. She had mused that thought, telling her father that she'd be content just to get the vote, but the idea had played around in her head. Now, however, her future was taking a very different road.

But everything has happened so fast, and I don't even know much about Patrick's likes and dislikes. We haven't even had a real outing together—one just focused on the two of us getting to know each other. I don't even know if he'll attend church with me.

At the sound of the front door opening, Camri forgot about her concerns and jumped to her feet. Judith stopped playing, and all gazes looked toward the entryway hall. It was if everyone held their breath.

Patrick stepped into view, and Camri thought she might cry. He was drenched from the rain but looked no worse for the wear. He reached out and drew a young man to his side. Camri frowned. Where was Liling?

Caleb crossed the room as the young man took off his hat. Shiny black hair fell across his shoulders, and only then did Camri realize it wasn't a young man at all. It was Liling.

"Mrs. Wong, Mr. Wong, come see." Caleb motioned them from the corner, where they couldn't see their daughter.

Mrs. Wong got up and started toward Caleb, then stopped. She reached for her husband's hand. They walked together, seeming almost afraid, keeping their gaze to the floor.

"It's all right," Caleb assured them. "God has answered our prayers."

Mrs. Wong looked up first and then Mr. Wong. Liling had stepped into the room. The clothes she wore were much too big for her, and her garish makeup was streaked and smeared from the rain. Even so, her expression was one of such happiness that Camri's eyes filled with tears.

"Mama," Liling whispered.

Mrs. Wong looked at her daughter with an expression of pure love and held out her arms. Liling hurried into her mother's embrace, and both women began to sob.

Mr. Wong looked at Patrick and bowed. "God made you to answer our prayers."

Camri could no longer stand the distance between them. She hurried to Patrick and threw her arms around him. He held her close for a moment, then pushed her away.

"I'm soakin' wet."

"I don't care." She looked up at him. "I'm so glad you're back safe."

"Ye should be in bed asleep. Ye have church tomorrow."

"Today," Caleb interjected. "Somehow, I don't think any of us will be making it."

The Wongs were whispering to each other in Chinese. Camri could see that Liling's rebellion and subsequent fall into ruin no longer mattered. Her parents loved her, and just like the father of the prodigal son, they welcomed her home with open arms.

Mr. Wong looked at Caleb. "We go now, take care of our daughter."

Caleb nodded. "Of course. Liling, we are so glad to have you here with us."

The young woman looked up. Her tears continued to fall. "I am grateful to be here." She glanced back at her mother. "So grateful."

Mr. Wong took her arm and led her from the room. Mrs. Wong followed close behind, pausing only a moment to look at Patrick. She smiled and reached out to pat his arm.

"You always welcome in our family. We give you many thanks."

"I was glad to help," Patrick replied.

Mrs. Wong nodded and followed her family without another word.

Camri took hold of Patrick and drew him to the fire. "You warm up, and I'll go get you a towel."

"Better still," Caleb said, "come upstairs and have a hot bath. I'll get you some of my clothes to wear. You can stay the night with us."

Camri nodded. "You may have my room, and I'll share with Judith or Kenzie."

"You can sleep with me," Judith said, leaving the piano. "I have the bigger bed."

Patrick looked as if he might protest, but then gave a nod. "Thank ye, I'm not of a mind to head back out into the rain."

Camri longed for him to stay and talk, but she knew the wisdom in getting him warmed up and dry. She watched the two men walk away and gave a sigh. Everyone was back safe and sound, and she could rest easy.

"I'm heading to bed," Kenzie said as she passed by Camri. She paused and gave Camri a weary smile. "I'm so glad everything worked out. I have to admit I despaired of us ever finding your brother alive. When he came home and told us his story, it renewed my faith. Then, seeing how God managed things this evening . . . well, it's given me a great deal to think about. Even when things seem completely hopeless, I must remember that God is still able to deliver."

Judith gave a nod. "Pastor Fisher said prayer changes everything. I can see now that it really does."

Camri put her arms around both women. "It truly does. Thank you both for helping me through this very difficult time. I'm so blessed that God put us together."

The threesome hugged, then Kenzie and Judith headed upstairs, leaving Camri alone.

As tired as she had been earlier, Camri now felt wide awake. She went to the fireplace and stretched out her hands. The front of her dress was still damp from embracing Patrick, but she didn't care. He was here and he was safe. Nothing else mattered. All of her plans for the future could be reordered, so long as Patrick was a part of them.

The next day Camri awoke to find the sun shining. After days of heavy rain, it seemed the weather had cleared. She stretched and then remembered that she was sharing the bed with Judith. When she looked at the other side of the bed, however, she found that Judith had already risen.

"Goodness, what must the time be?"

Camri got up and looked at the clock. It was half past noon. She'd never slept so late in all her life. She dressed quickly and made her way downstairs, where she found the others gathered around the dining room table, eating.

"We were beginning to think you might never wake up," Caleb said with a grin. "I thought perhaps I would have to send a handsome prince to awaken you with a kiss."

"How scandalous of you," Camri said, kissing Caleb atop his head. She looked at Patrick and smiled.

Mrs. Wong appeared with a pot of coffee. She poured Caleb a cup, then went around the table to check everyone else's cup. "You need anything more?"

Caleb shook his head. "I think we have food enough for ten more people, Mrs. Wong. Thank you."

She looked at Camri. "You want tea or coffee?"

"Tea is just fine, Mrs. Wong. Thank you."

Camri took her seat and considered the variety of food. Mrs. Wong had made eggs, bacon, and fried potatoes, not to mention biscuits and gravy. There was also a large plate of fruit and another of cheese. Next to that were cold roast beef and ham, as well as a basket of sliced bread for sandwiches. It made for a lovely brunch.

"My goodness, Mrs. Wong, you really outdid yourself." Camri reached for a biscuit as the housekeeper set a cup of tea beside her plate. "Thank you."

"You very welcome," Mrs. Wong bobbed her head twice then disappeared. For a woman who'd been up as late, if not later, than Camri, she was certainly full of energy.

"Judge Winters plans to pay us a visit after church," Caleb said before Camri could even take a sip of her tea. "He called quite early to say he has news for us."

She felt a sense of relief. "Good. I'd hate to have to wait much longer to hear what happened. I do hope there's no chance of Daniels being set free."

"I hope not either," Caleb answered. He dug into his plateful of food. "However, if Ruef is connected to Daniels, as he implied to Patrick, there's no telling."

"But if Daniels is released from jail, he will try to find Liling and Patrick." Camri couldn't keep the worry from her voice.

"Aye, he might well send someone to look for me anyway," Patrick said with a shrug. "He has plenty of friends who aren't in jail."

Camri put down her tea. "You say it so casually. This is terrible. I hadn't thought of that possibility. What shall we do?"

Caleb chuckled. "We finish our meal."

Eating seemed a perfectly logical way to pass the time, and despite her concerns, Camri soon found herself caught up in the conversation.

"So have you two set a date?" Caleb asked, looking at his sister and then Patrick.

"No. We've scarcely been able to talk about anything but finding Liling and seeing justice done." Camri smeared butter on her biscuit. Her concerns about how little she and Patrick knew about each other came back to her.

"Well, with that behind us, I'm sure you'll have plenty of time to make your plans," Caleb said.

She cast a quick glance at Patrick, who seemed to be paying no attention to the conversation. "I'm sure we will."

The doorbell sounded, and Mrs. Wong darted past the dining room and down the hall. When she returned, Judge Winters followed just behind.

"Judge Winters to see you," she announced.

Caleb started to rise. "Come in, Judge. Would you like a cup of coffee?"

The older man waved Caleb off. "Stay in your seat, and no coffee for me. We are dining with my daughter and son-in-law, so I'll make this brief."

"Won't you at least sit down?" Camri asked.

He smiled and shook his head. "Another time, perhaps. I just wanted to let you know that Daniels and the rest of his men from the dance hall are in jail. The place is closed down, and the young ladies have been cared for."

"'Tis good to hear," Patrick said before anyone else could speak. "And what of the sailors?"

The judge frowned. "Most of them will be just fine. Two died. The medication Daniels gave them apparently had an adverse reaction."

Camri could see the grief in Patrick's expression. His jaw clenched, and he looked away. No doubt he felt guilty about not being able to save them.

The judge seemed to sense this as well. "Son, you did all you could. You saved two dozen men from certain slavery and possible death. It is a sad shame that two should die, but that shame is on Daniels, not on you."

"Aye," Patrick whispered, "but I was hopin' to see them all to safety." He let out a heavy sigh.

"The judge is right," Caleb said. "And while I share your grief over losing two men, I think we must look at the bigger picture. This is just the start of putting the practice of shanghaiing to rest, closing down the Barbary Coast, and seeing Ruef pay for his crimes."

"That's right," Judge Winters interjected. "In the last couple of days, I've managed to speak to several men who haven't yielded to Ruef's demands. Men of power. They agree the time has come to put an end to Ruef and the mayor's corruption."

"We'll have our work cut out for us," Caleb said, looking to Patrick. "Are you still of a mind to help?"

Patrick nodded. "Aye. I'm more than ready to see the likes of them behind bars."

Caleb got to his feet. "Judge, thank you for coming to let us know."

"There is something else. Something I meant to mention before now."

Caleb's brow arched. "By all means, speak."

"Henry Ambrewster arranged his will with me, as well as business papers that named you a full partner in the business."

"Aye," Patrick said, nodding. "I saw them m'self. He told me all about it."

Caleb was stunned. "I . . . he never said anything about it."

Judge Winters smiled. "He told me he thought you the finest young attorney he'd ever known."

"I feared he thought me corrupted by the likes of Ruef and his men."

"Henry was a smart man and a good judge of character. He had his faults, to be sure, but he made a sound decision in this matter. Not only that, but he left you the bulk of his estate."

"What?" Caleb shook his head. "But what of his family?"

"He had no children, and his wife died some time back. The rest of his family has more than their fair share. I think he hoped to give you a leg up. The amount is substantial."

"I don't know what to say."

"Well, for now it's unimportant. I'll come again sometime this week, and we can discuss where you want to go from here. We've a battle—nay, a war on our hands that won't be easily won. Men all over this town have paid dearly at the hands of Abraham Ruef. It's time we rallied our forces and figured out a strategy. For now, I bid you all a good day. I hope you have a chance to get out and enjoy the sun."

Caleb excused himself to walk Judge Winters out while the others commented on the news.

Camri placed her napkin on the table. "I suppose I misjudged Henry Ambrewster."

"As did I," Patrick added.

"I can't imagine inheriting money," Judith said, shaking her head. "How wonderful for him."

Kenzie scooted back in her chair, causing Patrick to jump to his feet to help her. Camri smiled at his gentlemanly conduct.

"If you'll excuse me," Kenzie said, giving Patrick a nod, "I believe I will take the judge's advice and go for a walk in the sunshine."

"Oh, do let me join you," Judith said, jumping up. "It's been forever since we had nice weather."

The two left Patrick and Camri alone in the dining room. He helped her up and drew her into his arms. "And what about yourself, Miss Coulter? Would ye care to take a walk with an Irishman?"

"I would." She smiled up at him. "I have a great many things to discuss with him."

"I figured as much." He gave a chuckle. "Since when don't ye have plenty to say?"

She might have feigned insult and pushed him away, but now that his arms were around her, she had little desire to be rid of him.

"So say what ye will." He looked at her with such an expression of love that Camri almost forgot her concerns.

"It can wait until our walk."

"No. Let's be discussin' it now and save spoonin' for the walk."

"Spooning in broad daylight? We would be the talk of San Francisco."

This made Patrick laugh all the more. "You're avoidin' the point. What is it ye want to talk about?"

"There's plenty. For example, we've not had a true courtship.

There's been all this trouble with Daniels and searching for my brother, but in all that time, we've not really been able to court."

"And that's important to ye?" he asked.

"Yes. I think it must be." She searched for the right words. "I don't want to act in haste. Judith and Kenzie asked me if we'd set a date and where we'd be married, and it only reminded me that I know very little about you."

"Aye. The thought has come to my mind as well."

"It has?" She felt a sense of relief. "I'm glad. It's not that I don't want to marry you, because I do. I love you, Patrick."

He grinned. "And I love ye too."

"I'm happy to set a date for our wedding, but I think we should probably give ourselves a little time."

"Then we're of like minds," he replied. "Ye see, I would gladly have asked the judge to marry us here and now, but it wouldn't be right. I have nothin' to offer ye, and I can't be marrying ye without havin' a proper home to take ye to. And I won't have that unless I get back my business."

Camri lowered her face so he couldn't see her frown. She hadn't considered all of this. What he was saying made it sound as if it would be a very long time until they could marry. Maybe even years.

He lifted her chin. "Now, don't ye go frettin'. It won't take all that long, and while we're waitin', we can be courtin'."

"Sometimes, I think you can read my thoughts."

"Most of the time, I can." He grinned. "Like right now, I'm thinkin' ye'd like to be kissed."

"Oh, you think that do you?" She tried hard to sound aloof, even disapproving, but it wasn't working.

Patrick tightened his hold on her. "I think that and more." He gave her a very brief kiss, hardly more than a peck. "I'm thinkin' that ye're the most beautiful woman in the world." He gave her another kiss, this one just as abbreviated. "And I

think ye might well be the smartest woman I've ever known."
Again, he pressed his mouth to hers.

Camri found herself weak in the knees. Her pulse raced.
This man had such power over her emotions. "I feel like I've
been looking for you all of my life," she whispered. "Searching for something I didn't even know was missing. Something
I definitely couldn't find in a book."

"Aye." He chuckled. "I'll be enjoyin' gettin' to know ye."

She smiled and wrapped her arms around his neck. "In that
case, let me introduce myself. Good afternoon, sir. I am Camrianne Coulter." He looked at her, puzzled, prompting her to
ask, "And you are?"

"Yers," he whispered just before lowering his mouth to hers.
This time the kiss lasted for a very long time.

Tracie Peterson is the award-winning author of over one hundred novels, both historical and contemporary. Her avid research resonates in her stories, as seen in her bestselling HEIRS OF MONTANA and ALASKAN QUEST series. Tracie and her family make their home in Montana. Visit Tracie's website at www.traciepeterson.com.

Sign Up for Tracie's Newsletter!

Keep up to date with Tracie's news on book releases and events by signing up for her email list at traciepeterson.com.

From Tracie Peterson and Kimberley Woodhouse

Katherine and Jean-Michel once shared a deep love that was torn apart by forces beyond their control. Reunited in the 1920s at the Curry Hotel in Alaska, have the years changed them too deeply to rediscover what they had? And when Jean-Michel's nightmares of war return with terrifying consequences, will faith be enough to heal what's been broken for so long?

Out of the Ashes
THE HEART OF ALASKA #2
kimberleywoodhouse.com

BETHANYHOUSE

More from Tracie Peterson

Visit traciepeterson.com for a full list of her books.

Grace Martindale loses her last vestige of security when her husband dies on the grueling trail west. Upon arriving in Oregon Country, she uses her midwifery skills to help the other settlers, including the Cayuse tribe, with the aid of fur trapper Alex Armistead. But peace between the groups is fragile, and Grace soon finds herself in more danger than she ever imagined.

Treasured Grace
HEART OF THE FRONTIER #1

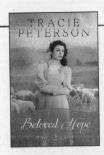

Hope Flanagan survived the massacre at the Whitman Mission, but at a terrible cost. Safe now, her mind and soul are healing. However, this peace is shattered when she is asked to testify at the trial of those responsible. As she confronts the pain of her past, an army lieutenant brings a ray of light into her life. But can she trust him with the truth?

Beloved Hope
HEART OF THE FRONTIER #2

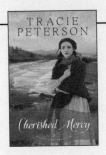

After surviving the Whitman Massacre as a child, Mercy still prays for peace between the native peoples and the white settlers of Oregon Territory. Longing for purpose, she travels to another mission to help a friend. There she meets Adam, a handsome young minister. When tragedy strikes yet again, Mercy and Adam must rely on their faith to make it out alive.

Cherished Mercy
HEART OF THE FRONTIER #3

🔥 BETHANYHOUSE

You May Also Like . . .

Vivienne Rivard fled revolutionary France and now seeks a new life for herself and a boy in her care, who some say is the Dauphin. But America is far from safe, as militiaman Liam Delaney knows. He proudly served in the American Revolution but is less sure of his role in the Whiskey Rebellion. Drawn together, will Liam and Vivienne find the peace they long for?

A Refuge Assured by Jocelyn Green
jocelyngreen.com

In 1772, Lady Keturah Banning Tomlinson and her sisters inherit their father's estates and travel to the West Indies to see what is left of their legacy. On the island of Nevis, every man seems to be trying to win Keturah's hand and, with it, the ownership of her plantation. Set on saving their heritage, can she trust God with her future—and her heart?

Keturah by Lisa T. Bergren
THE SUGAR BARON'S DAUGHTERS #1
lisatbergren.com

When dance hall singer Louisa Bell visits her brother at Fort Reno, she is mistaken for the governess that Major Daniel Adams is waiting for. Between his rowdy troops and his daughters, he's in desperate need of help—so Louisa sets out to show the widower that she's the perfect fit.

Holding the Fort by Regina Jennings
THE FORT RENO SERIES #1
reginajennings.com

◆ BETHANYHOUSE